He'd been gentle. So gentle...

Should it have surprised her? The second Mitch had touched her tonight, the soft heat of his palm had whispered memories to her.

Molly took another deep breath, trying to quiet the flutter that had started inside her the second he'd lifted her top to dress her wound. The bathroom had been far too cramped for the two of them. Definitely too cramped for the physical attraction she'd felt crackle across the narrow gap that had separated them.

"No." The sound of her voice forced back the images. And if that wasn't enough, Molly patted at the edges of the tape that held the bandage in place. It still stung, giving her a sharp bite of reality.

And the reality was, she was here to bring Mitch back to Chicago. Nothing more.

Dear Harlequin Intrigue Reader,

The holidays are upon us again. This year, remember to give yourself a gift—the gift of great romantic suspense from Harlequin Intrigue!

In the exciting conclusion to TEXAS CONFIDENTIAL, *The Outsider's Redemption* (#593) by Joanna Wayne, Cody Gannon must make a life-and-death decision. Should he trust his fellow agents even though there may be a traitor among their ranks? Or should he trust Sarah Rand, a pregnant single mother-to-be, who may be as deadly as she is beautiful?

Another of THE SUTTON BABIES is on the way, in *Lullaby and Goodnight* (#594) by Susan Kearney. When Rafe Sutton learns Rhianna McCloud is about to have his baby, his honor demands that he protect her from a determined and mysterious stalker. But Rafe must also discover the stalker's connection to the Sutton family—before it's too late!

An unlikely partnership is forged in *To Die For* (#595) by Sharon Green. Tanda Grail is determined to find her brother's killer. Detective Mike Gerard doesn't want a woman distracting him while on a case. But when push comes to shove, is it Mike's desire to catch a killer that propels him, or his desire for Tanda?

First-time Harlequin Intrigue author Morgan Hayes makes her debut with *Tall, Dark and Wanted* (#596). Policewoman Molly Sparling refuses to believe Mitch Drake is dead. Her former flame and love of her life is missing from Witness Protection, but her superior tracking skills find him hiding out. While the cop in her wants to bring him in, the woman in her wants him to trust her. But Mitch just plain wants her back....

Wishing you the happiest of holidays from all of us at Harlequin Intrigue!

Sincerely,

Denise O'Sullivan
Associate Senior Editor
Harlequin Intrigue

TALL, DARK AND WANTED

MORGAN HAYES

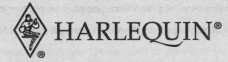

HARLEQUIN®

TORONTO • NEW YORK • LONDON
AMSTERDAM • PARIS • SYDNEY • HAMBURG
STOCKHOLM • ATHENS • TOKYO • MILAN • MADRID
PRAGUE • WARSAW • BUDAPEST • AUCKLAND

ISBN 0-373-22596-2

TALL, DARK AND WANTED

ABOUT THE AUTHOR

"Men and women finding love against great emotional odds and in the face of personal danger—that's what I attempt to deliver to my readers with each book," says Morgan Hayes. "For me, the combination of mystery and romance is the most fulfilling. With suspense and intrigue, I'm able to develop the compelling dynamics that, I hope, will keep my readers turning the pages not only to find out 'whodunit' but to discover how these characters are going to survive emotionally."

The inspiration for Hayes's suspense stories comes from her continued research in Baltimore, Maryland—primarily with the city's homicide unit. And quite often the inspiration for her characters comes from the admirable men and women behind the badge. With Mitch and Molly's story, there was the added inspiration of time spent in southwest Michigan at Shady Shores, a family-owned resort that hugs the shore of Dewey Lake just northwest of Dowagiac.

Hayes herself lives along the remote and rocky shores of Georgian Bay, Ontario, but admits that she needs the occasional dose of big-city life, and frequently travels to Baltimore and beyond. Ms. Hayes's book *Seduced by a Stranger* won the 1998 Romance Writers of America Mystery/Suspense Chapter's Kiss of Death Award, and in 1996 her second Harlequin Superromance novel, *Premonitions,* garnered a *Romantic Times Magazine* Reviewers' Choice Award.

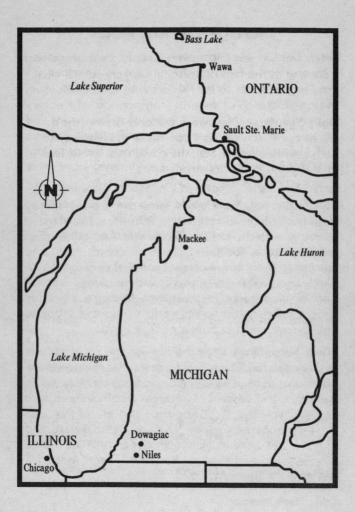

CAST OF CHARACTERS

Mitch Drake—He'd lost everything he held precious in life and now he was on the run. But with former love Molly Sparling by his side, his heart began to heal—and to hope.

Molly Sparling—She swore the only reason she'd sought out Mitch was as a cop doing double duty to catch a ruthless killer. Still, she couldn't help but feel like a woman in Mitch's strong arms.

Sergio Sabatini—Known in Chicago as "Slippery" Sabatini, this mob boss would do anything to keep himself out of the can—starting with the murder of the key witness in his case, Mitch Drake, and that meddling cop, Sparling....

Leo Sparling—His only daughter, Molly, meant everything to this retired lawman, but even he couldn't keep her safe from the dangers on her trail.

Sergeant Karl Burr—He knew Molly was a maverick and so he let her have her head. But was Molly's "uncle" Karl getting in over his head?

Detective Adam Barclay—Molly's partner on the force and her sole confidant—but could he truly be trusted?

Tom Sutton—This good cop's murder spurred Molly on—but could she have saved him from the evil that stalked him?

Rachel McCloud—Tom's former partner in Vice was a top dog detective, but just how much did she know about Tom's murder?

In memory of Alice Nevins…
avid reader, shining light and boundless soul.
May her enduring spirit live on in the memories of all
those who call Shady Shores their "other home."

And for Susan Bergey and Robyn Landers,
whose endless generosity and card table
made this book possible.

Chapter One

Mitch eased his hand around the cool brass of the door-knob. He turned it noiselessly, feeling the bolt slide free of the catch.

He didn't start when he heard one of the officers clear his throat behind him. He'd expected it.

"Uh, Mr. Drake, you weren't actually thinking of leaving, were you?"

Mitch turned in time to see a third officer round the corner to join the other two in the room. Expectation replaced the previous boredom that had marked all three of the officers' faces from the moment they'd arrived for duty at the safe house one week ago.

"As though I could go anywhere in this?" Mitch responded, nodding to the back window. Except for the narrow path that had been trampled down during the officers' frequent smoke breaks, the small, fenced-in yard was buried under a good three feet of snow. Chicago had been socked by one of the worst New Year's storms it had ever seen. Five straight days of freezing temperatures, nonstop flurries and winds that drove the snow into waist-high drifts, closing highways and more than half of the city.

"Why don't you guys go back to the game?" He could hear the Bulls game still blaring from the TV in the other room. "I'll be ten minutes."

"Look, Mr. Drake. It's the D.A. who makes the rules, not us, okay? And rule number one is we're not supposed to let you out of our sight."

"I won't be *out* of your sight. I'll be right outside. Now, if one of you wants to join me, you're more than welcome. I'm going for a smoke."

"But you don't—"

"I do now." He snatched up the pack of Camels left on the Formica-topped kitchen table, and tapped one cigarette out into his palm as though he'd done it a thousand times before. And when one officer tossed him a plastic lighter, Mitch caught it in the air, nodding the man an insincere "thanks".

He half expected one of them to scramble into his coat and come out after him. But no one did. The door slammed shut in its frame as Mitch stood against the full force of the gale that blasted around the side of the split-level bungalow.

No matter how bitter cold, he was grateful for the privacy. There'd been precious little of it these past few months, with a new safe house every couple of weeks, and a constantly changing team of officers breathing down his neck at every move as though *he* was the one waiting to go on trial.

Turning up the collar of his leather bomber jacket, he stepped off the snow-packed deck and ventured down the steps to the first low drifts. He buried his hands in his pockets, crushing the cigarette in the process, and followed the six-foot-high fence. Snow packed into the sides of his leather shoes. Icy wind bit at his exposed skin and whipped at his hair. He didn't care. At least it made him feel alive.

And—after eight months of safe houses, not to mention the two months prior to that recuperating in hospital—it was hard to remember what "alive" was anymore. Hard to remember there had ever been a life before this nightmare. Harder still to remember life with Emily.

He stopped at the far end of the yard, sheltered somewhat by the fence, and let the wind wrap its chill around him.

One thing he *would* always remember, however, was that night—the night his life had ended in one wrong turn, a detour directly to hell. Closing his eyes against the driving snow, he could, in an instant, conjure up every last detail of that night. The events unfolded before his mind's eye like some stuttering, overplayed movie reel—the grand opening of the Carlisle Office Complex he'd spent three years designing and building, the project that sealed his reputation and success in the world of architecture, a night of high society and glamor, of celebration and champagne. But the most vivid image, beyond all the glitter and opulence of the evening's events, was Emily—her glowing beauty, that shimmering smile of joy, her laughter and her words.

"Look at this, Mitch. All this—" she'd whispered, waving one slender hand at the grandeur around them. *"It's unbelievable, and all of it is yours. You did this. I am so proud of you."*

She'd kissed him then, oblivious of any onlookers. It was a passionate kiss that Mitch knew he'd remember to his grave, because it had been their last.

Within three hours of that kiss, everything he had known and loved was gone. They'd left the opening early. Emily, in spite of all her good cheer and exuberance, hadn't been feeling well. Mitch could still remember the unseasonable warmth of the spring night air wafting through the car's partly open window as they left the city center behind them.

If not for the road construction, they would have been safe in their bed, his body molding to Emily's curves as he held her through the night. Instead, there was the detour sign, followed by a wrong turn. And then that dark street—made even darker now by the memories.

Emily had asked if he was lost. There was no time to answer. The sports car's headlamps panned to the left as he took the turn, the light glaring across wet asphalt, illuminating the graffiti-covered wall of the overpass and finally capturing the small group of men.

They stood under the concrete arch, next to two dark-colored sedans, as the world spun into slow motion. Mitch couldn't be sure which came first—the piercing crack of the gunshot or the flare from the weapon's muzzle. Then there was the figure, crumpling to the shimmering pavement. And finally, the man…the man holding the gun. He'd turned, his deeply lined, sallow face forever etched in Mitch's mind.

Emily was speechless, but Mitch remembered how she'd clutched at the sleeve of his tuxedo, tearing at it as though prompting him into action. The gearbox ground when he forced the sports car into reverse, the engine whining as he accelerated back to the intersection.

He didn't need to glance in the rearview mirror to know they were being followed. And he hadn't needed to hear Emily's panicked observations as he steered for the on-ramp to the expressway.

They were already on him. Headlights blazing in the rearview, then disappearing below the mirror's field of view as the tailing car took its first crack at Mitch's bumper.

The small car was no match. The vehicle lurched, then swerved just as the battering sedan delivered another ram, and then another, to the ruined bumper. Mitch had already known they weren't going to make it to the expressway. One dark sedan was alongside them. A single sideswipe from the heavy vehicle tore the wheel from Mitch's hands. There was the agonizing squeal of metal on metal as the passenger side ground along the guardrail, and a spray of sparks lit up the night like a million stars. Then there was Emily's scream. And finally the gut-wrenching crack as the rail gave way, hurtling the tiny car into a headlong somersault down the earthen slope.

Mitch remembered little after that. Not until the blipping of hospital monitors and support machines. It could have been hours or days that passed before the detectives came. Time meant nothing once he'd been told of Emily. Eventually he'd been presented with a photo lineup, and now, after months of safe houses, Mitch wished to hell he'd never pointed out the man he'd witnessed firing the gun.

He had never actually seen a photograph of Sergio Sabatini until he'd picked him out of the photo array. But he'd certainly recognized the name the instant one of the detectives uttered it: *Slippery Sabatini*. What resident of Chicago *hadn't* heard of the notorious mob kingpin who'd spent the past fifteen years slipping through one judiciary crack after the next, evading every last criminal charge the Chicago Police Department tried to pin on him?

As though life without Emily hadn't been bleak enough, from that moment on, Mitch's life had literally disintegrated. First there had been the weeks of recovery in hospital under heavy police guard. And then, when Sabatini's slick, high-priced lawyer managed to convince a judge that his client was established in the community with a family that depended on him, and was, therefore, in no way a flight risk, Sabatini easily met the million-dollar bail. On that same day, Mitch was moved to the first safe house. And the next. And the next. He'd lost count after the twelfth or thirteenth, in the same way he'd lost count of the number of trial delays and the D.A.'s excuses for each one.

Now, ten months later, it was easy to lose sight of the real reason he'd subjected himself to it all—*Emily*.

With numbing fingers, Mitch drew his wallet from his back pocket. He ignored the razor-sharp wind that cut at his frozen hands as he flipped the leather wallet open. The one-inch photo behind the crinkled plastic was several years old, but Emily's beauty had never changed—from the day he'd met her in college her eyes had never ceased to shine, and her smile had only brightened over the years.

Mitch caressed the plastic over the photo with the pad of his thumb before closing the wallet and returning it to his pocket.

He *was* doing the right thing. In the end, in spite of everything he'd been through, it *was* the right thing. Only *he* could avenge Emily's death; only *his* testimony could put her murderer behind bars. There was no one else. Just him now. Up until three months ago, the D.A. had had two others lined up to testify against Sabatini, two witnesses who had seen the cars force Mitch's off the ramp that night. But now they were dead, or at least presumed so after their mysterious disappearances, which were currently under investigation by the CPD.

No, a conviction in the Sabatini trial lay solely in Mitch's hands. And yet how many times had he caught himself wishing he'd died along with Emily that night? So what if Sabatini went to prison for consecutive life sentences? It couldn't change the past. *Emily was dead.*

Mitch wiped the melting snow from his face and turned to look back at the safe house.

After all the safe houses, and after the trial, even after a conviction…what kind of life did he really have to go back to, anyway? Without Emily, it was hardly worth it.

He tilted his head and leaned against the fence, gazing up at the whirl of snowflakes. But it was images of Emily that swam before his mind's eye.

And it was at that moment, the instant he'd started to straighten from the fence, intending to head back to the house, that the frigid silence of the late afternoon was shattered. One second there was quiet, and the next the world was ruptured by a violent explosion. It tore through the flimsy structure of the safe house, ripping it into a million fiery pieces that spewed out in as many directions.

Instantly the air was thick, churning with the heat of the blast, alive with the hiss of the inferno that consumed the small house. Flames licked at the heavy sky, their heat blistering along Mitch's skin as his lungs took in the first wave of acrid smoke.

It was the second blast that knocked Mitch off his feet. It hurled him back against the fence under another shower of burning debris, and pitched him into utter blackness.

MOLLY SHOULD HAVE expected the mass of reporters and media vans camped outside Police Headquarters. Coverage of the explosion that had destroyed the safe house in Huntington was all over the news.

She'd been numb from the second she'd stepped out of the shower this morning, padded into her bedroom and seen the photo of Mitch flash across the TV screen. She'd been numb as she drove through the city and parked her car in the police garage around the corner; numb when she'd shoved change into the slot of the newspaper box and taken out a *Tribune*. She was still numb as she elbowed her way past the media and up the steps to the doors of Headquarters.

Even sitting down at her desk in the far corner of the Homicide unit, Molly was still in a haze of disbelief. Ignoring the chaos of phones and other detectives around her, she shrugged off her suit jacket and unfolded the paper. The front page of the early edition offered even less information. At least the TV report had suggested only three bodies were recovered from the late afternoon blast that had ripped through the Huntington bungalow. And unless Witness Protection was working under a new rule with less officers posted, that could mean...*could* mean there was still one survivor. Which one, though?

Her gaze scanned the rest of the page, scrutinizing the photo of the wreckage and finally stopping at the black-and-white image of Mitch. It wasn't a good photo. Grainy and blurred. He looked directly into the camera, his lips curved in the same sexy smile that touched the corners of his eyes. And in spite of the poor quality of the photo, there was no mistaking that something in his eyes—a light, a spark. She'd never been able to describe that look, but it was the same one that had always managed to trip her pulse and bring that rushing swell to her heart. It was the same look she had felt so certain would forever be reserved for her, and her alone.

Molly gave herself a mental shake. How was it possible that twelve years couldn't erase that sensation? Especially when the romance had lasted barely a quarter of that time? Then again, who was to say that at age seven she hadn't already been in love with "that Drake boy" down the street?

Mitch Drake, the much-celebrated architect behind the new Carlisle Office Complex and now a protected witness for the prosecution in the upcoming murder trial against Sergio Sabatini, is among those presumed dead in the Huntington explosion. Police are withholding comment until investigators have assessed the scene, and the medical examiner's office has identified the remains....

Molly swallowed the bitterness of bile threatening to rise to her throat. *He couldn't be dead. Not Mitch.*

She needed answers. Glancing across the squad room to her sergeant's office, she wasn't surprised to see his door was shut. With officers dead, the brass would be all over this case, and no doubt Sergeant Burr was either on the phone or in conference.

She stared again at the newspaper photo of Mitch. How was it possible for him to look even better than her memory made him out to be?

It was the same photo the *Tribune* had already used countless times in reference to the upcoming Sabatini trial. In it Mitch's hair was longer, and he sported a mustache and a trimmed beard. Molly had seen the combination on him only once, when he was nineteen, back from Boston after his first year of college. She hadn't had to say anything about the new look. Mitch had known almost immediately by her expression that she didn't like it, and he'd shaved for her that summer. Their last summer...

When she'd kissed him goodbye in September, how was she to know it would be her last?

"So you heard the news?"

Molly looked up. Adam Barclay, her partner, lowered himself behind his desk. His blond hair was damp and windblown. No doubt he'd slept in again and been forced to make yet another mad rush across the city so as not to miss roll call.

She nodded, then eyed the coffee cup he lifted to his lips as the steam circled his handsome face. "I don't suppose you brought me one of those?"

"Sorry. So what's the word then?" He nodded to her paper and she tossed it onto his desk.

"It's the early edition. They know even less than the vultures out on the front steps."

"Walden told me in the elevator that they got only three bodies, and the M.E.'s been working on 'em all night. Sarge talk to the squad yet?"

"Not yet."

"Well, this has definitely got Sabatini written all over it. First those other two witnesses and now Drake." Adam shook his head with obvious frustration. "I wouldn't be surprised if the D.A.'s office tosses the entire case now. Without Drake they've got nothin'."

Molly refrained from comment. There was far too much truth in Adam's suggestion.

"Thing that gets me," Adam continued, "is how they manage to keep this architect guy out of Sabatini's hands for ten months, and then, bammo. How do you figure Sabatini got the location? The way I hear it they were moving Drake every couple of weeks, and the Witness Protection guys were so tight-lipped about it, I doubt that even *we* could have found out where they were stashing him. If you ask me—"

But whatever theory Adam hoped to articulate was dashed the second Sergeant Burr's door swung open. The man's growling voice brought the clamor of the squad room to an instant hush.

"Sparling. In my office." With his large frame filling the doorway, he barely afforded her a glance before turning back to his desk.

"Sounds serious," Adam murmured.

But it was more the abruptness in Burr's voice that made Molly reach for her suit jacket and pull it on. Sarge rarely used surnames, and when he did, it was no time for informalities. Tugging the edge of the jacket over her gun's holster, Molly caught Adam's "good-luck" glance before she headed to the open door.

"What's up, Sarge?" She stepped into the narrow office.

"Take a seat."

As she did, Molly was struck by the pallor of his complexion. Exhaustion racked his face, and all of a sudden he looked much older than his fifty-five years. No doubt Sarge had been one of the first people called after the explosion late yesterday. He'd probably been up all night.

"I guess I don't need to tell you what this is about."

"The Sabatini explosion."

He nodded solemnly. "The verdict's still not in on whether this was a Sabatini hit."

"What have they got so far?"

"Three bodies…or what's left of them. Just got a call from the M.E.'s office. He's finally confirmed the identities of the three officers posted to the safe house."

Relief didn't come close to describing what flooded through her just then. *Mitch was alive.* She leaned back into the vinyl-cushioned chair across from Sarge's desk, about to release the breath of tension she'd been holding when the gravity of Sarge's expression reminded her this wasn't just about Mitch. Three officers were dead. Killed in the line of duty.

"As for Drake, the witness, they haven't found his body yet, but he's gotta be dead. There was nothing left of that house. And if he wasn't in it when it blew, you can bet Sabatini got to him first. Hell, we'll probably never find his body. But right now, we've got three officers dead. We're gonna see some heat on this one, Molly, and I want you on the team."

"Sir?"

"You're my best. I want you to get out to Huntington and start working with the Bomb Squad."

"Sarge, I really…I'm not sure—"

"What is it, Molly? Your caseload? Adam can pick up the slack on your other cases."

"That's not it, Sarge. In fact, you know I'm all caught up." Just like she always was, Molly thought. Every one of her cases was closed, with only two having outstanding warrants. And why not? Considering the number of overtime hours she put in, she could have closed all of Adam's cases on top of her own. For a year now, the only thing in her life *had* been work.

"So what's the problem?" Sarge asked again, his voice

adopting the more personal tone she was accustomed to hearing from him whenever they were alone together. ''I would have thought that thorn in your side was digging a little deeper ever since you'd heard about the explosion. Bad enough Sabatini's going to walk away from another murder charge, but three officers, Molly... I would have thought—of all the detectives on this unit—you'd be itching the most for the chance to get Sabatini on this one.''

''I know. It's just—''

''Molly, listen to me.'' Sarge rose and circled his desk, propping himself against one corner so he stood in front of her. This wasn't her sergeant talking now. It was Karl Burr, her father's old patrol partner, the man who'd taught her to swing a bat when her father had given up, the man who had helped build her tree house when she was six, the man who'd filled in at parent-teacher's night the time her father was sick, the man she'd called ''Uncle'' for years because it best defined their relationship.

He reached out and placed one large hand on her shoulder. ''I'm offering you this opportunity,'' he continued, ''because I know you want Sabatini. Ever since that son of a bitch killed Tom, I've held you back from anything to do with Sabatini. I didn't think you were ready. I thought the grudge was too deep for you to maintain a healthy and safe perspective. But it's been over a year now. I think you're ready.''

Yes, it had been over a year. But it hardly seemed long enough to get over the murder...no, the *execution* of her former partner. Then again, how much time *was* enough? Especially when she'd been the one who could have saved him?

Every day of the past year, she'd tried to put the haunting memories behind her, tried to forget. But not a day went by that Molly hadn't remembered, that she hadn't thought about Tom Sutton, her first patrol partner and closest friend.

They hadn't been partners the night Sabatini had had Tom murdered, but she'd known the risks Tom was taking. He'd come to her the day before, then called her again only an hour before he'd been shot. Working undercover Vice, he said he'd found something on Sabatini, something that might actually "stick" once and for all. And Tom had turned to Molly for help.

Only…she'd been too late.

"Molly?" Sarge prompted her. "Are you telling me you're not ready?"

"I'm not sure, Sarge," Molly said finally, noting how confusion deepened the lines in his face as he folded his arms across his wide, barreled chest.

But it wasn't just Tom she was thinking of now. There was Mitch.

Mitch was alive. He had to be. She had that gut feeling— the same one Tom had taught her to heed above all others.

Yes, Mitch was alive. And it was Mitch who was the ticket to seeing Sabatini behind bars. It was Mitch's testimony that would finally do it. She couldn't waste her time working potentially dead-end leads with the Bomb Squad. She needed to find Mitch. And she needed to find him before Sergio Sabatini did.

"This doesn't have to do with that search-and-seizure warrant, does it? It was a good warrant, Molly," Sarge was saying. "You know you weren't to blame for those charges against Sabatini being thrown out."

Another deep twinge of guilt. "You know I was, Sarge. But that's not why I can't join the team."

"Why then?"

"I need some time off."

"What?"

"I was planning to ask you before all of this broke," she lied. "Besides, you know I haven't had a single vacation day in almost a year. I'm due."

"But *now?*"

"Now more than ever. I'm burned out, Sarge. My cases are all closed. It's the perfect time. I need a break. It has nothing to do with Sabatini."

For a second, as she watched his eyes narrow into a scrutinizing stare, she wondered if he saw through her lie. Molly Sparling *never* needed a break. And the fact that she was asking for it now *had* to raise suspicions.

She expected him to demand what she was up to, to ask her flat out if she intended to go after Mitch. But he didn't. Instead, he let out a long breath, shook his head and resumed his seat.

"All right. Whatever you say, Molly. I only figured I'd give you the opportunity before anyone else on the squad. I'd thought... Well, forget it. If you say you need time, then you need time. Besides, your father already thinks I work you too damned hard."

Molly returned the rare smile that twitched at the corners of Karl Burr's mouth, the same smile she was quite certain only *she* had ever been privy to over the years he'd commanded the squad.

"Get your vacation slip to me. I'll sign it. You can start today, if you like."

"Thanks, Sarge."

"Don't thank me, Molly. They're your days. 'Bout damned time you took some off." He picked up his mug, the CPD logo on it lost behind his big hand as he lifted it to his lips.

When he opened the first file on his desk, Molly studied the top of his head, a mass of salt-and-pepper hair that seemed more "salt" than "pepper" these days. She wondered if it was due to age or stress, or more likely a combination of both. Still, there'd been no convincing him to join her father in retirement. Karl Burr was married to the force; more than that, he was committed to his squad.

"You'd better get that slip before I change my mind, Sparling," he muttered, not looking up. But Molly could see the quiver of a smile on his lips before she turned to the door.

"I REALLY WISH you'd reconsider, Mitch."

Mitch shook his head, heaving the last of Barb's bags into the trunk of the rental car.

"I'll be okay," he assured her again, closing the lid.

"You know I'm going to be worried sick about you up here alone. It's not safe. You should go to the police."

They'd been over this at least a dozen times already, and Mitch had figured that by now Barb Newcombe, one of his closest friends in college, would have remembered his stubbornness.

"I'm not going to the police, Barb. I went to them once, and it almost got me killed. I'm better off keeping a low profile up here."

She gave him a look, her blue eyes making the sternness appear even sharper. He'd seen that look too many times in the past couple of days.

He forced himself to smile then, and reached out to brush snow from her shoulder. "I'll be fine," he said, trying to assure her again.

"Well, you've got my numbers in Chicago. You call me…for whatever reason. Just call to let me know you're okay, 'cuz I know you won't answer the phone."

"I'll be fine," he said again, feeling like a broken record.

She studied him for a long moment as the snow tumbled down around them in the still air. To his right, he was vaguely aware of the sun setting behind the distant line of firs, but even the slight blush of orange in the sky did little to warm the cold that settled over the northern landscape.

And then, as though Barb had at last given up trying to

persuade him to do the logical thing, she threw her arms around him and gave him a hug.

"You've got the keys to my Blazer. And I've left you some more cash on the kitchen table," she said, stepping back and lifting a hand to stop his objection before he could voice it. "Take it, Mitch. You can't risk using your credit or bank cards. Think of it as a down payment. I'm considering an addition to the house."

She smiled and walked around the car. When Mitch joined her, she turned to him once more.

"Be careful, Mitch. Promise me."

"I promise. Everything's going to be all right." And Mitch wished he could believe his own words.

She nodded, touching his cheek with one cold hand. "By the way, I like you without the beard and mustache, you know?"

"Yeah?"

"You should have shaved it years ago. And the hair…"

Mitch ran one hand across the short cut. It was definitely a different look than the one he'd sported the past few years. One he hoped would buy him some anonymity up here in the relatively secluded northern Ontario wilderness.

"…it suits you," she finished. She flashed him a parting smile and folded herself elegantly into the driver's seat of the rental car.

"Just be careful, Mitch," she added one more time before rolling up the window and popping the vehicle into reverse.

He watched her back the car out the drive, giving her a quick wave as she turned down the side road and disappeared out of sight. Even after the sound of the engine was swallowed up by the dense, snow-covered forest, Mitch stood in the drive, recalling the many words of warning Barb had given him over the past couple of days.

She was right in a lot of her fears. There *was* only so

long he'd be able to hide, only so long he could run from Sabatini. And it wasn't as though any of this nightmare was going to just go away on its own.

Eventually, Mitch turned back to the house nestled in the firs and pines. From its rocky perch, it overlooked frozen Bass Lake, sheltered from most of the other cottages and houses that clustered along its shore. Barb's house couldn't exactly be classified as a cottage, even if it didn't quite measure up to the grand expectations both she and Mitch had talked about back in college. But when Barb finally made CEO of a software company in Chicago, she'd held Mitch to his college promise to design her lakeside retreat.

The two-story, wood-and-glass structure was easily one of the most impressive in the lakeside community, he thought with pride as he headed up the front steps. Now more than ever Mitch was grateful he'd talked Barb into adding the spare bedroom to the initial plans; he'd made good use of it for the past three nights.

Nothing had felt better than that extra bed after the full day he'd spent on a Greyhound from Huntington all the way through Sault Ste. Marie and on up to Wawa, followed by a one-hour car ride after Barb picked him up at the terminal.

He'd had a whopping headache by the time they pulled into the hidden driveway, but he'd known it was more on account of the blow he'd sustained from a flying plank during the explosion than from the long hours sitting in a cramped coach.

Reaching the wraparound porch, he lifted one hand to his forehead and fingered the neat piece of gauze that covered the healing gash. It had bled fiercely when he'd scaled the fence of the bungalow's backyard. He mustn't have been unconscious for long, he'd decided. He'd already staggered a good three or four blocks from the safe house before he'd heard the wail of sirens.

He knew then that, unless he had a death wish, he couldn't return to Chicago, and even before he located the bus terminal in Huntington, he'd already decided he had to come here. He could trust Barb. No one else. Not even the police, it seemed.

There was *one* person on the Chicago police force he might be able to trust with his life. He couldn't count the number of times he'd thought of Molly during the past few days. Then again, how was that any different from the past twelve years? In all that time, not a day went by when he *hadn't* thought of her, when he hadn't wondered about calling her, seeing her. But in all those years, he'd never had the courage. Nor had he ever been able to think of the words to apologize for what he'd done to her.

Chapter Two

Molly gripped the wheel of her Jeep Wrangler a little tighter and eased her foot off the gas as she maneuvered the vehicle into a sweeping curve. The headlights skimmed across the high snowbanks, hinting at the dark trunks and dense underbrush beyond. Normally she'd enjoy a drive like this—twisting blacktop through the middle of the wilderness. But with the snow coming down even thicker now, and with the wind battering against the side of the Wrangler, the fun was lost to the struggle against the elements.

Not to mention the fact that she was exhausted. For almost ten hours straight she'd battled the slippery conditions of Highway 131, then traffic along the I-75 heading north through Michigan; she'd spent another three past the Canadian border, fighting whiteouts and snow-covered roads the entire way. The thrill of the drive was long gone, replaced with anxiousness as Molly glanced down at her gas gauge.

"Bass Lake, eh? Oh yeah, that's just up the road a few kilometers," the proprietor of the last convenience store had advised, and he'd proceeded to give her directions that had convinced her she'd make it there on the quarter tank of gas.

But "a few kilometers" had translated to miles. And those miles had been added to when she'd missed the snow-plastered sign and the turnoff, and ended up driving a good twenty minutes beyond before realizing the mistake and having to backtrack.

The needle of the gas gauge dipped even farther below the *E* as she banked the Jeep through the next curve. Molly cursed. Why hadn't she heeded that voice of warning in her head when she'd considered stopping a couple of hours ago to scout for a motel?

Because her gut had told her not to. Her gut told her Mitch was alive, and that she had to get to him before Sabatini did. Her gut had led her to Mitch's closed-up architecture firm in the Jackson Boulevard Complex, where she'd rifled through his files and Rolodex, and found Barb Newcombe's name and the address of her summer place in Ontario. And Molly's gut had told her that of all the possibilities, it was his college friend's cottage Mitch would most likely run to.

Of course, it wasn't her gut that was running on empty and was about to die along this deserted stretch of godforsaken, freezing road, Molly thought, cursing again.

She'd called Barb Newcombe's secretary yesterday afternoon in Chicago, and managed to find out that the CEO had taken an extended New Year's vacation in Canada and wasn't expected back to work until the day after tomorrow. The chance of Mitch being at Newcombe's cottage with her had seemed even more likely after that, and Molly had started packing.

She'd almost finished by early evening when Adam had shown up at the door of her apartment. He hadn't waited for an invite, but pushed his way in, demanding to know what she was up to and why she hadn't responded to any of his attempts to page her.

"Yeah, right, Molly," he'd said, standing in the doorway of her bedroom as he'd watched her shove more clothes into her overnight bag. "You aren't visiting your aunt in

Cleveland. Unless, of course, you always pack your off-duty for family reunions.'' He lifted one fleece sweater to reveal the compact Walther 380 tucked in its ankle holster. ''Hell, you probably don't even *have* an aunt in Cleveland, do you?''

Molly ignored the question, praying he wouldn't search further and find her on-duty weapon in the bag as well.

''Adam, would you do me a favor?''

''Nope.''

''Adam, come on, it's just—''

''No way.'' He shook his head, and Molly followed him into the cramped living room, where he attempted to pace.

She'd always thought Adam Barclay was built like a linebacker for the Bears, and in her small apartment, he looked even broader as he tried to maneuver around the clutter.

''You've got a key to my place,'' she continued, adopting a plea in her voice. ''Just come in and feed Cat once a day? Please?''

''That ungrateful bag of—''

''Please?''

''Only if you tell me where you're really headed.''

''I can't do that, Adam.''

''You're going after *him,* aren't you?''

The question shouldn't have surprised her. After all, practically everyone in the Homicide Unit—especially her partner—knew of the deep-seated grudge she held against Sabatini. How could Adam *not* have guessed what she was up to?

''I don't know what you're talking about,'' she stated.

''The architect. Mitch Drake. You figure he survived the bombing, that he's alive and hiding out someplace. So you're going to single-handedly bring him in. The unwilling witness.''

''And how do you arrive at that conclusion?''

"Come on, Molly, I've been your partner three years, and in all that time you've never taken a vacation. I think I can figure it out. So…what d'you think you'll get for this stunt—bringing in the one witness that can finally put Sabatini behind bars? Assuming you can pull it off, that is. You aiming for another bronze star?"

The rancor in Adam's voice had confused her. "Why are you so bothered at the thought of me taking a little vacation time to follow a personal hunch?"

"Oh, I don't know." His voice had sharpened. "Maybe because I don't want to lose my partner?"

She'd thought she saw a glimmer of concern sweep across Adam's face then.

"Come on, Molly." He softened his tone, as though still hoping to convince her. "This is insane. Sabatini isn't your crusade, and you're not some one-woman crime squad, as much as you've been trying to act like it ever since Sutton's murder. Even if this Drake guy *is* alive, it's suicide to think you can bring him in on your own, against Sabatini's men. And I'm tellin' you, if Sabatini hasn't already had the guy executed, you can bet he's got every hired thug of his out there lookin' for him. Leave it to Witness Protection or the Fugitive Squad or whoever it is they've got searching for Drake."

"I'm just going to take a few days and see what I can come up with, Adam. That's all."

"You're just going to take a few days and get yourself killed, is all. Just like Sutton, for God's sake. Guess you learned more from your former partner than I gave you credit for, huh?"

"Look, Adam, I appreciate your concern. Really, I do. But I have to do this. I have to try. Mitch…he…if he is alive, he's running scared. He's not going to trust anyone now."

"And what makes you think he'll trust you?"

"Because...because he and I have a past," she admitted before she could change her mind about sharing the personal tidbit.

Her gaze had involuntarily flitted to her fireplace. It was so brief, but Adam caught it. He looked to the framed photo of her and Mitch, barely out of high school, in one another's arms. She didn't know why she kept it there on her mantel, but anytime she tried to put the photo away she wasn't able to.

"Adam, I have to at least *try*. If anyone is going to be able to find Mitch and convince him to testify...it's me."

But now, as Molly strained to see the next road sign through the mounting snow squalls in her headlights, she was beginning to doubt what she'd told Adam. And as she slowed to make the turn toward Bass Lake and felt the first sputter of the Jeep as it accelerated on what could only be fumes at this point, Molly silently prayed that her past with Mitch *would* have some power in convincing him to return to Chicago and do the right thing.

It wasn't just to see Sergio Sabatini behind bars, Molly realized as she spotted the distant glimmer of lights beyond the thumping wipers. Mitch's life depended on it.

BARB'S WORDS HAD PLAGUED Mitch all day. He'd shoveled snow, split some firewood, even changed the oil in the Blazer. And all the while he'd weighed the wisdom of doing as Barb suggested and going to the police.

Still, he'd not been able to see any reason for doing so. Returning to Chicago to testify against Sabatini would have no affect on his own life, anyway. It would do nothing to change the fact that Emily was dead and his career was over. The only reason left for testifying now was to ensure Sabatini didn't kill any more innocent people. But how was it that he owed anyone anything?

Bitterness had consumed him several times throughout

the day. It would clutch at his heart and start the small, familiar fits of anger he'd felt far too often over the past ten months. What *did* he owe anybody, after what he'd been through, after everything he'd lost?

By early evening, after spending an hour wandering through the house, reacquainting himself with his past design, he'd finally settled down by the fireplace. He'd picked up a pad of paper and a pencil and started sketching possible plans for the addition Barb had mentioned. What else did he have to do except bide his time? Wait for Sabatini's men to find him...

The sketching, however, had done little to take his mind off his situation. In fact, it only served to remind him of the work and the life he no longer had back in Chicago.

Mitch lowered the pad and pencil at last. He checked his watch: almost 11:00 p.m. The living room lay in shadows, the only light coming from the fireplace and the lamp next to the wing chair he'd occupied for the past several hours. The classical CD on the stereo had finished long ago, and the entire house seemed to have been swallowed by the silence of the surrounding wilderness.

He might not have heard the neighbor's German shepherd otherwise. But there was no mistaking the anxious bark from the next lot. Mitch set his sketches on the coffee table and moved across the dimly lit room. He approached the east window with caution and fingered open one of the shutters to peer into the darkness.

It was the thin beam of a flashlight through the thick, swirling snow that caught Mitch's eye first. With such low cloud cover, the night was black, but he could just make out the silhouette of the figure behind the flashlight. It was impossible to tell if it was a man or woman who struggled through the mounting snow, but there was no mistaking the person's seemingly determined route—straight down the drive toward the front door.

Maybe it was paranoia, but the name Sergio Sabatini jumped to the front of his mind. It was too late at night for lost or stranded tourists, and even if it *was* just some hapless soul, Barb's was certainly not the first—and definitely not the most obvious—house along the lakeshore road.

It was that thought and a renewed sense of self-preservation that spurred Mitch away from the window and into action.

MOLLY COULDN'T PUT a finger on the bad feeling that had started in the pit of her stomach from the moment she'd seen Barb Newcombe's name on the mailbox, but the feeling had risen steadily with each step she took toward the virtually unlit house. A dim but warm light slipped through the shuttered windows of a single downstairs room, flickering through the driving snow. The only other light came from the front porch.

As she mounted the steps, Molly switched off her flashlight and shoved it into a pocket of her anorak. She brushed herself off, removing one glove and wiping at the melted snow on her face while she stared at the set of double front doors.

The bad feeling moved up from her stomach and clutched at her lungs. She took a deep breath to try to calm it.

It wasn't like the feeling she would sometimes get while working a case, moments before something went very wrong. And it was different from the kind that had saved her skin on more than a couple of occasions in the line of duty. But it was definitely a "feeling."

Maybe she was tired.

Then again, maybe she was just worried, Molly rationalized. Worried about the kind of reception she might receive from Mitch after all these years.

She lifted a hand to one door and knocked solidly.

She waited.

Nothing happened.

Again she knocked. And again, nothing. The cold, black silence of the night, so different from the bright lights of Chicago, only added to her sense of unease as she reached for the door's brass handle.

And that unease intensified when the latch moved freely and the door swung open. Maybe it *was* one of those gut feelings she was having, Molly thought as she took the first tentative step into the house and lowered her knapsack to the floor. Something definitely felt wrong.

What if Sabatini had gotten to Mitch first? The thought sent a hot prickle of fear along her skin. Lifting the bottom edge of her anorak, she unclipped the holster at her hip and removed her duty weapon. The Glock's grip was cold, and her fingers shivered along the icy nickel as she drew back the slide.

She refused the urge to call out Mitch's name. If Sabatini's men *had* already found the house, there was the chance they were still on the premises. She certainly couldn't afford to announce herself, she thought, taking another step into the dimly lit foyer and nudging the door closed behind her.

Vaguely, she was aware of the interior, the predominance of pine, the spaciousness of what had initially appeared to be a small house, and the tasteful, expensive decor including huge plants that thrived in the abundance of natural light that undoubtedly flooded through the floor-to-ceiling windows and the several skylights overhead during the day. The curved staircase reached up toward a darkened second floor, and to her right was the living room.

A warm glow flickered across the hardwood floors from the blazing fireplace. The only other light was a reading lamp beside an empty chair. As Molly moved cautiously through the room, she spotted the sketches on the coffee table. Architectural sketches.

Mitch *was* here. Or, at least, he had been.

Molly tucked a stray wisp of hair behind her ear and looked to the hearth. If Sabatini's men had found Mitch, it had been very recently. She'd not seen any headlights in her long walk from where the Jeep had finally run out of gas, and the fire had been recently stoked. So maybe they *were* still here.

Like a sixth sense, the bad feeling gripped her again. It shivered its warning along her spine and caused the fine hairs at the back of her neck to bristle. Tightening her grip around her weapon, she started down the shadow-filled hallway to what she guessed was the kitchen.

But Molly didn't get far. Barely two steps through the arched doorway, a blinding pain stopped her in her tracks— a pain that seared along the base of her skull and pitched her to her knees. For one wavering moment, Molly was aware of the floor's ceramic tile, cool against her cheek. And in the next, blackness swallowed her.

ALL OF A SUDDEN the chunk of firewood in his hands seemed unbearably heavy—heavier than it had before he'd swung it high and felt its reverberating, almost sickening contact with the woman's skull. With a small twinge of guilt, Mitch set the makeshift weapon down next to the body sprawled across the kitchen floor. He hadn't thought it would be that easy when he'd taken up the piece of firewood and slipped into the kitchen before the first knock at the door.

His grip had tightened around the wood as he'd listened to her move through the front hall, then the living room. And when she'd rounded the corner to the kitchen, stepped through the doorway past his hiding spot, and he'd seen the light from the living room glint along the metal of the gun she held in her hand, he'd needed no more incentive. Mitch had swung.

Maybe he'd brandished the log a little too hard, though, he mused now as he turned on the kitchen lights and knelt beside her unmoving body. Thankfully there was no blood, but what if he'd broken her neck?

Part of him knew he shouldn't care; after all, she'd come here to kill him. If he hadn't attacked her first, she would have turned that gun on him. Still, she was a woman, and he had just struck her with a blow beyond anything he'd considered himself capable of inflicting on another human being.

Mitch slipped his hand beneath the collar of the woman's anorak to the soft skin along her throat. Relief swept through him. There was a pulse.

In the harsh glare of the kitchen's overhead fluorescents, Mitch was surprised at her small stature. When he'd seen her shadowed figure come through the arched doorway, her back to him, she'd looked bigger somehow. Or maybe it was the gun that had made her appear more formidable. But now, with her face turned away and her arm splayed out across the tiles as though she were reaching for him, she looked almost fragile.

Taking a deep, fortifying breath, Mitch reached for her. He grasped her shoulders in his hands and slowly eased her limp body over.

He wasn't certain what came out of his mouth first: a curse or her name. But as he stared into her face, disbelief washing over him, there was no stopping the string of expletives that escaped his lips.

Her complexion seemed pale—almost frighteningly so— and Mitch felt for her pulse again.

"Come on, Molly. Snap out of it." His voice filled the silence of the house, panic causing it to waver. "Molly, come on. I know you're tough. Don't do this to me. You're going to be all right. Come on, honey.''

But there wasn't so much as a moan or a twitch. She was out cold.

He should take her to the hospital, Mitch reasoned. But how could he? Even if anonymity wasn't a crucial factor in his life right now, the closest ER had to be a good hour away at least, and that didn't take into account the storm.

God, if he'd only known it was her. What was she doing here? How had she found him? Why hadn't she called out for him? What had possessed her to just walk in with her gun drawn? And then Mitch was cursing her all over again as he unzipped her jacket. He checked her pulse a third time.

Beneath the dark green fleece lining, she wore a form-fitting thermal top tucked into her jeans. It puckered around the leather strap of her gun's empty holster, drawing suggestively over the gentle swell of her breasts and her delicate rib cage. Mitch watched the fabric pull slightly as she took another shallow breath.

Twelve years… They'd certainly been good ones to Molly, he thought, staring into her face. The rounder lines that had been there in her youth had been replaced with more angular, mature features that accentuated the extraordinary bone structure beneath. Mitch was reminded of all the photos he'd seen of Molly's mother. And when he looked at the seductive curve of Molly's slightly parted lips, full and still moist, it was as though the years hadn't passed, as though it was only yesterday that he'd tasted that tantalizing mouth.

Reaching out to brush back a stray wisp of dark hair, he touched her cheek. So soft. Like silk. He could still remember the feel of her skin…its softness against his, the supple curves of her body molding into his, the eager heat of her passion melding with his until he'd hardly known where his longing had begun and hers ended....

"Come on, Molly," he murmured again, trying like hell to push the torrid memories back. "If you can hear me, you've gotta snap out of this. You're scaring me, honey. Do you hear me? Molly?"

He leaned even closer to her, not sure what to do next, but knowing that he had to get her off the cold, hard kitchen floor. And that was when he smelled her—subtle traces of jasmine mingling with that intoxicating scent that was undeniably and forever Molly. The years melted away...they were in her father's house, in Molly's bedroom. She'd lit candles, while old Elton John tunes played on her stereo. She'd been bolder that night than she'd ever been, knowing her father was working midnight shift at the precinct. In twelve years, Mitch had never forgotten the tantalizing smile that had played on her lips when she'd shed the short, silk kimono, letting it fall to the floor as she stood naked before him, her skin glowing in the candlelight, her dark hair tumbling over her tanned shoulders and the shadows playing along each seductive curve, while he lay on her bed...waiting.

It was the last time they'd made love, one week before fall semester started, the night before he'd had to return to Boston. The last time he'd ever seen Molly...

"Molly, please..." he begged her again, but this time he slid his arms beneath her and gently lifted her delicate body from the floor. "Please, honey..."

God, she had to be all right, Mitch prayed. She *had* to be.

Chapter Three

Molly was aware of the pain first. The dull throb stemmed from the base of her skull and spiked upward. Then she felt the heat—a radiating warmth against her left cheek—and she could hear the low crackle of fire in the hearth.

The memories came together like scattered pieces of a puzzle. She'd walked through the house, seen Mitch's sketches on the coffee table, moved down the hall with her gun drawn, and finally there had been the blow and the blinding pain. Silently, she cursed herself. Yes, she'd certainly done a good job of walking directly into someone's trap.

Sabatini's trap? It had to be. She pushed back the instantaneous surge of panic. His men must have gotten to Mitch first, then had probably left her for dead.

But...the last thing she remembered was the cold, ceramic tiles of the kitchen floor. Even without opening her eyes, she knew she was on the leather sofa she'd seen in the living room. Why would Sabatini's men move her?

"How do you feel?"

In twelve years...no, in a *million years*, she'd never forget his voice. Its deep, resonant tone slipped through the silence, smoothing out the sharper edges of her pain and wrapping itself around her like a lover's embrace.

The only thing more seductive than that was the sight of him.

Mitch sat less than three feet away, perched on the edge of the coffee table. He leaned forward with his elbows braced against his knees. His forehead creased and those dark eyes narrowed with what appeared to be genuine concern.

Molly blinked several times, gradually bringing him into focus. She had to be dreaming.

It wasn't the Mitch of the photos she'd seen over the years—always dressed to the nines in hopelessly crisp suits and expensive ties as he endured the limelight his success garnered, or even donning a hard hat at some groundbreaking event for a new Drake construction, still wearing what appeared to be an Armani.

No, this was the Mitch of Molly's memories, of twelve years of recurring dreams and fantasies. That rugged handsomeness, that overwhelming masculinity, dressed in a rumpled denim shirt over a sparkling white T tucked into a faded pair of jeans...

And his hair... It was cropped short. The mustache and beard were gone as well. The warm glow of the fire softened his sharp features—the square chin, the strong jawline, those chiseled lips and that perfect nose with the smallest of clefts at the tip. But it was his eyes that riveted her and seemed to have stolen her ability to speak as she watched them reflect the flames' dancing light.

This was the Mitch she knew, the Mitch she'd made love to and believed would be with her forever. This was the Mitch she'd kissed goodbye as she saw him off to college twelve years ago. This was the Mitch who had smiled as he'd driven off to Boston, and out of her life....

"Are you okay?" he asked.

She managed a nod, but her eyes never left his.

"Talk to me, Molly," he prompted again, the lines of

worry etching even deeper. "Are you all right? How do you feel?"

"Like I've been clubbed over the head." Her voice cracked and she cleared her throat. The simple act sent another shot of pain searing through her.

"I thought I was going to have to drive you to a hospital."

"I'm fine," she lied, and attempted to sit up. But the effort was more than she'd anticipated. Her vision blurred again and dizziness swept over her.

She should have expected Mitch to reach for her then—strong hands grasping her, guiding her up and then lingering on her shoulders as though assuring himself that she was all right. More than that, however, Molly should have expected the almost instant physical reaction her body had to his touch.

"I'm fine," she said again, brushing his hands away.

He backed off, but only briefly. From the coffee table he picked up an ice pack and settled onto the sofa next to her. She could smell the faint trace of aftershave on him—something she'd not smelled in years, and yet it seemed as familiar as yesterday. She fought back the memories.

"How long have I been out?"

"Not long. Fifteen minutes…maybe twenty."

He reached behind her, attempting to settle the ice pack against the tender and throbbing source of her pain. Molly winced and reflexively reached up to take the pack from his grasp.

"I told you I'm fine."

She heard the release of his breath before she saw him shake his head.

"How could I forget?" he asked, a frown quivering at the corners of his mouth. "Just as stubborn as your old man."

She watched him lift a hand and run his fingers through

the short-cropped hair, as though he expected to find long locks of black hair still there.

"So I guess I have you to thank for this goose egg?" Molly bit her lower lip as she eased the pack against the injury, feeling the initial burn of the ice.

"What do you expect when you come creeping through the dark? And with a gun drawn, no less?"

Molly caught his quick nod to where her Glock lay on the coffee table. She cringed at the idea that she'd so easily lost her on-duty weapon. Yes, she'd certainly messed up. If it had happened in the line of duty, the incident would have been written up in a heartbeat.

"I did knock," she said.

"Yeah, well, you should have announced yourself." There was a definite edge to his tone. But the anger wasn't at her, Molly realized then. It was more at himself, for having struck her the way he had. And judging by the residual dizziness and the pain hammering through her head, it must have been a damned good swing. She could only imagine what had gone through his head when he'd seen her drawn gun coming through the kitchen door.

"So what the hell are you doing here, Molly?"

"You have to ask?" She shifted the ice pack and tried not to wince again.

"You're wasting your time."

"Whether or not you testify is up to you, Mitch. All I want to do is ask that you reconsider what you're doing."

"And what *am* I doing?"

"Honestly? I'd say you're committing suicide. Thinking you can stay out of Sabatini's reach. It's insane. After all, *I* managed to find you. It can only be a matter of time before Sabatini's men catch up with you as well, and you're a fool if you think you can hold your own against them. You're not safe, Mitch. No matter *how* much firewood you have," she added.

"And you're saying I'm safe in Chicago?"

"Certainly safer than running, yes."

He stared at her for what could only have been seconds, but caught in those dark eyes, it felt like an eternity.

"Well, I'll take my chances," he said at last. "Like I told you, you're wasting your time."

In the intensity of his stare she thought she saw resentment, anger, and beneath that...a kind of resignation, a glimmer of defeat that frightened her. When he drew himself to the edge of the sofa eventually, and turned to look at the fireplace instead, Molly studied his profile. But she could still see that sense of hopelessness she'd glimpsed. It was the look of a man who didn't care whether he lived or died. And Mitch Drake was the *last* person she'd ever expected to see it in.

No, the Mitch she'd grown up with was a strong man. A man who loved life, who had never let anyone or anything cut him down or hold him back. She'd fallen in love with that strength, that vitality, probably before she was even old enough to understand those qualities. And later, in high school, it was that love for him that had left no question in her mind as to who she wanted to be with, who would be her first lover.

She'd been Mitch's first, too. Sure, she knew he'd kissed a couple of other girls on occasional dates before she had dared to profess her feelings. But Molly knew, beyond a doubt, that Mitch spoke the truth when he'd sworn that night on a blanket along a stretch of Lake Michigan beach, under a full sky of stars, that Molly was his very first. *His first and only,* he'd vowed.

They'd dated through his senior year and then Molly's while Mitch started college in Boston. And in their last summer together—before Mitch went for his second year at Boston and Molly joined the Academy as her father had done—they'd made grandiose plans for their future, even dared to speak of marriage a few times. But Mitch had wanted to finish school first so he could afford to buy her a real ring. Even back then Molly had wondered if there was more to Mitch's holding off than the cost of a diamond ring, because he knew her well enough to know that she would never have worn something as precious as a diamond.

Then, through their grapevine of friends, Molly had learned of Emily Buchanan, a girl Mitch had met during his second year of college. Molly had learned he was bringing his new girlfriend home during the Christmas break, and she'd made it a point to escape Chicago for the holidays, leaving her father on his own and heading to the slopes with friends just so she wouldn't have to see or speak with Mitch. And when she returned to the city to start her new life as a patrol officer with the CPD, Molly had vowed she was through with Mitch, through with the dreams and the hopes. She'd returned his few letters unopened, and didn't respond to any of the phone calls he'd placed to her father.

And then, three years later, when she'd heard the news of Mitch's marriage to Emily, Molly had at last come to the painful conclusion that it had never been a matter of Mitch not being ready for marriage all those years earlier. It had never been a matter of timing, or money for an engagement ring. It had simply been a matter of her not being "the one."

Even so, it hadn't been easy seeing the pictures in the papers and the magazines over the years as Mitch's reputation grew in Chicago and the architectural world. Harder still to look at that one photo in which he'd posed with his new wife on his arm at some Chicago high society event. Emily had been everything Molly wasn't—tall, elegant, poised; not some tomboy down the street Mitch had grown up with, pitching stones at old factory windows and racing their matching CCM bicycles through trash-cluttered back streets.

No, she certainly hadn't been "the one," Molly resolved yet again as she watched Mitch stand and cross the dimly lit room to the fireplace.

There was no missing the way he favored his left leg, the slight limp seeming uncharacteristic of his obviously sturdy, muscular build. Molly was reminded of the crash ten months ago that could very easily have claimed his life. She should have been used to the guilt she felt now; after all, it had plagued her ever since she'd heard about the accident and hadn't made the effort to see Mitch. Not that she would have necessarily been allowed in to see him at the hospital or even been able to find out the location of the safe house if she'd tried. And not that she would have known what to say if she *had*.

She watched him throw another log onto the fire. A burst of sparks sprayed out and up the flue.

"I...I'm sorry, Mitch," she murmured now. "I'm sorry about the accident. About...your wife." The words sounded flat, even though she'd meant them.

His back was to her, but she could see the rigid tension that straightened his spine then and tightened his shoulders. And when he turned to her again, there was no mistaking the pain that darkened his face. He rubbed at the gold wedding band, and Molly couldn't help thinking it was a completely unconscious habit of his.

In the uncomfortable silence that fell over the room, Molly tried to imagine the kind of loss he'd suffered. Yes, she'd lost her mother years ago to cancer, but she'd been only four, too young to have known her, too young to fully comprehend the loss.

And then, just as quickly as it had appeared, the dark pain in Mitch's expression was gone again, as though maybe she'd only imagined it. The wall came up and masked his features in a way only Mitch could manage.

Molly remembered the first time she'd seen him do that—so skillfully construct walls around his emotions. They'd been ten years old when they'd found his dog at the side of the road, killed by a car. Mitch had carried the collie in his arms the whole six blocks home, and it was only days later that Molly had at last seen him cry.

That memory, and many others, flashed before her mind's eye as Mitch stared back at her. Only when he cleared his throat was she able to return to the present.

"Where's your car?"

She lowered the ice pack and tried to draw herself to the edge of the couch. Another cruel wave of pain surged through her head, and the room threatened to spin again. "About a mile back, at the side of the road," she answered, remembering the long, cold walk. "I, um, I underestimated. Ran out of gas."

"Well, you can't leave it there. With this snow, the plows'll be through at least once tonight," he said, turning from the fireplace. "I've got a spare tank. I'll drive you out there."

SOME OF THE COLOR had returned to Molly's face before they'd left the house, and she seemed to have regained her equilibrium. But from the moment she'd reholstered her gun and pulled on her anorak and boots, she'd been silent. Even now, in the passenger seat of Barb's Blazer, she said nothing, only stared out the windshield into the mesmerizing swirl of snow.

Mitch could only imagine her thoughts as he backed the vehicle out the drive and nosed it south along Lakeshore Drive. *Was she remembering as well?* No, Mitch thought, more likely she was thinking about the years that had separated them. Was it resentment that turned down the corners of her mouth now? he wondered as he snatched another quick side glance. Was it bitterness and anger, harbored over the years because he'd never been able to offer her an explanation?

In spite of the sickly green glow of the dash lights, her features appeared soft and innately feminine. Still, her angular profile had maintained that strong, almost fierce look of determination he'd always remembered. The loose ponytail that drew up her dark hair revealed the delicate curve of her neck, leading to the regal jawline—the same jawline he'd so often watched jut out with that unparalleled Sparling stubbornness.

Another glance and he caught the determined chin, the tight yet exquisite lips, the fine, straight nose, the subtle hollow below her cheekbone, and those gently arched eyebrows. But even with his gaze directed out to the mounting storm beyond the windshield once more, Mitch could see Molly's eyes. They had long since been burned into his memory—exquisitely wide, and dark...almost black, like a bird's, Mitch had often thought.

In the confines of the vehicle, it was impossible not to remember the early days of their relationship: the summer evenings at the drive-in theater, when he'd sneaked the same side glances at her and hoped to sneak a kiss as well. The late-night drives home, and then sitting outside her father's house with the porch light still blazing. That's where he'd kissed her the first time, at 1:00 a.m. on May 16, in the front bench seat of his father's old Plymouth.

It hadn't mattered that he'd kissed other girls before then; with Molly it had felt like the first. From the moment he'd leaned across the seat, buried his fingers in her thick hair and drawn her mouth to his, Mitch had known it was more than just another kiss. *Much* more. There was no comparing, because *that* kiss, and every one they'd shared after that, had always felt like...coming home.

Mitch's body responded to the memories, and he tried instead to shift his focus to the road ahead of them, keeping the Blazer steady through the accumulating drifts. The weatherman's predictions had certainly been accurate. Between the heavy snowfall and the unrelenting wind, whatever tracks Molly had made in her walk to the house had long since been covered or blown clear. Mitch was grateful that Barb had left him with the four-wheel drive and rented a car to get back to Chicago.

"So the police know I'm alive?" he asked finally, needing something—anything—to break the heavy silence between them.

In his peripheral vision he caught the flash of Molly's eyes, but the second he tried to meet her stare, she looked away again.

"No," she answered flatly, her soft voice almost drowned out by the Blazer's fan and the thumping wipers. "They think Sabatini got to you first."

"But you didn't?"

She shook her head.

"Why?"

"Call it a gut feeling."

"So you came all this way on the department's budget?"

"No. This is my vacation time, Mitch. *My* budget. I wanted to find you."

Was it possible? he wondered. Could Molly have driven all the way from Chicago just for him? Out of concern for his safety and well-being?

No. The truth of the matter was Molly was a cop. Vacation or no vacation, as a cop she'd searched for him, and as a cop she wanted him to come back to Chicago. *To testify.*

"So how did you find me?"

"I broke into your office," she said, so matter-of-factly she made it sound like standard police procedure. "Went through your Rolodex. Process of elimination. Figured that of all the places you'd run to, I'd find you here.''

He saw her nod past the windshield.

''My Jeep's just around the next turn. I thought I saw headlights.''

''Probably the plow,'' he suggested. But if there had been a plow or another vehicle it was gone by the time he steered around the bend and caught sight of the Jeep's four-way flashers.

Mitch drove past the vehicle and pulled the Blazer to the shoulder of the road as well. Leaving it idling, he stepped out into a blast of icy air. In spots where the wind had blown the road clear, the packed snow squealed under his boots as he took out the gas can and walked back to the Jeep. There was no other sound; the heavy blanket of snow over the dense forest muffled the jangle of Molly's key ring as she unlocked the gas cap, and the clank of the can as Mitch brought it up and fitted the nozzle.

Holding the flashlight in one hand, Molly lifted her collar and tugged her scarf up under her chin against the biting cold. Mitch didn't know why she unzipped her anorak from the bottom just then and fumbled underneath as though checking her gun's holster. If he'd had time to think about it, he might have taken the gesture as a warning. He might have thought Molly sensed something that he didn't. Or…he might have wondered if she'd expected what happened next.

But the thoughts had barely begun to form themselves in his mind when they both heard the low rumble of an engine. Together they turned in time to see the sudden glare of high beams as a vehicle careened out of the darkness and around the corner. Momentarily caught in the headlights of the Blazer, the dark-colored SUV accelerated along the snow-covered road.

"What the hell? It's coming right at us!" Molly shouted above the revving engine.

But Mitch didn't need any warning. Instinct drove him. There was no time to wonder what lay in the darkness beyond the snowbank to his right. Anything was better than the grill of the oncoming vehicle. He dropped the empty gas can, and before it even hit the road, he'd snatched Molly's hand in his.

He cleared the bank before she did, dragging her after him, up and over the hard slope and into the soft, deep snow beyond. Vaguely he was aware of branches whipping at his face and an exposed boulder gouging into his back as he rolled with Molly. And finally, his own wind escaped in a gasp, knocked out of him as she landed on him.

In the same instant, above the engine's roar came the gut-wrenching sound of impact. It was followed by the scream of metal grinding against metal, of tortured steel and shattering glass.

He heard Molly's curse as she bellied up the bank, and when he joined her, peering over the top, the Jeep was a good forty feet from where it had been parked. It wasn't until the assailing four-by-four slowed to a stop farther down the road and finally turned around that Mitch was able to see the damage it had inflicted on the smaller vehicle. In the other vehicle's headlights, it was clear Molly's Jeep had been spun around, the driver's side crushed and the windows smashed out.

Again he heard Molly curse, but this time she followed it up by lifting the edge of her anorak and taking out her gun. In the brief glare of headlights, he could see the determination in her face as she gripped the weapon in one gloved hand.

"Molly, what are you doing?!"

"What does it look like?"

"It might have been an accident."

"I hardly think so. Get down, Mitch," she ordered, pulling back the slide of the semiautomatic.

"Molly, what the hell—"

But he didn't need to ask, nor did he need to hear Molly's explanation behind the defensive stance she took, her body pressed along the snowbank, her elbows propped against the hardened surface as she brought the gun up. He, too, watched the four-by-four slow as it neared their hiding place, and when the passenger window rolled down, Mitch was shocked to see the weapon in the man's hand.

"Get down," Molly warned him once more, a mere second before the night erupted in gunfire.

There was no telling which shots were which then. To Mitch, it sounded like a virtual torrent of bullets. A war zone. From where he crouched just below the top of the slope, he could almost hear the small missiles piercing the air above him, striking trees and ricocheting off boulders in the darkness beyond. When he snatched a look at Molly, he saw she was holding her position at the top of the embankment, one round after the next exploding from the black muzzle of her gun.

Mitch could only imagine that her shots were far more accurate, because as suddenly as the gunfire had begun, it ended. There was the rev of the four-by-four's engine and the grinding of huge tires against the frozen road as it sped off.

But Molly wasn't finished. Far from it. Mitch heard her mutter something about them getting away, and in a flash she was on her feet.

"Molly, no! Let them go." He snatched at her coat, hoping to stop her, but it was pointless. She tore loose and charged down the snowbank to the road before he'd even caught his balance.

In the roadway, Mitch winced with each earsplitting shot

as Molly let off several more rounds at the fleeing vehicle. And that was when he smelled the gasoline.

Behind them, only one of the Jeep's hazard lights continued to blink through the inky darkness. The four-by-four must have struck the Wrangler's fuel tank.

"Molly!" But his voice was lost to yet another shot as the four-by-four's taillights disappeared around the bend.

"Molly!" he shouted again.

The blast of her final round echoed through the woods. It was followed by the quiet, yet unmistakable whisper of a fire igniting. In the next second there were flames. Over the low crackle, he heard Molly curse again, turning to the vehicle as though she hoped to rescue some of her belongings.

"Molly, no. Come on!" he shouted above the hiss, tugging at her coat.

She'd lowered her gun, and in the intensifying red-orange glow of the hungry flames that already engulfed the driver's side of the Jeep, Mitch saw the shock in her expression. The heat of the flames, searing against his own cold-numbed skin, seemed to hold her back.

The air was swollen now with the heat of the fire. Flames licked higher and higher into the stormy night, fanned by the wind.

"Molly, now! It's going to blow!" This time when he grabbed at her coat, Mitch didn't let go. He half dragged, half ran with her away from the Jeep and down the empty road, uncertain how much distance was needed.

It wasn't enough.

There was the low whoosh of gas igniting, followed by an earth-shattering explosion that hurled both of them to the cold ground. The shock of the blast rippled through the air around them, followed by a wave of thick, acrid heat and a storm of flying shards that rained down around them.

"Are you all right?" His body covered hers, and when

he raised himself enough that she could move, Molly rolled over and sat up. She brushed snow and grit from her face and stared back at the burning wreckage, the flames reflecting in her wide eyes.

"Are you all right, Molly?" he asked again, taking her by the shoulders.

She managed a nod and instantly scanned the snow-covered ground. Locating her gun, she brushed it off as well.

"Yeah," she said at last, "I'm okay. I think...I think we need to get out of here."

"I couldn't agree more."

It was when Mitch started to stand that he spotted the two figures in the roadway. Twenty...maybe twenty-five yards away, they were no more than silhouettes in the flickering glow of the fire, but there was no question as to their intent. Each of them carried a gun, and each approached with the steady determination of hired killers.

Chapter Four

He'd saved her life. Not once, but twice now. And Mitch seemed bound and determined to do it a third time, Molly thought as he tore at her sleeve.

This time, however, Molly needed no prompting. With one eye on the two advancing men in the roadway, she nudged Mitch to the side of the road. She winced against the searing pain along her right side. She'd felt it for the first time up on the embankment, and hoped it had been a rock or a stick that had caused the injury. But now it felt warm. Hot, in fact. And Molly wondered if she might have actually taken a bullet during the rain of gunfire.

Hurriedly, she reached under her anorak with her bare hand, certain she felt the slipperiness of blood as she groped for her Glock's extra ammunition clip.

"Over the bank," she whispered harshly, jamming the magazine into the grip of her semiautomatic.

Even at fifteen yards, she could feel the singe of the flames as the two of them stumbled across the road. Vaguely, she was aware of various parts from her Jeep strewn about them from the explosion. She and Mitch had been lucky.

But there would be no counting of blessings if she didn't get them out of there...and fast. Sabatini's men were serious—*dead* serious. The guns they wielded were nothing short of illegal. To her trained ears, even in the heat of the gunplay only moments ago, she knew the men's weapons were fully automatic.

With the cold, wet Glock in one hand, and Mitch holding her other, Molly relied on his strength to drag her to the top of the embankment. On the other side, the snow was deep and loose, swallowing them almost to their waists. Molly needed no words. Mitch seemed to understand she had a plan. She moved ahead of him and led the way back toward the section of the road where they'd left the Blazer idling.

Molly could only pray that Sabatini's thugs didn't expect them to be brave enough to come back right at them with little more than the embankment for cover. But what other option did they have? Stumble through the deep snow and the storm into the middle of the bush? And then what? No, their only option was to get to the Blazer.

Staying in a semicrouch, Molly pushed her way through a tangle of branches and saplings. She could feel Mitch right behind her. He'd caught her more than a couple of times as she nearly tripped over hidden rocks and fissures in the earth beneath the thick snow.

They had to be close now. If Sabatini's men had kept up their pace, then they should be parallel to them. Only a few yards separating them. A few yards and a snowbank. Molly realized she was holding her breath, as though the men on the roadway would actually hear her over the roar of the fire that steadily consumed her Jeep.

Still, she didn't dare peer over the bank to confirm her guess. They had to keep moving. Only now, she gestured to Mitch to go ahead. Testifying aside, she was here to protect him, and protect him she would. No matter what happened, if Sabatini's men wanted Mitch, they'd have to go through her first.

For a panicked moment, she thought she heard their

voices. Shouts over the crackle of the flames. And any second she expected to see one of the men crest the snowbank, his gun blazing. But…nothing happened.

With Mitch ahead of her now, the going was a little easier. She followed the path he cut, ignoring the snow that jammed down the tops of her boots and blew under the collar of her anorak. She wasn't sure where her gloves were; she'd removed them when she first took out her gun. Her hand was numb around the weapon's rubber grip. Sore even. She hoped she'd be able to fire the Glock when and if it came to that again.

A transient wave of relief swept through her when she heard the low sound of the Blazer's idling engine. Sabatini's men could easily have tampered with the vehicle, but instead they'd passed it by, obviously more intent on finding Mitch. Perhaps even thinking the explosion had taken care of their business for them.

Molly snagged the edge of Mitch's coat. He stopped. Waiting for her next move.

With extreme caution she eased herself to the top of the bank and peered over. She scanned the roadway behind the Blazer. There was nothing visible but the burning Jeep. And then, finally, she saw them. The first man had obviously spotted their footprints and seen where they'd scaled the snowbank. He was already halfway up, stumbling over clumps of ice and gravel. His counterpart was right behind him.

"They're onto us," she whispered to Mitch. "Come on—" she nodded to the Blazer "—you take the wheel. Circle around the front. And the second you're in, floor it."

She didn't need to wait for his nod of acknowledgment. Mitch was right behind her. Together they scrabbled down the crusty bank, a small avalanche of frozen snow cascading around them and onto the roadway. There was no way of knowing whether it was their movements or the sound of the Blazer's doors opening that alerted the men, but in the same instant that Molly landed in the passenger seat, the black night erupted around them for a second time.

Bullets sliced the air, some exploding against hard-packed snow, while others struck deeper in the forest where the road curved to the left.

"Go, Mitch!" Molly shouted between bursts of gunfire. "Drive!"

But he hardly needed motivation. There was the unmistakable whack of one bullet striking what had to be the Blazer's steel bumper. And then another. And another.

Before he'd even slammed the door, he'd jammed the car into first gear and his foot was on the gas. The wide tires spun, throwing snow and gravel up against the vehicle's underbelly, until they found purchase.

Molly looked at the passenger-side mirror. In the flickering illumination of the fire, she saw the two figures. Their pursuit by foot was no match for the accelerating vehicle, and when Mitch steered into the curve, Molly could no longer see them.

In the dim glow of the dash lights there was no mistaking the tension in Mitch's face. Molly had heard about his valiant attempt to escape Sabatini and his men that night ten months ago—the high-speed chase to the expressway and the violent tactics used by the pursuing men to force him off the road. She'd seen the police photos of the wrecked sports car and remembered wondering how anyone could have survived in it.

As she watched Mitch's knuckles whiten around the Blazer's steering wheel, she could only imagine the kind of fear he was reliving now. He didn't check the rearview, but concentrated on the road as the gunfire from behind continued.

Ahead, just past the curve, Molly spotted the thugs' SUV

at the shoulder. Exhaust curled up from the idling vehicle, caught in the glow of the rear lights.

"Stop," Molly ordered as they neared it.

"What? Are you insane? They're—"

"Stop," she said again.

"Molly, they're right behind us." Amplifying his concern, another burst of gunfire erupted around them.

"Just stop!"

She heard him curse as she started to open the door, and—with no choice—Mitch brought the Blazer to a skidding halt. She was out of the car in a flash. Icy wind blasted against her. With freezing fingers, she tightened her grip on her gun while she grappled at the door handle of the other vehicle.

She had no idea if there was a third man behind the tinted windows of the four-by-four. She could only pray.

Flinging open the door on the driver's side, Molly brought her other hand up to her gun, prepared to fire. But there was no one inside. As another rain of bullets pierced the air, Molly reached across the driver's seat and turned the key. The heavy engine shuddered and died, and in the same second she tore the key from the ignition. Mitch shouted something then, but over the gunfire there was no making out the words.

Behind them she thought she could just discern the two figures running up the middle of the road.

"Molly! Let's get the hell out of here!"

This time she heard Mitch. She turned, reaching for the Blazer's door handle, but not before hurling the keys to her right, deep into the forest and the snow. She'd barely landed in the passenger seat when Mitch gunned the engine and they sped away.

MITCH HAD TO TAKE the roundabout way back to Barb's house in order to avoid Sabatini's thugs. It entailed a good twenty minutes of driving, the buffeting wind and snow making the going even slower. And although there wasn't any sign of headlights in the rearview mirror, Mitch's heart rate didn't slow one bit. Even after he closed the garage door, his pulse raced and the adrenaline continued to lick through him.

The snow was coming down thicker as he and Molly made their way to the house. He tried to take comfort from that. If Sabatini's men *did* have a second set of car keys, the tracks left by the Blazer would be covered in a matter of minutes. They'd have to search the entire community along Bass Lake, and that was providing they even knew Mitch was here.

Still, Molly didn't seem willing to take a chance. Before he'd closed the front door behind them, she kicked off her boots in the foyer and started to move through the house, turning off lights. She hadn't said more than a dozen words during the drive back. Then again, he hadn't been any conversationalist himself. He'd been practically speechless, thinking about what he'd just witnessed, amazed and shocked at the extreme courage Molly had displayed tonight. It was a side of her he'd never seen, even though he should have expected it from her.

Molly had always been somewhat fearless. Bold and spirited. Always prepared to do battle for whatever person or cause needed defending. He hadn't been at all surprised to learn about the bronze star she'd received from the police department. It had been four…no, five years ago, when she and her patrol partner had single-handedly saved the life of a convenience store owner during an armed robbery while they'd been off duty.

But seeing Molly tonight, atop the snowbank, firing one round after the next, and then racing out into the spray of bullets to steal the thugs' car keys…

It was like a movie, Mitch thought. Only the bullets had been real.

Very real.

He shuddered now at the thought of how the night could have taken a very different turn. No, he shouldn't consider how close they'd both come to being killed tonight. Mitch focused his attention instead on the fire in the hearth. He stirred the ambers with a poker and was just reaching for a fresh log when Molly stopped him.

"Leave it," she instructed. "Let it die. Turn up the furnace if you need to, but if they *do* come looking for us tonight, we want the house to look empty."

"You think they will?"

"Maybe not tonight. I'm guessing they didn't have a spare set of keys. But I'm sure they'll be rolling before long. Let's hope they wait till morning to start searching."

Mitch turned from the fireplace. Molly stood in the middle of the living room, facing him. And for a moment, illuminated by the warm glow from the hearth behind him, she looked nineteen again. It was one of the images that Mitch had carried in his mind all these years...of her standing in the middle of her bedroom with the light of a dozen candles dancing across her face.

Molly stared back at him, and he wondered what memory, if any, she was conjuring up herself.

"I, uh, I need to use your washroom," she said at last, obviously feeling awkward at the sudden silence.

"It's upstairs. To the left."

He watched as she tossed down her scarf and lifted her anorak over her head. It wasn't until then that Mitch saw the blood. There was only a hint of it on the dark-colored anorak, but beneath it, and the green fleece under that, the startling crimson stain had spread across the snug-fitting thermal top.

"Jesus, Molly, you're bleeding!"

''I know.'' Her tone sounded so matter-of-fact. However, Mitch thought he detected a slight waver in it.

In a second he'd crossed the room. Before she was able to cast aside her jacket and fleece, Mitch was gently tugging the top from the waist of her jeans. It was soaked, as was the heavy denim. He thought he heard her quick intake of breath and sensed her body stiffen as he lifted the top farther. The hearth provided enough light for him to see the blood glistening against her skin, and the dark, ragged tear in the flesh of her midriff.

''You got shot?''

''I guess so.'' She looked at the wound herself now, and let out a small groan.

''How bad is it?'' he asked.

''It's fine.''

''Fine, my ass. Look at all the blood!''

''Mitch, really. I'm all right.'' She inspected the injury again. ''It's just a graze. It looks worse than it is.''

''Come on.'' He took her hand in his, refusing to let her protest further, and led her to the stairs.

In silence she followed him.

How was it that people never changed? Molly was just as stubborn now as she had been at ten. That was the first time Mitch had witnessed her unparalleled stoicism. Never a whimper. Never a complaint. Not from Molly Sparling.

They'd been out at Fisher's gully, climbing trees, playing some ridiculous kid's game that he couldn't even remember anymore. Molly had slipped, and fallen a good twelve feet. She'd had a nasty scrape along her cheek, and Mitch had figured that to be the reason behind the tears he'd seen well up in her eyes. But she hadn't shed a tear. No, not Molly.

They'd walked all the way back to his house, at least a mile or more. And only there did he find out she'd actually dislocated her shoulder. Even then, he wouldn't have known had it not been for his mother's insistence on driving her to the hospital so it could be reset.

Molly was definitely one of the toughest. Always had been.

Mitch stopped when he reached the bathroom at the end of the hall. He flipped on the lights and parked her next to the sink while he rummaged in the cupboard underneath for the first aid kit. And when he stood, Molly was already unbuckling her gun's holster and gingerly sliding the leather straps over her shoulders. He saw her grimace as she lifted the edges of her blood-soaked top and pulled it over her head.

In spite of the ghastly injury and the dark crimson smears across her stomach, Mitch couldn't prevent his gaze from taking in the full sight of her. Standing before him, wearing nothing more than the pair of faded jeans and the delicate white lace bra, she was an image directly from his fantasies. Her olive-colored skin looked as radiant as his memory had kept it all these years, and he could almost feel its softness under his fingertips, even though he hadn't touched her yet.

Molly had certainly grown up. Where she'd been more angular as a teenager, she now possessed the rounded and seductive curves of a woman. The shyness and modesty of her youth were gone as well, replaced with a bold confidence.

She was beautiful. Even *more* beautiful than his memory had made her out to be.

Mitch fought back a groan that echoed the pull of desire he felt deep inside. And as if the sight of Molly wasn't enough, there was the smell of her.

Jasmine.

In all these years, that one scent held more memories than any other for Mitch. He wondered what it was—if it was her soap or her shampoo—because he knew Molly never wore perfume. Even the small, expensive bottle he'd bought for her sixteenth birthday had hardly seen any use.

Mitch wasn't sure how long it took him to tear his gaze away from her and sort through the first aid kit for the cotton swabs and alcohol. She said nothing as he started to wipe at the blood, dabbing her skin gently, working toward the glistening gash. And as he got closer, Molly placed a hand on his shoulder. It rested there at first, but the second he touched the swab to the ragged tear in her skin, he heard her quick intake of breath and felt her fingers dig into his muscle.

"Sorry."

"It's all right," she whispered.

Perhaps it was the long silence, or the way it was broken by the seduction of her voice... For the first time Mitch wondered if there was someone in Molly's life. He didn't know why he hadn't questioned it before, but now that he thought of it, he realized there *had* to be, even though she wore no ring. With her beauty, her strength, not to mention her unbelievable magnetism, it was insane to think that there *wasn't* someone in Molly's life.

"I'm going to have to call my partner back in Chicago in the morning." Molly broke the silence, and Mitch wondered if she felt the same awkwardness he did in the close quarters of the bathroom.

"With this storm," she continued, "I doubt the local authorities are going to find my Jeep, let alone do anything about it until morning. It's probably a small police force up here, so I'm sure it'll take them some time to run my tags. Hopefully Adam can get ahold of them before then and calm them down a bit. I don't think we should take the risk or the time to speak with them ourselves."

"Well, I'm certainly not going to be around long enough to talk to them," Mitch told her. "I'm packing up and getting out of here just as soon as I get a bandage on you."

"Why?"

"Why? Why the hell do you think?" He stopped swabbing long enough to look up and meet that mesmerizing gaze of hers. "We've just been shot at—and even *that* is a gross understatement. I don't know what your theory is on this, but *I* don't think it's such a good idea to stick around and wait for those two to come knocking at the door."

"They're not going to come around here, Mitch. At least, not until tomorrow at the earliest. We're okay for tonight."

"How can you say that?"

"It's late. And it's a good-size community here. They don't know where you are, so they'll have to start knocking on doors."

"How do you know what they know?"

"Because if they knew where you were, Mitch, they would have gotten to you already. And they certainly wouldn't have been waiting around for us back at the Jeep."

"You're saying they followed your Jeep, and then lost you when you came in by foot?"

"Most likely. Yes. That's why they were waiting. They knew I'd be coming back for my car."

He sensed the stiffening of her spine, and felt her fingertips dig a little deeper into his shoulder as he brushed the cotton swab across the gash a final time.

"So they followed *you* then. Probably all the way from Chicago," he suggested, cutting a piece of gauze and ripping off several sections of tape.

She hesitated before whispering, "I guess."

Mitch shook his head. He was silent until he'd taped the gauze over her injury. Only then did he stand and face her.

"I don't believe this," he said. "I was safe here. Nobody knew where I was. And then you show up, and all of a sudden I have Sabatini's men all over me, trying to run me down, shooting at me. For God's sake…''

''I'm sorry.''

''*Sorry?* That's all you can offer? You brought them here, Molly. *You* did. Didn't you even know you were being followed?''

She shifted then, obviously uncomfortable being the focus of his scrutiny. He could see her shoulders tense and a muscle flex along her jaw as she crossed her arms over her chest.

''I'm a good cop, Mitch.''

''I'm sure you are. But you can't deny that it's because of you Sabatini's men found me.''

''They would have found you anyway. You're just lucky I got here first.''

She seemed so confident with the statement that Mitch wondered if she *was* right. Maybe it would have been only a matter of time before Sabatini's thugs found him up here in Canada. And without Molly…he certainly wouldn't stand much of a chance against their firepower.

He cast a glance down at the heavy, black semiautomatic on the rose-colored vanity. It seemed so out of place. Molly obviously sensed his line of thought then. With a visible degree of physical discomfort, she leaned over to lift the cuff of her jeans. He shouldn't have been surprised at the sight of the weapon strapped to her ankle.

''I know you hate guns,'' she said, ripping at the Velcro fasteners. ''But I want you to keep this one with you.''

The gun was more compact than her Glock, and the polished nickel gleamed when she turned it over in her hand. Molly had always displayed an ease around guns. Mitch accredited it to the fact that her father was a cop and had made it a point to teach both her and Mitch how to shoot when they were teens. Mitch had hated those trips to the gun range...except for the fact that he'd get to spend more time with Molly.

"I know you know how to use it," she stated, lifting the weapon toward him.

He was already shaking his head. "I don't want to carry one."

"Mitch, you have to. It's too dangerous for you not to. Take it." She forced the weapon into his hand. "If I have my way, you won't have to use it. Now, if you don't mind, you could dig out an extra sweater for me. And maybe a drink. I could use something to dull this pain a little."

Chapter Five

The second Mitch walked out the door, Molly breathed a sigh of relief. The bathroom had been far too cramped for the two of them, she thought now, turning to face herself in the mirror. Too cramped for the memories, and definitely too cramped for the physical attraction she'd felt crackle across the narrow gap that had separated them.

She took in another deep breath, trying to quiet the flutter that had started inside of her the second he'd lifted her top. Shifting to catch the light, Molly inspected Mitch's handiwork.

He'd been gentle. *So* gentle.

Should it have surprised her? Hadn't Mitch always been the most tender man she'd ever met? Ever since they were kids, she'd always thought of Mitch that way. And later, when they were lovers…well, granted, there hadn't been many others, but no man had come close to comparing to the tenderness Mitch had always shown her. She'd been reminded of that the second he had touched her tonight, one hand resting lightly on her hip as he cleaned her wound, the soft heat of his palm whispering memories to her.

"No." The sound of her own voice forced back the images. And if that wasn't enough, Molly patted at the edges of the tape that held the bandage in place. It still stung like hell, giving her a sharp bite of reality.

And the reality was she was here to bring Mitch back to Chicago. Nothing more.

"Did you say something?"

Molly jumped at the sound of his voice.

"No. Nothing." She turned in time to see him fill the door frame.

"Here." In his hand he held a flannel shirt and a wool sweater. "I'm not sure what you'd prefer. These are mine, but Barb's got an entire closet full of clothes. Maybe you ought to go through it and find yourself some things. You can have these in the meantime."

"Thanks."

He hesitated then, handing her the clothes and lingering in the doorway as he seemed to take a final hungry gaze. It was only once his eyes met hers that Mitch cleared his throat and stepped back.

"I'll...I'll go downstairs. Pour us some drinks."

"Thank you," she said again. She watched his broad shoulders when he turned down the hallway, and listened to his fading footfalls on the stairs.

Molly flinched again at the sharp pain in her side as she slipped the flannel shirt over her shoulders. She buttoned it, the soft fabric sliding through her fingers, as she breathed in the scent of Mitch—fresh and masculine. It lifted from the shirt's collar, bringing with it too many deep and long-denied desires.

When she met her own gaze in the mirror, Molly took a long, hard look at herself. Mitch had every right to be angry with her for bringing Sabatini's men to his doorstep. *How could she have let it happen? How had she not noticed a car tailing her all the way from Chicago?*

But she knew how. She'd been so intent on finding Mitch, her mind so fixed on seeing him again, that she'd not paid much attention to her rearview mirror. Then again, why should she? Why should she have even suspected she'd be followed up here? How could Sabatini have found out about her? Yes, it was a well-known fact—even by Sabatini himself—that Molly would do just about anything to get him.

But how had he known what she was up to?

"Would you prefer Scotch or brandy?" Mitch called from the bottom of the stairs.

"Uh…Scotch would be great," she answered, hurriedly straightening the shirt and running her fingers through her damp hair. Taking a last look at herself, Molly snatched up her Glock and its holster from the vanity and headed downstairs.

She found him at the fireplace again. He held one glass in his hand, and the glow of the dying flames reflected in the amber liquid as he swirled it around in the tumbler.

He said nothing when he handed her another glass from the mantel. Even when she thanked him, he was silent.

Molly took a sip from the tumbler, feeling the smooth liquid warm her throat. Any second now she expected to feel the alcohol dull the edges of her tension. She needed that, she decided, and took another long sip.

"Are you okay?" she felt compelled to ask him at last.

He nodded, his stare still fixed on the embers. Tilting back his own glass, he finished off the Scotch and turned to her at last.

"I'm sorry about your Jeep."

Molly shrugged. "It's only a car. I'm just glad we weren't in it. Thank you, by the way."

"For what?"

"For saving my life back there."

"Well, I think *I'm* the one who should be doing the thanking."

She watched as he crossed the living room and poured himself another shot.

"So does your sergeant know you came all the way up here to get me?" he asked.

"No. The police don't know you're alive. They suspect Sabatini got to you before the explosion."

"Good."

"Mitch, you...you can't keep running. You know that, don't you? You can't hope to elude these guys on your own. Sabatini's too powerful. After those two thugs, there will be four. Then six. He'll have a whole army of hired men out looking for you if he has to. He won't stop until you're dead."

"Well, the *police* certainly weren't able to keep me out of his reach, were they?"

"We don't know that for certain yet. The Bomb Squad and Arson...they're still investigating the explosion. They don't know yet if it was even deliberate."

"Oh right, and now you're going to tell me it could have been the gas line?"

"Maybe."

"Not too damn likely. You didn't see that explosion. *I* did. And that wasn't any ruptured gas line. At least, not accidental."

Molly tossed back the rest of her drink as well now. What would it take to get through to him?

"Listen, Mitch, you have to come back to Chicago. If three officers in a safe house couldn't protect you, then how the hell am I supposed to, single-handedly out here in the middle of nowhere?"

"I wasn't in need of protection until you showed up," he reminded her, his tone sharpening with accusation.

What else could she say?

"Why did you really come all the way up here?" he asked coldly. "To protect me or bring me in?"

She studied him then, holding his scrutinizing stare until he looked away. "Why should I even bother answering that? You're not going to believe me anyway, are you, Mitch? When you look at me you just see another cop, don't you? You think the only reason I'm here is to bring you in. You won't, for an instant, believe that I might be here because I'm concerned for your safety. Because I still care."

But Mitch didn't seem to have heard her last remark. Or, at least, he'd chosen to disregard it.

"So what did Sabatini do to *you,* Molly?" he asked coldly. "What kind of thorn does he have in *your* side that would make you drive all this way, hmm?"

"Fine! You're right. I do have a thorn in my side about Sabatini, okay? A deep one."

"I'm listening."

It was Molly's turn to look away. She didn't want Mitch seeing the emotion she knew came to her face whenever she thought of Tom and remembered that dreadful night. She reached for the bottle of Scotch and poured herself another drink.

"Molly?" he prompted again.

"He killed my partner. In cold blood."

"I'm sorry."

"Tom Sutton," she continued. "We were partners on patrol together for almost five years. We went on to separate investigative units after that, but we were always close. He was working undercover Vice at the time, over a year ago. Tom had been digging for evidence against Sabatini and his gang on a number of felonies, from money laundering to illegal gambling. And…when he got in too deep, Sabatini had him murdered. Shot in the back."

At last the Scotch was numbing her senses. But it wasn't enough. Molly took another drink.

"We've never been able to bring any charges against

Sabatini in Tom's murder. Probably never will. But if there's a way that I can bring him to justice—even on something unrelated—I will, Mitch. I'll do whatever it takes. Including bringing you back with me to Chicago.''

There was something in his stare then, something behind those dark eyes that made Molly believe he was on the verge of agreeing. But then Mitch started to shake his head. He downed the last of his own drink.

''Except…I'm not testifying,'' he said at last, turning from her.

''How can you *not?* After what that monster did to you? After what he did to…''

She'd almost said it.

Emily.

But even though she had stopped herself, the name floated through the air as clearly as if she'd spoken it.

When Mitch turned this time, even the shadows of the living room couldn't conceal the pain Molly saw in his eyes.

''And what makes you think that even if I *did* testify against Sabatini, I'd be safe? His reach goes beyond prison walls, Molly. Do you think I don't know that? Do you think I'd be fooled into believing that—even if the D.A. managed to get a conviction—I'd be safe? That I can go about my life as though nothing had happened? Come on, Molly. I might not be a cop, but I know how the system works.''

''Okay, you have a right to those fears. But that 'system' is set up to protect you, Mitch.''

''Oh, right. You mean some Witness Protection program?''

''Of course. There are all kinds of—''

''Witness Protection?'' he interrupted. ''*Please.* Do you know *anything* about me? Anything about my firm and its success?''

Molly nodded. Even if she'd not followed his career

through the media, she would have known of Drake Designs' success. Mitch had seen to that. An invitation to the grand opening of Chicago's new Carlisle Office Complex had been mailed to her, care of the Fairfield Police Department. The envelope had been addressed to Detective Molly Sparling, Homicide Unit.

It was the invitation that had proved to Molly that Mitch had been keeping tabs on her as well over the years. Not only had he known where to find her, but he knew which unit she was with.

"Do you?" Mitch prompted her again.

"Yes, I do. I got your invitation."

"And do you have any idea what a name means in this business? Do you know what 'Mitchell Drake' represents in the world of architecture?"

Even if she'd known what to say in response to his mounting anger, Mitch didn't give her a chance.

"I've spent the past seven years building a reputation. And that reputation is synonymous with my name. Without the name, I'm nothing. So *please* don't try to placate me with suggestions that I start over, that I launch a new career. I've heard enough of that crap from the D.A.'s office already. It would take me years. And long before then I can guarantee you that Sabatini will have found me out, if by no other means than through my work. So, if you want to talk about Witness Protection, let's talk about the end of my career."

"And what's more important, Mitch? Your career or your life?"

"Life? Come on, Molly, I don't have a life anymore. My life was taken away the night I saw Sabatini shoot that undercover detective. Sergio Sabatini took my life away. So pardon me if I'm a little *attached* to my career right now. It's all I've got left, all right?" He turned his back to her then, facing the hearth.

Ten months in safe houses. Ten months of being jerked around by the D.A.'s office. Ten months of police officers watching your every move. *That* was the anger she heard from Mitch now, Molly realized.

That…and the loss of his wife.

"I'm sorry," she said at last, moving across the room to close the distance between them.

When she placed a hand on his shoulder, he didn't pull away as she expected he might. Under her fingertips she felt his muscles, tight and knotted. She didn't doubt the tension had been there for months.

"I'm sorry about Emily, Mitch." She squeezed his shoulder, but there was little obvious comfort in the gesture. "I know it was an incredible loss, and I'm sure it must seem like the end of the world, but…you've got a life, Mitch. You're alive. And you can choose to do anything you want with it. You'll get beyond this. I promise. You *will*."

But they were empty words. After all, how could *words* possibly console such a hurt? Such an emptiness?

Molly felt the muscles in those broad shoulders tighten even more, and when Mitch turned to face her, she couldn't remember if she'd ever seen such rage as she did from him now. For a brief second her eyes flitted from his to the tumbler he held in one hand. His knuckles were white around it, and she imagined the glass exploding under the force of his anger.

"Loss?" he asked, nailing her to the spot with those dark eyes. "What do you know about loss, Molly, hmm? How can you possibly know what it is I feel? To lose everything in one moment. All your plans, your hopes, your dreams…all gone in an instant. How can you know what that's like?"

And then, as though it had been brewing for the past twelve years, Molly felt the surge of her own anger. The years of resentment and bitterness rose within her. Her own broken dreams, the shattered heart, the unanswered questions...

"Geez, Mitch, how *could* I? How could *I* possibly know about having every last dream and hope stripped away?"

There was no mistaking the change that came over Mitch's face then. His eyes narrowed as he matched her stare, and his mouth tightened into a thin line. He understood exactly what she was referring to.

"I'm going to bed," he said at last, his voice so low she almost didn't catch the words.

Molly smelled the faint trace of his aftershave when he brushed past her. She turned in time to watch him stalk out of the room, running a hand over his short hair and shaking his head as he stepped into the hall and turned the corner. Then he was gone.

Immediately a sense of remorse came over her. She'd not been fair. Not at all. No matter how much she had believed she would be with Mitch for the rest of her life, a teenage romance could not possibly compare to the death of a spouse. Especially after eight years of marriage.

Mitch was right in saying she had no idea what that kind of loss was like. She'd been wrong to draw such a comparison. Selfish, even.

Molly set down her glass and contemplated the wisdom of going after him. She stared at the doorway, searching for the words she needed to apologize.

But, no. She wouldn't apologize.

She had her *own* wound. A wound that had been too deep for too long. A wound that had had the scab picked off of it every time she'd seen his picture or heard his name over the past twelve years. And now...just when she'd thought that wound had healed, it was ripped open all over again. Only this time it felt to the bone.

No. There would be no apology. Not tonight. And cer-

tainly not until she understood the hurtful decisions Mitch
had made twelve years ago.

THE ELECTRIC ALARM CLOCK on the guest room nightstand
turned over another number: 1:18.

Mitch wondered if the old clock was dying a slow death.
Surely the minutes couldn't be passing this slowly. For an
hour now he'd lain awake, wishing for sleep but coming
nowhere near. His head was running rampant with thoughts
of Molly.

He imagined her asleep in the bedroom across the hall.
Then again, it wouldn't surprise him if she wasn't able to
sleep, either. Far too many emotions were in the air between them. That had been amply clear to Mitch when he'd
seen the anguish in her face.

It had been lit by the dying glow of the hearth, but
there'd been enough light to see the pain that racked her
fine features. And in those wide, dark eyes of hers, Mitch
was certain he'd seen the glisten of unshed tears.

Maybe his words hadn't been fair. It wasn't for him to
say whether or not Molly could comprehend the kind of
loss he'd suffered, the emptiness he felt from Emily's
death. How was he to know what Molly had gone through
since he'd seen her last?

Or, for that matter, how could he know what she'd gone
through when she'd found out about Emily twelve years
ago? He'd been all of nineteen—too young and stupid to
realize it fully at the time—but now he could easily imagine
the hurt he'd caused her. After all, he'd heard nothing from
her after that first time he'd brought Emily home to meet
his family at Christmas. No matter how many phone calls
he made to Molly's father, Molly hadn't returned a single
one. And the letters he'd written attempting to explain had
all been returned, unopened, to his college dorm.

Just as well that she'd never read them, Mitch thought

now, recalling some of the lame excuses his nineteen-year-old self had tried on her.

I'm sorry, Molly. It's not you. It's me.

And:

Things are changing so fast. I have a new life here in Boston. It's so different. I miss you, and I wonder, if you were here, whether things might be different for us. But you're not. It's like you're from my old life, and I feel like I need to move on. I think we both do, Molly. For now, at least. I'll always love you, though. Please remember that. And maybe after college…who knows?

Lame excuses. And lies.

But how else to tell Molly that he'd found someone in Boston who was everything Molly was not? Someone who wasn't the tomboy he'd grown up with, the girl down the street….

Emily had been fresh, exciting, and yes, absolutely stunning. With all that Manhattan poise of hers, she'd captured him the instant he'd laid eyes on her in the front row of Structural Analysis class. And from the moment she'd turned to meet his stare, Emily had charmed him. That charm had only died the day she did.

It had been easier, at the time, to blame the distance for the end of his relationship with Molly. Emily was there; Molly wasn't. For a while he'd thought that if he'd actually *seen* Molly that Christmas, if he'd been reminded of the love they shared, he might have ended it with Emily, believing it had been nothing more than a fling, motivated by curiosity. But he hadn't seen Molly, and she had remained so out of reach. And then, eventually, he'd convinced himself that what Molly and he shared had been a sweet high school romance and nothing more. After that, things simply fell into place with Emily.

But Emily had known. Oh yes, even when he hadn't realized it, Emily had recognized that he'd never really lost his love for Molly. Especially when she'd found Molly's old love letters to him, saved from his first year at college; his first year away from home, away from Molly. Of course, Emily had found them only weeks before their wedding.

"If they aren't important to you, Mitch, why have you kept them?" she had asked.

Her shock had been so apparent. Emotions always were with Emily; another huge difference between her and Molly, who had always managed to keep that cool, calm exterior.

Emily's hands had been shaking so violently, several of the letters had slipped from her fingers and fluttered to the floor as she'd held them up for him to see.

"You're still in love with her, aren't you, Mitch? You probably never stopped loving her."

"I'm in love with you, Emily. With *you*. Molly is in my past. I haven't talked to her in…in years. It was over a long time ago."

But he remembered the look in Emily's eyes, and the way her lips had trembled.

"Emily, it's *you* I'm marrying, okay? It's *you* I want to be with."

"I wish I could believe you, Mitch. It's just…the way you've always talked about Molly… I—I don't want you marrying me if you're not in love with me."

"But I *am* in love with you."

Mitch never knew if Emily believed him that day. He'd taken the letters to the attic and buried them deep with other memorabilia. He'd made it a point to never mention

Molly's name again, and he never tried to contact her. *And* he'd prayed that Molly would never attempt to contact him.

But he'd always been aware of Emily's reaction whenever one of his parents happened to mention Molly while discussing Mitch's high school years. He'd seen that stiffening in Emily's stance and the stony expression that would grip her soft features. And now, after twelve years, he finally understood why Emily had reacted the way she had. Even though his desire and love for Emily had blinded him to it, *she* had sensed the undeniable connection he'd shared with Molly. And she must have known that that kind of connection was rarely lost.

Mitch rolled onto his back and stared at the thin sliver of light that slipped in over the top of his door from the hallway.

Yes, Emily had certainly had just cause for concern. He realized that now. Mitch recalled the wave of dark panic that had crashed over him tonight the instant he'd seen the blood on Molly's top and then the deep gash left by the bullet. He remembered the warmth of her skin under his fingertips as he'd held her waist, and then the feel of her hand gripping his shoulder.

It was electric. There was no other way to describe it. Nothing else like it. Yes, he'd loved Emily deeply. But in all his life, no one had affected him the way Molly could. One look into those dovelike eyes of hers, one glance at the smile curling the corners of that tantalizing mouth, one breath of her familiar scent, one touch of that silky skin…

Mitch tossed again, kicking at the sheets to free them from the foot of the bed.

No, he couldn't think these thoughts. He couldn't let himself believe there was anything left between him and Molly, no matter how remote. Molly was here for one reason—to take him back to Chicago. And he couldn't let that happen.

If Emily were alive, he might be willing to testify against Sergio Sabatini. He might even be willing to consider the Witness Protection program, because at least with Emily he might be able to accept Molly's suggestion that life was more important than his career.

With Emily in his life...he'd know what to do.

Mitch rolled to his other side. Through the darkness of the room, he looked past the window into the black night. He could hear the cold northern wind swirl around the house, driving icy snowflakes against the windowpane. Habit caused him to reach across the bed, expecting to find Emily's warm, inviting body next to him. Ten months... and he still sought out her presence. Especially at nights.

God, he missed Emily. What he wouldn't do to feel her again in his arms, to hold her against him, and know that everything was back the way it had once been.

Mitch closed his eyes, searching for a visual memory of Emily. But it was Molly's image that filled his mind's eye as he finally found sleep.

Chapter Six

With one hand tight around the phone's receiver, Molly lifted the other to her neck. Gently she massaged the knot of muscles there, but with little affect. She'd be lucky if she'd gotten four hours of sleep last night with all the tension she had felt from the day's events.

And now she had Adam to add to the tension. Across the long-distance lines, there was no mistaking the accusation and the worry in her partner's tone.

"I doubt there's a single thing you've done these past couple of days that even *resembles* police procedure," he snapped. "Are you *trying* to get yourself killed, Molly? If you don't manage to do that, you'll certainly screw yourself out of a job here with the department, you realize that, don't you?"

Molly had reconsidered the wisdom of telling Adam about the war last night with Sabatini's thugs, and about her wrecked Jeep. But she'd had to. She needed someone to help smooth things over with the local authorities. The last thing she could do was spend time in some police station explaining the goings-on from last night. She and Mitch had to get away from Bass Lake as quickly as possible. In fact, they needed to get right out of Canada and on their way back to Chicago. Sabatini's men couldn't be far from finding them.

"Listen to me, Adam. Please. Just deal with the Jeep for me, will you? You have the serial and tag numbers, right? And you'll call the local police up here? I can't deal with them right now."

There was a pause over the line, and she could visualize Adam at his desk, his elbow planted, his forehead resting in his hand as he massaged the tension from his scalp. Then there was the release of his breath.

"Molly, what the hell are you doing up there? You found Drake, right? So just bring him in."

"That's what I'm trying to do."

"Don't tell me—he's not willing."

"Would you be?"

"If I had Sabatini's thugs shooting at my ass, I think I would, yes."

Molly heard the shower stop.

Mitch had woken early as well. He'd walked by the open doorway of her bedroom a half hour ago, obviously believing she was still asleep, and had said nothing. The shower had started upstairs only a few minutes ago. Nothing changed, she thought. Mitch had always been one of the fastest shower takers she'd ever known...unless, of course, there had been a reason for him to stay in there.

Molly suppressed the erotic memory before it could take firm hold.

"I still think you should talk to Sarge about this," Adam was saying, whispering this time, and Molly guessed that someone must have walked by his desk just then. She wished she'd been able to call him at home instead.

"I don't want others involved, Adam. Not right now." This time it was Molly's turn to lower her voice, no longer having the shower for cover. "Too much police involvement and I can guarantee you Mitch will run. No. This is something I have to do on my own. At least for now."

"This is insane, Molly. *Completely* against departmental policy."

"I'm on vacation," she reminded him. "You're the only one here bound by policy, and…if you can't bring yourself to keep quiet, at least until I'm closer to convincing Mitch to testify, well, that's up to you. I guess I can't blame you. But I *do* trust you, Adam. I trust you'll do the right thing, and right now that means keeping this as low-key as possible."

Molly drew the receiver away from her ear slightly. She was certain she'd heard Mitch on the stairs. But there was only silence.

"I don't like this, Molly."

"I know you don't. But please just trust me on this, will you?"

He mumbled something that she couldn't make out, but she knew he'd agreed.

"And one more thing," she asked.

"What?"

"I…I need cash."

"I knew it."

"Listen, Adam, I can't afford an electronic trail right now, okay?"

"Fine, but why do I get the feeling that you're referring to *my* cash?"

"Come on, Adam. You know I'm good for it."

"How much?" he asked resentfully.

"A few hundred. Whatever you can get your hands on."

Molly pulled open the first drawer of the side table and rummaged inside. It was in the second drawer that she found a map of Michigan.

"I need you to wire it—" quickly she trailed her finger along the most logical route, gauging the distance and the driving time "—to Mackee, Michigan. Can you get it there for this afternoon?"

"Which bank?"

"How should I know? Any bank, Adam. Just get it there. And then call me on my cell phone."

There was silence.

"Please?" she added, hoping to soften the tension she heard in her own voice then.

Finally, she heard his compliance. With little more than a "Talk to you later," Adam hung up.

She could count on Adam, Molly thought as she returned the receiver to its cradle. He was a good detective. A good partner. And even if he might complain bitterly, he'd be the first to break policy if it meant helping her out.

"Who was that?"

Molly nearly sent the phone flying off the side table. She spun around, startled to see Mitch standing in the doorway. He'd shaved, and his hair was still wet. He wore a white T-shirt under a camel-colored sweater that folded over the waist of his faded but fresh jeans. With his arms crossed over his chest, he leaned against the doorjamb. There was no telling how long he'd stood there, or how much he'd overheard.

"Who was that?" he asked again.

"My partner in Chicago."

"You told him where we are?"

"Of course I did. I need him to deal with the local police in regards to my Jeep."

"And you think that's wise?"

"I trust my partner, Mitch. If that's what you're asking."

He seemed to take a moment to scrutinize her, as though wondering whether he could trust *her,* before shaking his head at last.

"You can trust who you like, Molly. But given everything that's happened, *I'm* not about to trust any cop."

"What are you getting at?"

"Just that they weren't able to protect me before, and I'm not about to rely on them again."

"And that includes me?"

It was clear he didn't want to answer that one. Silently, he straightened away from the doorjamb and crossed the hall to the spare bedroom.

Molly followed. She stopped at the foot of the bed when she saw the knapsack and the few folded clothes. Next to them lay the Walther 380 she'd given him last night.

"You're leaving?"

"Of course I am. You think I'm going to sit around and wait for Sabatini's men to come knocking?"

"Good. I'll be ready in a few minutes myself."

"You're not coming with me."

His tone was flat, almost severe then, and he seemed determined not to meet her gaze.

"What do you mean, I'm not coming? Mitch, you're not going anywhere without me. It's not safe for you—"

"The way I see it," he interrupted, directing his focus on his packing, "you don't have much of a choice. After all, it wasn't *my* Jeep that got totaled by Sabatini's men last night."

"Mitch, don't be crazy. On your own, you can't possibly hope to—"

"I can take care of myself, Molly. Besides, how foolish would it be of me to let you come along when it was *you* who brought Sabatini's men to my doorstep in the first place?"

And then, as if on cue, the peal of the doorbell shattered the silence of the house. They both jumped. No doubt Mitch's heart was racing as rapidly as hers.

With her own gun still tucked away in her bag where she'd put it last night, Molly reached for the Walther. The handsize semiautomatic fit neatly into her palm, the cool nickel against her skin giving her a reassurance that nothing else could.

"I'll get it," she murmured.

But Mitch was right behind her as they headed down the stairs. He stopped at the living room window overlooking the front porch, and carefully angled one louver of the blinds.

When Molly looked at him then, she could actually see the relief that slackened his shoulders.

"It's only Dale," he said

"Who's Dale?"

"Dale Holcomb. Next-door neighbor. Nosey as hell."

"You're sure it's him?"

"Yes."

"All right then." Molly lifted the back of her fleece top and tucked the compact semiautomatic into the waistband of her jeans. Only after straightening the top did she reach for the door handle.

Dale Holcomb was a round man, made rounder still in appearance by the down-filled parka he wore. With the hood up, his face was circled by a halo of what was most likely rabbit fur, and what little face there was to see had already turned rosy in the cold.

"Oh. Hello?" Surprise lifted his voice as a puff of vapor momentarily obscured his face. "Just wondering if you folks heard all the commotion. Wondered if perhaps you knew anything."

"Commotion?" Mitch asked, stepping forward. He crossed his arms over his chest against the cold.

"Oh, yeah. Lots going on. More excitement than we've seen in these parts for years."

"What happened?" Molly asked, and received an inquisitive once-over from the man.

"Dale, this is my friend…Catherine. From New York."

"Oh, listen to him. 'My friend,'" she mimicked, giving

Mitch a playful shove and placing herself in front of him. "He's so shy about it. We're actually engaged. He just can't seem to say the word. It's *fiancé,* darling." She flashed a wide smile for Dale's benefit and leaned back against Mitch's chest.

It may have appeared perfectly natural from Dale's point of view, and to Mitch it must have seemed like a cover, but the gesture had been pure strategy. Molly hated the open doorway. They were completely vulnerable. They may as well be standing out in an open field for all the protection the porch offered. Who knew where Sabatini's men were? And since she wasn't about to invite Dale in for a neighborly chat, her best hope was to cover Mitch. She nudged him back inside as far as possible and placed herself between him and any potential assault.

"Oh, well, hey, congratulations," Dale offered.

"Thank you. So, you were saying about the commotion?"

"Oh yeah. Last night apparently. The wife and I didn't hear anything, but they're saying there was shooting. And an explosion even. Can't believe we didn't hear *that.* Cops say there was a car blown up, and—"

"The police?"

Dale looked to Mitch. "Oh, yeah. They're going around the lake, door-to-door, asking if anyone knows anything. Thought I'd let you folks know they'll be a'knocking."

"Thanks for the warning."

Molly felt Mitch attempt to step away from her, but she followed, keeping her back against his chest. And when Mitch reached for the door handle, Dale took the cue.

"Okay, well, you folks have a good day then. Let me know if you hear any other news, eh?" Giving them a final nod, he turned to waddle across the porch, his snowmobile boots squelching on the fresh snow.

Molly took a quick scan of the immediate area—the tall

pines, their boughs weighted with snow, the gentle slope leading down to the lake, and then the wide, open expanse of ice with a black-blue sky hanging low overhead. They couldn't stay here. Safety in numbers was good for only so long. And who was to say that the door-to-door knocking was really being conducted by local authorities, and not by Sabatini's thugs?

"WE'RE GETTING OUT OF HERE right now," Molly said, closing the front door against the raw cold.

"If you'll recall, that *was* my plan."

"Yeah? Well, your plan's changing. I'm going with you, Mitch, and I'm not wasting time arguing about it."

Mitch allowed Molly to push past him in the foyer and head to the living room. He considered arguing anyway, but was beginning to wonder if perhaps she was right. He couldn't handle Sabatini's men on his own. Eluding them after the explosion in Huntington had been easy; Sabatini hadn't expected him to survive, so he'd had a time advantage. But this small community was the only one in a twenty-mile radius. It couldn't take much for Sabatini's thugs to figure out that Bass Lake was the most likely hide-away, and once they were here, very little time to narrow down the possibilities.

That wasn't the only reason Mitch felt an urgency rise within him. There had been Molly's tactic at the doorway. He'd known exactly what she was doing, positioning herself between him and any possible threat. He'd sensed her fear that Sabatini's men might already be closing in on them, and he'd seen it in her eyes seconds ago when she'd scanned the horizon before closing the door…as though she expected to see them walk down the drive.

And if Molly was nervous, well, maybe he should heed that cop's sense of hers. Maybe he did need her. For now…

"We're heading to Mackee," Molly said from the living

room, and when he joined her she was folding the Michigan map and tucking it into the small shoulder bag that was her only luggage.

"I know you think you'll still convince me to return to Chicago," he began, but Molly didn't let him finish.

"Right now, returning to Chicago isn't my main concern, Mitch. Getting us out of here *is*."

She shoved several other items into the already crammed bag, and glanced around the room as though she might have left something behind. When her eyes met his at last, Mitch was surprised at the anxiety he saw there. It was so unlike Molly to become flustered, and now she appeared on the verge.

"If you want to waste time arguing how you won't testify against the man who is currently trying to have you killed, fine. But I have to at least try to get us as far away from Sabatini's men as possible. Drive me as far as Mackee. We'll pick up the cash my partner is wiring, and then we'll talk, all right? If you're still insistent on going your own way from there, then fine. I'll catch a train or whatever."

But as Molly held his stare, Mitch knew that there was no way she would climb on a train and leave him on his own. No, she intended to use every minute of the drive to Mackee to convince him that returning to Chicago was the right thing. As he watched her head up the stairs, Mitch knew it could be a very long day.

IT HADN'T TAKEN THEM long to get on the road, especially since Mitch seemed resigned to Molly's demands. He'd been silent as he dug out another knapsack and the two of them packed a few of Barb's clothes. Silent still as he'd closed up the house, locked the doors and started the Blazer.

Leaving Bass Lake behind them, they'd passed several

incoming police cars. Neither said a word. From the passenger seat, Molly had spent the first hour watching Mitch's white-knuckled grip on the steering wheel. It eased only gradually as they passed through Wawa and finally headed south on Highway 17.

For three hours they barely spoke, concentrating instead on the changing road conditions and the rearview mirrors. Only when they reached the border without a sign of a dark SUV tailing them did Mitch seem to relax somewhat. Still, he refused to let Molly take a turn at driving, obviously needing that sense of control he got from having the wheel in his hands.

It was around Kinross that Molly finally dozed off. She'd tried to fight her exhaustion, but between the drone of the Blazer's defroster and the large vehicle's gentle rocking, it was a losing battle. And if not for Mitch waking her two hours later as he steered them into Mackee, Molly might have continued to sleep much longer.

He reached across the seat and nudged her shoulder. Molly started slightly, taking a second to recall where she was. Sitting straighter in her seat, she squinted against the late afternoon sun's glare on the wet blacktop.

"We're here already?"

Mitch nodded, pushing his sunglasses a little higher on the bridge of his nose.

The sight of him sitting behind the wheel sent a flood of memories through Molly. How many times had she gazed across the front seat of a car to watch Mitch drive, one elbow propped against the window as he steered, while the other hand rested on the stick shift? It was so familiar. So comforting.

She couldn't remember the last time she'd fallen asleep in a car. In fact, Molly was quite certain she hadn't done that since her last drive with Mitch. Countless times as teenagers, Mitch and she would head out of the city on road trips. From the start Molly had always felt secure in his presence, in his driving, and she'd often fallen asleep across the bench seat of his father's Plymouth, her head resting in Mitch's lap while he stroked her hair.

The memory caused her to look over at Mitch again, half expecting to see the teenager she'd fallen in love with.

"How are you feeling?" he asked, lowering the mirrored glasses to meet her stare.

Yes, Molly thought, the eyes were definitely the same, but the mouth was sterner, and the lines in his face testified to the time that had passed and the wisdom that had been gained by those years.

"Good. Thanks," she replied. But the truth was her neck was killing her. Molly massaged the stiffness that had settled there again over the past couple of hours. "What time is it?"

"Almost four. I thought, since we're supposed to get the money here, we'd stop for a bite to eat. You hungry?"

"Starving."

He nodded again, edging the Blazer onto the main street. He was silent again for the next ten minutes, maneuvering through the downtown traffic until finally pulling into the lot of a diner at the west end of town.

In a booth at the back of the greasy spoon, they ordered, and Molly began to shed several of her many layers of clothing. The hours of silence in the car had created more tension than they'd started off with this morning, Molly realized now, not knowing what to say. Mitch, as well, shifted on the vinyl-covered cushion and fidgeted with the car keys on the Formica tabletop, obviously uncomfortable with the ongoing silence.

Molly watched his hands, admiring the strong fingers that still had a deep summer tan. How easy it would be to close her eyes and remember the way those hands had felt so many years ago. But she couldn't do that to herself.

Her gaze lifted to his face. He seemed deep in thought as he stared down at the table, and there was no mistaking the aura of defeat that seemed to sag his shoulders and deepen the lines across his forehead.

She liked to think that it was the sight of him, that it was sympathy and nothing more, that caused her to reach across the table and place her hand over his. But Molly couldn't be sure.

What she *could* be sure of was the feeling that swept through her then, the same one she'd felt last night when Mitch had touched her. *Desire.*

And yet it was more than that. It was like coming home again, after too many years.

He stopped fidgeting with the keys.

"Mitch?"

She waited for him to lift his gaze.

"I'm sorry," she said. "About everything. I know it can't have been easy…these past ten months. Being shifted from one safe house to the next, having no one…"

He waited for her to finish, but Molly didn't know what to say. After all, it may have taken some work, but she might have been able to arrange to see Mitch. Somehow. She could have been the one to be there for him. If she'd tried.

"Well, I guess what I'm saying is, if you need to talk, I'm here."

The corners of his mouth lifted slightly, creating a tired but genuine smile. He murmured, "Thanks," and Molly felt his hand shift beneath hers, as though he intended to hold hers in return.

It was the shrill warble of her cell phone that made them start then, their hands separating as they both sat straighter in the booth.

Molly flipped the phone open.

"Yes?"

"Molly, it's Adam. I've got your money for you," he said through a wall of static that forced her to shield her other ear.

"What bank is it at?"

"Huh?"

"Which bank?" she repeated, attempting to keep her voice as low as possible. Bad enough that her phone had caught the attention of several patrons; she hardly needed the content of her conversation broadcasted.

"Nations Bank. Branch number 8739 in Mackee, Michigan. You there yet?"

"Yeah, we made it."

"The branch is supposed to be on the corner of Robertson Drive and Main Street. That's all I could get out of the woman. You need their phone number?"

"No. That should do it. Robertson and Main, right?"

"Uh-huh."

"Okay. I got it. Thanks, Adam. I owe you."

"Yeah. Like I ain't heard *that* one a million times," he muttered. "So where you headed from there?"

"I'm not sure."

"Have you convinced Drake to come in?"

"I don't think so." Molly glanced up from where she'd written the bank's location and met Mitch's intent gaze. "Not yet, at least," she added.

"Any sign you're being followed?"

"Doesn't appear to be, but we're being cautious all the same."

There was a brief silence, during which Molly knew Adam was waiting for someone to move past earshot in the Homicide offices. "Listen, Molly, if you...if you need a hand, I can look into taking some days off myself. I don't like the idea of you bringing him in on your own. You need backup."

"We'll be fine, Adam. Really. I think I can handle it."

But Molly knew she didn't stand a hope in hell against Sabatini's men. She'd been lucky last night. *Damned* lucky. She could hardly hope for that kind of luck a second time around if Sabatini's men did find them. At the same time, she knew there would be no convincing Mitch of anything if anyone else was involved. "But thanks," she added, before turning off the cell phone and laying it next to the salt and paper shakers.

Mitch was shaking his head when she looked across to him next.

"What?" she asked.

"I don't like you trusting him with so much information," he said.

"Adam? He's my partner, Mitch. I have to trust someone."

"Well, maybe the someone shouldn't be a cop."

"And why not?"

"You don't see it?"

Molly shook her head. "What am I supposed to see?"

"A police connection to Sabatini. How else do you explain his thugs knowing to follow you here, or Sabatini finding the location of the safe house? And how else do you figure Sabatini knew he had to protect himself by killing your former partner?"

It wasn't a new theory to Molly. She'd turned that one over in her mind too many times to count. Especially after Tom's murder. How else could Sabatini have known that Tom was undercover, let alone that he'd been closing in on the mobster?

Tom was easily one of the department's best undercover detectives, and Molly had spent numerous sleepless nights wondering how Tom might have slipped up and revealed himself. But what if it hadn't been a slipup on Tom's part? What if someone else had tipped Sabatini off?

To think that one of their own could be leaking information to Sabatini...it was too frightening to imagine.

And yet someone else in the CPD must have had the same suspicions. Otherwise, Mitch's safe house wouldn't have been relocated every two weeks with such secrecy.

"Maybe it's even someone in your own unit," Mitch suggested. "I mean, in order for Sabatini to know to follow you, he must have been tipped off by someone who not only knew you were taking a vacation, but knew you were likely to use that time to try to find me."

"If you're suggesting that Adam—"

"Hey, I'm not pointing any fingers here. I just don't think it's safe to trust *anyone* right now. You can't know what information's being overheard or passed on. Who all knows you've taken time off?"

"Everyone on my squad. Probably everyone in the unit, in fact."

"And who would guess that you'd use that time to look for me?"

Sitting in this diner in the middle of rural Michigan, Chicago seemed a lifetime away, but Molly thought back to that morning only three days ago. *Who might have overheard her request for vacation on the morning after the safe house explosion?* The sarge's door had been open. Anyone...everyone there that morning would have heard. And the squad room had been full.

"Who?" Mitch prompted again.

"Everyone, Mitch. They all know the beef I have with Sabatini."

"Well, like I said, I don't think it's safe to trust *anyone*. And that includes your partner."

Molly was shaking her head as their food arrived. Only when the waitress left the table did she lean over her plate and lower her voice.

"I trust Adam, Mitch. He's been my partner for three

years. And right now I *need* him. I can't do this on my own.''

"Do what? Protect me?''

"Yes. You and I…we don't stand a chance against Sabatini's men. Last night…last night we were lucky. But if those men catch up with us again, I can't promise we'll be that lucky a second time.''

She reached across the table, pushing aside her plate so she could take Mitch's hand in hers again. She was grateful when he didn't pull away.

"I need to get you to Chicago, Mitch,'' she pleaded. "I know it sounds as though I'm trying to drag you into the belly of the dragon, but it's the safest alternative, really. I can't protect you on my own. Not out here.''

Mitch's hard gaze seemed to soften somewhat then, and Molly wondered if he was about to agree. But instead, he withdrew his hand from her grasp, took up his cutlery and nodded toward her plate.

"Maybe you should eat something, Molly,'' he said flatly. "Then we can get the money and find someplace to stay for the night.''

"Mitch, please,'' she begged one last time, "we *have* to go back. If there *is* someone on the force leaking information to Sabatini, I can't possibly hope to figure out who it is if I'm running around up here. I need to be in Chicago to launch an investigation into it.''

"Fine. I'm not arguing,'' he said as he speared a fry with his fork. "We'll find a place to stay, and in the morning we'll go to the train station so you can look into the schedule. Now, why don't you eat so we can get out of here?''

Chapter Seven

Dinner sat heavy in Molly's stomach. It wasn't the greasiness of the diner's food, however. It was her nerves that caused the low rumbling, she realized, pocketing the cash Adam had wired.

As she crossed the foyer of the Nations Bank, she knew the teller's eyes were on her. Molly had been on edge from the moment she'd stepped through the door, and she was sure the teller had to be wondering what her story was. Nervously, she'd surveyed the bank while the young woman had counted out the money, and when she'd finally taken the cash, Molly's hands had been shaking. After the dinner conversation and the suggestion of a police leak, she half expected Sabatini's men to descend upon her.

Added to that anxiousness, Molly worried about Mitch. He'd refused to come in with her. At first she'd believed it was out of a determination to keep a low profile, but now Molly was struck by another thought—what if Mitch hoped to take off? Leave her?

Pushing open one of the double glass doors, Molly cast a panicked glance across the small lot. Relief spread through her when she spotted the snow-covered Blazer. She lifted the collar of her anorak against the biting cold. It was getting dark. Headlights glared against the wet pavement. Through the mounting snow, she spotted Mitch's silhouette behind the wheel of the Blazer, and when the wipers swept the windshield clear, she met his stare.

She was being paranoid, thinking that Sabatini's men could find them so soon. She trusted Adam. Why had she allowed Mitch's doubt to affect her?

Still…an edginess was good. She shouldn't let her guard down. There was no telling who Sabatini's source was or how quickly the information traveled. And there was certainly no way of knowing beyond a doubt that Sabatini's men hadn't kept a low profile and actually followed them from Bass Lake into Michigan.

"No problems?" Mitch asked when she opened the door and pulled herself up into the passenger seat.

"No problems."

She settled in as Mitch nosed the Blazer out of the lot and into traffic. Removing the cash from her pocket, she counted out several bills.

"Take this," she said, handing him the money. "It's just a few hundred, but I want you to have it in case we get separated."

He seemed reluctant, but accepted the cash, tucking it into the inside breast pocket of his parka.

"So, any suggestions for tonight? Would you like to find someplace here in Mackee?"

Mitch shook his head and checked the rearview mirror. "No. I think we should get at least a little way out of town. Your partner knows we're here, and I'm sorry, but I don't want to count on him being the only one knowing."

"Fair enough. So do you have something in mind?"

"I know a place." Again he looked at the rearview, and Molly wondered if he saw something. "My parents took me skiing up this way once. I don't know if you remember."

Of course she remembered. How could she forget? Mitch had been sixteen and she fifteen. It was around the time when she'd been deciding Mitch was far more than just the boy down the street. And when Mrs. Drake had suggested Molly come with them on their Christmas-break ski trip, she'd seen it as an opportunity to finally ask Mitch what he felt about her. She'd spent the entire three weeks prior to the trip imagining the romantic getaway, rehearsing the things she wanted to say to him, to finally ask him.

And then, the day before they were to leave, with her bags packed and their contents painstakingly chosen, Molly had sprained her ankle playing basketball in gym class. No matter how hard she'd tried to convince her father she was fine, she'd barely been able to hobble across the room, let alone hope to shush down the slopes in northern Michigan. So instead of the romantic experience she'd fantasized, Molly had spent that Christmas at home in front of the television while her father had worked a double shift at the precinct.

Oh yes, she remembered.

"I think it's only about an hour out of town, unless this weather gets worse," Mitch was saying, checking the mirror again. He squinted, and Molly saw his grip tighten around the wheel.

"What is it, Mitch? Is someone following us?"

"Could be," he said quietly, as he took a right off the main street. "He's been on us since the bank."

Molly checked the passenger-side mirror, squinting also against the glare of headlights. She studied the grill of the dark-colored four-by-four as it came closer, waiting for the next streetlamp to offer more lighting. As though the Illinois tags weren't enough of a clue, the battered condition of the front bumper made it perfectly clear who was following them now.

"Any suggestions?" Mitch broke the tense silence.

"We have to lose them. As long as we're in town,

they're not likely to make a move. I doubt they're willing to risk having witnesses.''

Mitch made a lane change around a slow-moving truck. The black SUV followed suit.

''So, are you still convinced there isn't a police leak?'' Mitch asked, studying the in-town traffic ahead of them.

''They could have been following us all along.''

''No one was following us, Molly. Six hours on the road, I think I'd have seen some sign of them.''

''Then how else? For them to get to the bank... I got off the phone with Adam less than an hour ago. They would have had to be in Mackee already.''

''They've had all day to get to Mackee,'' Mitch said coldly, making another lane change. ''They didn't need to *follow* us. They probably already knew where we were headed this morning. In fact, they might have even hit the road before we did, maybe only minutes after you hung up the phone in Bass Lake after telling your partner to wire the money here.''

''I can't believe that, Mitch.''

''You don't have to. But the proof is right there.'' He nodded at the headlights in the rearview mirror. ''Now, unless you have any suggestions on how I should lose these two, you'd better hang on.''

Molly saw the amber light first, then felt Mitch's foot on the accelerator. The four-by-four didn't hang back. It shot forward, coming close enough that Molly could almost make out the driver's face, but then dropping back again once it had cleared the intersection.

She held the grip on the passenger side door as Mitch jammed the Blazer into third and cranked the wheel to the right, cutting off a snow-covered sedan. A horn blasted, and the driver of the sedan flashed his high beams several times. Still the four-by-four kept up with them.

The late afternoon traffic was thick—a blessing and a

curse. The driving was slow, but with enough vehicles on the road for cover, there was a chance of outmaneuvering Sabatini's men. It was all in the strategy. And Mitch seemed to have one.

Molly remained silent in the passenger seat, keeping one eye on the side mirror and another on the layout of streets. At the next set of lights, Mitch braked for the red light. Leaving a couple of car lengths between them, Sabatini's men stopped as well. Molly could only guess that it was fear of being identified later that caused them to hang back, because there was no concealing the fact that they were tailing them.

And then, as though a godsend, a maroon-colored compact nudged forward from the right-hand lane to fill the gap between them and Sabatini's men. Through the SUV's tinted windshield, Molly saw a flurry of movement from the driver's side; she was certain it was the driver slamming his fist against the wheel. But before she'd even begun to smile, Mitch came down heavy on the accelerator.

With the traffic light still glaring red, Mitch lurched the Blazer out into the middle of the intersection. Molly gasped, bracing herself against the passenger door, as Mitch cranked the wheel to the right. The heavy vehicle slid dangerously on the slushy surface as he cut across the right-hand lane. Horns blared. There was the squeal of tires across wet pavement, and in seconds Mitch had the Blazer tucked safely into the northbound traffic.

He was calm behind the wheel, Molly noted when she glanced over at him. He checked the rearview again, assuring himself, as she already had, that Sabatini's men were caught in the snarl of vehicles at the light. Several more intersections and numerous turns later, Molly was certain there was no way Sabatini's men would find them.

"I'm impressed," she said eventually, as Mitch gunned

the engine and they sped past the Come Again sign at the town limits. "You handled that well."

She watched a muscle flex along his square jaw as his gaze remained fixed on the road ahead of them.

"Just luck," was all he said.

"It was more than luck. You're a good driver, Mitch."

"Yeah? Well, I guess I wasn't that good ten months ago."

He didn't speak after that. And Molly could think of nothing to say herself. No words of comfort could possibly ease the pain she saw in his hardened expression.

He blamed himself. That was evident in the dark silence that fell over him now. Again the image of the battered sports car filled Molly's mind. The passenger side had sustained the greatest damage. Then again, the fire crew had done their share of destruction in their futile attempts to rescue and revive Emily.

Molly had seen the photos: the blood on the seats, the dash, the shattered windshield. And she'd read the reports indicating that Mitch had still been conscious when the rescue crews arrived on the scene. Had he known then that Emily was dead? Pinned upside down with his seat belt restraining him inside the twisted metal wreckage…had he seen her, called to her, tried to touch her as he waited for help?

Molly couldn't imagine the horror.

"It wasn't your fault, Mitch," she murmured in the silence.

"What wasn't?"

"Emily's death."

"You weren't there, Molly. So please, don't try to tell me I couldn't have done something different, that I couldn't have outdriven Sabatini and his men. Don't tell me I couldn't have saved Emily." His stare out the windshield remained fixed. "You weren't there," he repeated, and fell silent.

Molly settled back in her seat. There was nothing she could say or do to ease the pain so apparent on his face.

For twenty minutes they drove in the falling darkness. Countless times Molly checked the passenger side mirror, but the road behind remained empty. Only a thick swirl of snow churned in the vehicle's wake.

MITCH'S MEMORY WAS BETTER than he'd given himself credit for. He'd had to backtrack only once before he'd located The Pinery—the modest resort his parents had taken him to over fifteen years ago. It was dark by the time he'd steered the Blazer into the resort's drive, and beyond the lights of the main office, the wooded hillside was speckled with the warm illumination of the couple dozen cabins.

Molly had gone in alone to register, and when she'd returned to the Blazer, she told him she'd paid in cash and used the name Smith. She'd been given directions to the last available cabin, but even so, they'd spent more than a few minutes trudging through the snow to find it.

Now, at last warm from a hot shower, wearing a pair of fresh jeans and a heavy flannel shirt, Mitch squatted before the hearth of the small stone fireplace and stoked the embers. Over the low crackle of the flames, he could hear the shower running in the adjacent bathroom. The sound of the spray, the water drumming against porcelain…too many images leaped into his mind: Molly naked, her dark hair hanging in wet tresses around that delicate face, the water sluicing over her slender body and glistening on her olive skin.

The image, of course, was aided by memory. Vivid memory. A memory he knew would not die until the day he did. Nineteen years old. Home from college for the holidays. Her father had been on shift and Molly was home, anxiously awaiting Mitch's return from Boston. Only he'd been early.

From the foyer of the Sparling house, he'd heard the shower. He'd climbed the stairs, shedding his hat and scarf and coat along the way. The erection he'd felt straining against the fly of his jeans had surprised even him, especially since he'd felt it long before he'd stepped into the steamy bathroom. Once there, he'd eased back one edge of the vinyl curtain and promptly lost his breath.

It was bad enough he hadn't seen her in two months, but then to see her like *that*... Steam wrapping around her, water running over each curve and seductive angle, her face lifted, eyes closed, to meet the hot spray...

Of course, he'd never meant to scare her half-stupid.

Her gasps had turned to laughter, and eventually she'd stopped cursing him. And then...nothing had compared to the love they'd made in the shower...and out.

Mitch stood up from the hearth now, restraining an inner groan as he felt the familiar throb deep in his loins. He glanced over his shoulder. A wide bank of steam billowed out through the partly open bathroom doorway, and he wondered if Molly had left the door ajar for fear that he might decide to run.

Crossing the small room to a low dresser, he lifted the complimentary bottle of white wine from its cooler. He peeled the foil from its neck and worked the bottle screw into the soft cork. He filled two glasses, then downed half of his in one toss before turning to survey the one-room cabin.

He recalled Molly's reaction when she'd first opened the door of the small split-log structure. Mitch had watched her eyes scan the cramped room, then fall to the double bed against the west wall. Her gaze had stayed there for some time before Mitch had brushed past her with their two knapsacks and closed the door against the cold. Yet she'd said nothing, only offered him first turn in the shower.

Yes, the cabin was certainly smaller than he remembered. Then again, the two-bedroom cabins like the one he and his parents had stayed in had all been booked. This one was definitely cozier. And far more romantic. He'd always dreamed of bringing Emily to The Pinery for a second honeymoon. But whenever he might have been able to sneak away from the firm for a few days, Emily had always had some pressing deadline for the magazine. In eight years of marriage, their schedules had rarely been in sync. It was one of his deepest regrets. They should have made more time.

Emily. Ironic, Mitch thought now as he tossed back the rest of his wine, how after he'd finally recognized the preciousness of life, it was too late to share it with the woman he'd loved.

Mitch hadn't heard Molly enter. He started when she cleared her throat, and he spun around to see her cross the room toward him. Barb's clothes were easily a size too large for Molly, but not large enough that they masked the tantalizing curves just beneath the flowing silk-and-wool sweater she wore over a pair of heather-gray tights. She'd already spied the poured wine and took up her glass from the dresser before moving to the fireplace.

"Thanks." Her voice was a deep, sensuous whisper.

Or was the seduction just his imagination?

With the light of the fire setting her freshly washed skin aglow, Mitch's thoughts threatened to run wild again. *No.* He had to tame those rampant musings. The only basis for them was a teenage romance. And besides, he thought again as his gaze flowed over her, caressing each suggested curve with his eyes, surely Molly belonged to someone already. Back in Chicago, some lucky man was no doubt sitting by his phone, waiting for it to ring with news that Molly was safe.

Still…she *hadn't* called anyone other than her partner, Mitch thought. And surely she would have called a boy-friend or fiancé…or husband? After all, wouldn't he want to know she was safe?

Unless, of course, over the years, Molly had become her father. With Leo Sparling as her only parent and family, it was just as likely that she'd followed in her old man's footsteps and grown up to let "the job" mean more to her than anything else in life.

"This is nice wine," she said, breaking the silence.

Mitch took up the bottle to join her as she snuggled into a corner of the small love seat before the hearth. He refilled his own glass and topped hers up before lowering himself to the rug. Using the love seat as a backrest, he drew up his legs. The wineglass dangled between his fingers as he balanced his wrist on his knee, the dancing flames casting a hypnotic reflection in the pale golden liquid.

"How are you feeling?" He turned enough so he could see her, and when she obviously saw his gaze drop to her waist, where she'd taken the bullet last night, Molly nodded once.

"I'm fine. I put on a fresh dressing. Thanks for leaving it out for me."

"So was that the first time?"

She sipped her wine. "The first time…?"

"That you've taken a bullet."

"I didn't 'take a bullet,' Mitch. It grazed me. But yes, that was certainly the first time I've been shot *at*. I've been kicked and punched, beaten, thrown through a plate glass window and even been run down by a suspect's getaway car. But last night was definitely the first time I had bullets flying at me."

He studied her as she gazed into the flames, seemingly

entranced. She lifted one hand, her fine fingers combing several wet tresses from her forehead. The warm glow of the fire softened her features, radiating delicate femininity and vulnerability. Definitely a sharp contrast to the fearless woman who had held her own against two of Sabatini's thugs armed with automatic weapons.

"You were lucky," he said.

"We both were."

"Thank you, Molly. For saving my life."

A slight nod accompanied the fleeting smile that touched her lips, but she said nothing. The crackle of the fire and the wind battering occasionally against the windowpanes were the only sounds in the cabin for a long spell.

"So is it worth it?" he asked eventually.

"What's that?"

"Getting Sabatini. Does it mean so much to you that you're willing to be shot at? Risk your life?"

She paused, as though needing to think through her answer, but given the obstinance he knew was hers and the tenacity he saw fixed in her expression, there was no doubt that Molly had made up her mind long ago.

"Yes," she said. "It's worth it."

"But why you? Can't someone else nail him? Why does it have to be *you* who brings Sabatini to justice?"

"I already told you. He killed my partner."

But there was more to it than that. Mitch could tell by the way her mouth tightened and how she avoided eye contact, staring into the fire instead. And he could tell by the whitening of her knuckles around the bowl of her wineglass.

"What else, Molly? Why do you *really* want Sabatini so bad?"

Still she refused to meet his stare. She took a sip of wine instead and stared at the swirling liquid in her glass.

"There's more than you're telling me, isn't there?" he

pressed. "Something possessed you last night when you went after Sabatini's men. I saw it."

The image of her behind that blazing gun, charging down the embankment, firing one round after the next...it would stay with him forever.

"There was a rage in you, or something. I don't know what. Was Tom...were you and he—?"

"No. Tom and I were friends. Good friends. Nothing more."

"So why then? Why this one-woman crusade?"

She shook her head, her gaze dropping again to her wine. Still she said nothing. She took another sip as though requiring the alcohol to loosen her nerves and break down the wall of silence she so obviously kept up.

"I guess, last night, I...I wasn't entirely honest with you about what happened to Tom," she said eventually.

"You told me Sabatini had him murdered."

"I think Sabatini did it himself. Shot him in the back, after he'd stripped Tom of his weapon. I can only guess the scenario that went down that night. But the point is, it should never have happened. Tom came to me for help. He told me he was in deep, and that he needed me. Only...I didn't get there in time."

She stared at the fireplace, but in her eyes Mitch could see that she was far away from this cabin in the woods in northern Michigan. She was back in Chicago, speeding down dark streets, desperate to reach her former partner and friend.

"I found him behind a warehouse, next to a Dumpster in a filthy alleyway. He was lying on the wet pavement, trash all around him. And...he was still alive when I got there."

Mitch thought he saw the trace of a tear threaten to slip from those dark eyes of hers.

"The hole in Tom's chest... God, I tried everything, but

I couldn't stop the blood from pouring out of him. He died in my arms...just before the paramedics arrived.''

"I'm sorry, Molly.''

A smirk of self-condemnation twisted her lips as she shook her head. "There's more,'' she said darkly. "The charges against Sabatini... We had the son of a bitch for murder one. As close to open and shut as you can get with Sabatini. I even had Tom's dying declaration. Only...I screwed up.''

"You were in charge of the investigation?''

"My sergeant was. Any cop shootings are handled by a sergeant. But I was the secondary detective. I was the one doing the legwork and the paperwork. I was the one who wrote up the search-and-seizure warrant on Sabatini's estate. I thought...I thought I'd been so thorough. I figured I'd thought of everything, crossed all my t's and dotted every i on that warrant. I had more than twenty uniforms going over Sabatini's place the next morning with fine-toothed combs, and guess where we found the murder weapon?''

Mitch shrugged.

"In his damned car. It was right there, under the driver's seat. God, Sabatini was so smug about it all. He just drove that Cadillac in through the gates with a dozen cruisers parked right there at his front doors. Stepped out of his car and didn't so much as flinch when one of the officers pulled the weapon out from under the seat. It was as if the son of a bitch knew.''

"Knew what?'' Mitch prompted her.

"He knew the gun would be deemed inadmissible. He knew...*somehow* he knew what my search-and-seizure warrant covered, and I'd forgotten to include the damned Caddy. Because he drove in after we'd already begun the search, and because I'd failed to specify the vehicle in the warrant, it was essentially off-limits to us.''

"So the murder weapon was thrown out?"

Molly nodded.

"But why couldn't they have gone to trial on what you had? On Tom's statement?"

"The D.A. didn't like it. Said it was all we had, and it wasn't enough. Tom…hell, *every* cop on the force wants Sabatini. The defense would have shot down the dying declaration, making it seem that Tom…or even *I* had been trying to set up Sabatini. The statement would have worked only with the murder weapon."

"So the D.A. threw the case out?"

Again she nodded. "Said it was a lost cause. Not worth the money of a trial."

This time it was Mitch's turn to nod. Now he understood the woman who had returned fire against Sabatini's men last night, the woman who had driven all the way up from Chicago on the slim chance that she might find him, and then convince him to testify. It was clear to Mitch that Molly would do just about anything to see Sabatini behind bars. And, before the long string of safe houses, and before he'd realized that even the police weren't able to protect him, he *too* would have done anything to see Emily's murderer put away.

He expected Molly to launch into another attempt to persuade him to return to Chicago, but she didn't. Instead, she slid off of the love seat and joined him on the rug. Crossing her legs, she sat close, cradling her wineglass in one hand as she ran her fingers back through her damp hair.

"Tell me about that night, Mitch. When Sabatini ran you off the road. What did you see?"

"It's all in the police reports, Molly. I'm sure you've read them more than a few times."

"Yes, but maybe…maybe by talking about it again, you'll remember something else. Something useful."

"Useful for whom?" There was no biting back the resentment he heard in his own voice. "*I* certainly don't need to relive that night again."

"Please, Mitch?"

God, but those dark eyes of hers wcrc wide and deep enough to get lost in. When Mitch looked at her now, it was as though the years slipped away. They were teenagers again, sharing intimacies, secrets, dreams. Only this wasn't a dream. The dark memory of that night was very much a reality.

"For me?" Molly prompted. "Please?"

If she hadn't taken his hand in hers then, he might have been able to say no and mean it. If he hadn't gazed into those dark brown eyes for as long as he had, he might have been able to look away and pretend that she was just another cop who didn't care what happened to him, as long as the D.A.'s office got their witness. But this was Molly. And her request sounded more personal than professional.

He glanced down at their hands, his nestled between the softness of her palm and the warm bend of her knee. With her thumb she stroked the curve of his wrist, and when she slid her fingers between his and squeezed his hand with a reassurance that was far too familiar, Mitch knew there was no holding back. For ten months he'd done just that, and now, in light of Sabatini's recent attempts, he did need someone to talk to. Someone who knew him. Someone…who cared. And as he sat beside her, swallowed by her consuming gaze, there was no doubt in his mind now that Molly cared.

He told her about the opening of the Carlisle complex, how Emily hadn't been feeling well, so they'd left early. He told her about the detour, and then the wrong turn. And finally, about what he and Emily had seen in the headlights: the men, the cars, the blast of the gun and then the victim crumpling to the ground.

How many times had he relived that moment? The surge

of panic whipping through him as Emily clutched his arm and he'd known the men were taking pursuit. The glare of headlights in the rearview mirror, the squeal of tires on the wet blacktop and then the bone-wrenching crunch of bumper on bumper and the first realization that they were in real trouble.

"Do you remember any of the other men at the scene?" Molly asked him at last.

"No. Of all the photos they showed me, the only man I was able to point out was Sabatini." He grunted a laugh. "If I'd known then who I was identifying…"

"But they made no attempt to have you ID the other men?"

"Sure they did. I went through pages and pages of mug shots without success. After that, the detectives seemed satisfied that they'd gotten what they wanted—a positive ID of Sabatini. Besides, he was the man holding the gun."

"The other men, though," she asked, "do you think you'd be able to recognize any of them again?"

Mitch shook his head. Too many other images filled his mind from that night. The other men under that dark overpass hadn't been the focus of his memories. "I don't know. Possibly."

"How many were there?"

"I'm not sure. A half dozen maybe."

"And not one of them sits in your mind? Not a single face?"

"Molly, I don't remember."

"Hair color. Clothing. Anything…"

"No, it was dark. *They* were dark. Suits, trenchcoats. All dark."

"And you saw only Sabatini?"

"No. I told you, I saw them all, but Sabatini's face was the one I remembered."

"And no others?"

"For God's sake, Molly, will you stop? I *don't* remember. It was ten months ago."

"I know, Mitch. I only thought that—"

"Well, you thought wrong." He removed his hand from hers, and the second he did so Mitch could see the apology in Molly's expression. "Look, sitting here in a cabin in the middle of nowhere, conjuring up past images that I'd much rather forget—thank you very much—is *not* going to do anything for my memory. God, you're just as pushy as you always were."

He stood abruptly then, needing to put distance between himself and Molly. He leaned one arm against the mantel and gazed at the fire. Even with his back to Molly, he knew she was staring at him. And finally, through the long spell of silence, her voice reached out for him.

"Is that why you left me, Mitch?"

"What?" He faced her, and was surprised to see how her expression had softened. The cop was gone, replaced with the vulnerable Molly he'd so rarely seen.

"Did you fall out of love with me because I was pushy?"

"No. I didn't…. You weren't pushy, Molly." But what he'd almost said was: *I didn't fall out of love with you, Molly.* In fact, the words were so immediately on the tip of his tongue, it frightened him. Had Emily been right all those years? Had he never really fallen out of love with Molly?

"It's all right, Mitch," she was saying, as though reading his thoughts in the tight lines of anxiety he knew were etched across his forehead. "You don't have to explain. It was years ago, and we were both young. And…I sort of know what it's like, to a certain degree. I know how college opens up your eyes. I can understand how Boston would be so different from Chicago, so fresh, so new. You were young, impressionable. You needed to move on, try new things.''

''Molly, I...'' But he didn't know what to say. It was ironic: after years of longing for the chance to explain to Molly, he finally had the opportunity, and had no idea where to start.

''We've grown up, Mitch,'' Molly added. ''I can look back on it now and understand. It's all right. I've forgiven you.''

But he didn't want her forgiveness. He wanted Molly to get angry. He wanted her to call him every name in the book, to tell him what a louse he'd been for leaving her in the brash, immature way he had. In fact, he *needed* Molly's anger, Mitch realized then, as though it might be the only thing to erase the guilt he'd carried all these years.

''I only wish...'' It was Molly's turn to stumble for words. She lowered her gaze to the wine in her glass again, as though unable to face his stare. ''I only wish there had been a way to...you know, to stay friends through that time. It was bad enough losing you as my lover...as my soul mate. But to lose you entirely...''

''I tried, Molly. You *know* I tried.''

Only when he lowered himself onto the rug next to her once again did she dare to meet his gaze, and he was certain he saw the glimmer of tears behind those dark eyes.

''I left messages with your father. You sent back my letters unopened.''

He wanted to remind her that it was a two-way street, that she could have contacted him. But all through the years, he'd always known it was up to him to do the contacting, no matter how many letters she'd returned.

''And later?'' she asked. ''Why didn't you try later...once I'd had the chance to get over you?''

But the shimmer in her eyes made Mitch wonder if Molly had *ever* gotten over him.

"Later, once Emily and I were married…I couldn't contact you. Emily was…she was jealous of what I'd shared with you. She felt threatened. And…I wasn't about to upset my marriage. I loved Emily, Molly."

He watched her mouth tighten by a degree, as though she were fighting back the pain she'd harbored for years. Again he wished she would just let it out. Just scream at him…

But she didn't. Her voice was soft. "So what about the invitation then? The one you sent to me at Headquarters for the opening of the Carlisle building?"

She tossed back the last of her wine, but refused to set aside the empty glass. It was as though she needed something to play with in her hands, something to focus on so she wouldn't have to look at him.

Mitch reached over to take the glass, putting an end to her restless worrying. And when he took her hand into his, he felt its brief tremble.

"Actually, the invitation was Emily's idea. I guess she'd gotten to a point where she didn't feel as threatened by the idea of you. Or maybe she just knew what it would have meant to me to have you at the opening."

Molly moved her hand, and for a moment Mitch thought she was about to pull away. But she didn't. Instead, she wove her fingers through his, returning the gentle squeeze he gave her.

"It would have meant a lot to me, Molly. I wanted you to come."

"So was Emily right?"

"About what?"

"Was she right to be afraid of what might have happened if you'd contacted me?"

Mitch dropped his gaze. He studied their entwined fingers, the feel of Molly's small hand in his driving every last memory home.

"I don't know," he said finally.

But he *did* know. Now, looking at Molly, seeing in person the face he'd seen in his mind's eye every single day of his life for the past twelve years, Mitch understood Emily's fears.

Unable to look away from those mesmerizing eyes, Mitch lifted one hand and gently toyed with one stray lock of hair. It was damp between his fingers as he tucked it behind her ear. He watched Molly's eyes close, and when she pressed her cheek into his palm he felt a raw desire unlike any he'd experienced before.

He knew he was going to kiss her. Knew that nothing could possibly stop him now as he leaned toward her, the scent of jasmine like a beacon for him. And as Molly lifted her mouth to meet his, Mitch knew there was no turning back.

The first shock of familiar longing drove through him the instant his lips brushed against hers. The heat of her lips, the warmth of her breath across his cheek, the moist welcome of her mouth…it was like coming home.

And then, from home to heaven. The sweet seduction of her kiss—arousingly hesitant at first—exploded with the same passion he felt. Slipping one hand behind her neck, he drew her deeper into their kiss, tasting her desire as distinctly as the wine that sweetened her lips. The low ache that had already started deep inside of him swelled. He tried to swallow the groan that rose from his throat, but when he heard Molly's quiet whimper there was no holding back. The dam broke.

She shifted closer, kneeling before him so that their bodies touched. Eagerly, he swept his hands down past her shoulders, letting them flow carefully over her rib cage and the curve below it where he knew her bandage lay. When his hands reached her small waist, he cupped her hips, and drew her even closer against him, feeling the heat of her body through the thin, sheer sweater, sensing the familiar curves.

How was it possible that all of his yesterdays could just vanish? That the years could simply wash away as though no time had passed? They were on the beach. Lake Michigan. The low waves licking at the shoreline, a sky full of stars above them… He'd held her like this back then, kneeling on a blanket in the sand, clutching her to him. He'd thought he would burst with wanting her, too impatient to strip clothes, too anxious to unclasp buttons or fiddle with bra snaps.

He felt breathless…as breathless as he'd been back then, barely eighteen years old, on that nighttime beach with Molly, making love for the first time. He'd been torn then, between wanting her right away and taking his time to kiss and touch every last inch of her exquisite body.

Even now, with maturity and experience on his side, Mitch wanted nothing more than to be inside of her, to feel her body move with his in the familiar rhythm of their lovemaking. He wanted more than just the memories. He wanted to lose himself in Molly, and in the driving passion that had so evidently never died between them.

He quelled another groan as Molly took his hand in hers. He knew what she was doing even before she'd lifted the edge of her sweater and slid their hands beneath. He knew where she was guiding his hand seconds before he felt the brush of delicate lace and then the glorious weight of her breast in his palm. And *still* his breath caught in his throat.

He found the hardening nub just beneath the lace, and circled it several times with his thumb before kneading the supple roundness of her breast. Her skin felt ablaze under his touch, adding to his hunger to feel every inch of her, to feel her skin burn against his. Desire coiled deep inside of him. He wanted far more. *Needed* it, as though being with Molly was one of…no, the *only* necessity in his life right now.

WITH ONE HAND BRACED against Mitch's broad chest, Molly felt his deep groan vibrate against her palm before she heard it slip from his lips. The sound of it sent another hot wave of desire sweeping through her.

She wasn't sure who had made the first move, who had kissed whom, but the second Mitch's mouth brushed across hers, Molly had been lost. She'd responded with equal passion. Her world narrowed: the cabin, the fire in the hearth, the wind at the windows…everything melted away by the heat of yearning that settled deep in her body.

With her hand still over Mitch's, she pressed his palm even more firmly against her breast, urging the long, square fingers to caress her. But Mitch needed no urging. Relentlessly he circled her nipple with the soft pad of his thumb, and her imagination needed only the smallest of leaps to remember what Mitch's mouth had always felt like in that same spot, and how it had never failed to drive her wild with longing.

She could hear her own breathing, as ragged as Mitch's, as though neither of them could possibly get enough from one another with just a kiss. Then again, this wasn't ''just a kiss,'' Molly thought. This was twelve years of abstinence. Twelve years with nothing but memories of the one thing she'd once felt she would die without.

She wanted more. *Much more.*

And when she felt Mitch's body shift against hers, a stinging disappointment cut through her as she expected him to pull away. But he didn't. Instead, he shifted closer still…close enough that she could feel his arousal, that she could sense the incredible restraint quivering along each muscle as he lowered his mouth to the top of her shoulder. There he pressed several long, ardent kisses, each one more seductive than the last. Slowly, he worked his way up the curve of her neck, stopping only once he'd reached the sensitive area just below her ear.

Mitch knew the spot. And only Mitch. No one else in the sparse string of boyfriends she'd entertained over the years had ever come close to finding the one spot that Mitch had discovered. No, Molly thought, it was more like Mitch had *defined* it.

Countless times she'd pressed her fingertips to that same area and remembered the feel of him, his touch, his kisses. She remembered how—the last night they'd been to-gether—he'd spent so long caressing her and kissing her throat that she'd almost climaxed without him touching her anywhere else.

It had always been one of the most erotic memories she'd had of Mitch over the years. But now, suddenly, that same memory made her instantly stiffen.

What was she doing? How could she be kissing Mitch, allowing him to touch her? Allowing herself to desire him? *Mitch*—the one person who had hurt her the most in life.

"Molly?"

She didn't answer. Couldn't. Her heart was too busy skipping over itself as she caught her breath.

"Molly, are you all right?"

He took her by the shoulders now, easing her back enough so he could look at her. The genuine concern she saw in his face shouldn't have surprised her.

"I'm sorry," she managed to say at last. "I...we...that shouldn't have happened."

It was a struggle to stand. Her knees felt shaky, her mus-cles weak. She gripped the edge of the love seat for bal-ance, taking several steps away from Mitch. She needed space. More than that, she needed reason. How could she let herself be played the fool...twice? Mitch was in no po-sition for any kind of commitment after his wife's death.

She'd seen his grief firsthand, listened to him talk about the woman he'd loved. How was he anywhere *near* the point where he could entertain thoughts of being with another woman? Let alone the one woman he'd left so wantonly twelve years ago?

No. She would *not* be played the fool again. She'd come so close. *Too* close. Even now, turning to look at him, Molly wanted nothing more than to return to Mitch's embrace, to kiss him again, to make love to him and answer the urges that had raged through her from the moment she'd looked into his eyes again after all these years.

He stood as well now, and started to move toward her.

It would be too easy...

No. She needed to get Mitch back to Chicago. That's why she'd come. And the sooner she got him there, the sooner she'd be safe from temptation, from his seduction.

"Listen, Mitch. We...you can't keep running."

Confusion tightened his face as he no doubt wondered how she'd made the sudden leap from their passionate embrace to her role as cop.

"You have to come to Chicago with me. Please. It's not safe if you—"

"Whoa. What just happened here, Molly?" He waved a hand behind him, indicating the small area before the hearth. "I thought—"

"I'm sorry, Mitch. It shouldn't have happened. It...it was nothing, it just—"

"It was *nothing?*" His eyes narrowed as he shook his head. "It was nothing?" he asked again. "Or was it maybe your way of persuading me?"

"What? What are you talking about?"

"Persuasion, Molly. Is that it? Did you kiss me just now hoping to convince me to go back with you to Chicago?"

"No! Of course not. You *know* that's not true."

"I do? How?"

"Because you know me, Mitch. For God's sake, I wouldn't kiss you unless…"

"Unless what?"

She couldn't say it.

"Unless *what,* Molly?" he prompted again, this time closing the short distance between them. "You wouldn't kiss me unless…"

"Unless I was in love with you," she finally blurted, her voice sharp, almost accusatory in tone as she spun away from him.

His eyes were on her back. She was sure of it. And when she turned to face him again, she could see that her confession had rendered him speechless.

"Truth is," she admitted, "I never stopped loving you, Mitch, okay?"

She watched the firelight flicker across the strong angles of his face and illuminate the lips whose kiss still burned on hers. She guessed then, as he stared at her, that the shock she saw in those dark eyes was not so much caused by the content of her statement, but rather by the fact that she had admitted it.

She couldn't be sure how many minutes passed with Mitch standing in the middle of the cabin, staring at her, but eventually he turned away, silent as he picked up the poker. Only after he'd needlessly rearranged the burning logs in the hearth did he speak again. Still, he didn't seem able to bring himself to meet her gaze.

"I can't trust the police," he said at last.

"Then trust *me,* Mitch," she whispered, daring to place one hand on his shoulder. "Trust me."

And the look he gave her at last offered Molly the most hope she'd had yet of convincing Mitch to return to Chicago.

Chapter Eight

After so many beds in just as many safe houses, Mitch would have thought himself used to the jolt he experienced almost every morning when he awoke. This one was less pronounced than all the others over the past ten months, and the moment of not knowing where he lay was far more fleeting than those before.

He blamed it on the lingering scent of jasmine.

Then he blamed it on the feel of Molly in his arms.

Opening his eyes, Mitch turned his head so he could see her. She faced him, her eyes still closed, her lips parted slightly and her jet-black hair framing her peaceful features. With her cheek nestled against the curve of his shoulder, he felt her breath fan warmly across his bare chest. She stirred once, nuzzling her body tighter against him, but she did not wake.

They'd gone to bed with few words after their kiss. Mitch had offered to sleep on the floor, but Molly argued they should share the bed. They were, after all, adults, she'd said.

She'd mumbled something about staying on her side, and he'd heard a tinge of bitterness in her voice when she suggested that she'd refrain from any "persuasion tactics."

And yet here she was—asleep in his arms.

He wanted to blame it on habit. After eight years sleeping with Emily, he had naturally been drawn to the middle of the bed sometime in the night and had taken Molly into his embrace. Perhaps even believing it was Emily.

But what then of the ten months he'd been sleeping alone? No, holding Molly in his arms this morning had nothing to do with Emily or with habit. It had everything to do with Molly, and the passion he'd felt rise within him once again last night. It had to do with him wanting her more than anything he could remember wanting.

He let his gaze linger on her mouth. How easy it would be to lean over and steal a kiss from those enticing lips, to press himself against her soft, warm body and feel her awaken. Respond.

Almost as though aware of his rampant thoughts, Molly shifted again. This time a quiet moan slipped from her lips, the sound reminding Mitch only too vividly of their kiss last night. Instantly his body responded.

Restraining his own groan, Mitch carefully eased Molly's head from his shoulder and slid out from under the covers. She didn't wake. Even after he'd rummaged for his clothes and dressed, she didn't stir. And as he slipped on his boots her eyes were still closed.

He stood next to the bed, unable to take his gaze from her. Again he wondered if there was someone in Molly's life. There had to be. Why else would she have pulled away from their kiss? If she was still in love with him, as she claimed, why wouldn't she have wanted more last night?

And, quite suddenly, the thought of someone else with Molly—another man holding her and kissing her, making love to her—was too much for Mitch to bear. He turned and reached for the car keys. Grabbing his parka, he was out the door as silently as he'd sneaked from the bed.

The cold morning air offered him a new level of lucidity. He filled his lungs and let out his frustration in a plume of vapor that momentarily clouded his vision. As it cleared, he stepped from the cabin's porch. Sunshine pierced the canopy of tall pines and raked brilliantly across the fresh snowfall.

Several more breaths of the crisp air and Mitch wondered if what he'd experienced in the cabin last night, and again in his mind this morning, had been nothing more than a dream. But as the scent of Molly lifted off the collar of his sweater, Mitch knew it wasn't any dream.

Snow crunched beneath his boots as he headed to the Blazer parked down the hill from the cabin. In his gloved hand, he gripped the car keys a little tighter.

What did he hope to do? Drive away? Leave Molly?

In the blink of an eye he could remember the desperation he'd seen in her expression when she'd touched his shoulder and begged him to trust her. But could she protect him? More important, could she protect herself?

Mitch cast a glance over his shoulder back to the cabin. *I never stopped loving you, Mitch.* Her voice whispered through his mind as it had a thousand times throughout the night. The confession had shocked him, even if a small part of him had already suspected that might be the case. But— quite possibly—what had shocked him even more was the fact that, during their kiss, he'd wondered about his own feelings for Molly. What he felt with Molly in his arms was something words couldn't come close to describing. It was like finally finding your way, only you never knew you were lost in the first place.

Was he still in love with Molly? Had he been all these years? Or was last night's kiss simply a product of longing? Of a desperate need for physical contact? He couldn't rule it out. He missed Emily. He missed human touch.

Either way, whether it was love or need that drove his libido, he couldn't be with Molly. Sabatini's men had no interest in her. It was *him* they were after, and as long as she was with him, she was in danger. He couldn't let Molly risk her life for him.

Around him, the resort seemed to be waking. Other guests stepped onto their cabin porches with backpacks and skis, loading up their vehicles in preparation for a day of skiing or snowmobiling. *People on vacation,* Mitch thought, stopping at the driver's door of the Blazer. *People with lives.*

He forced down the now-familiar, sour taste of bitterness that rose within him. *Where was* his *life? And what were the chances of him ever reclaiming it?*

Involuntarily his gaze drifted back to the cabin where Molly slept. He wanted to be with her. Last night, for the first time in months, he'd felt alive. Her kiss had revived him. Her touch had given him hope when he'd forgotten what hope was.

But being here, with her…it was too dangerous. Ten months ago he hadn't been able to save Emily. He was hardly about to risk Molly's life now.

STILL DROWSY WITH SLEEP, Molly stretched. She didn't open her eyes immediately, but rather basked languidly in the rested feeling she'd not experienced in a very long time. For months she'd not slept a single night straight through, until last night, until she'd found the security of Mitch's arms.

Mitch.

With a gasp, Molly sat bolt upright. Her anxious gaze darted across the empty room as her hand slid across to his side of the bed. The sheets were cool. *Too* cool.

How long had he been gone?

Flinging off the duvet, Molly swung her legs over the edge of the bed. The floor was cold against her bare feet, but she hardly felt it in her panic to cross the room.

He couldn't have left, she argued with herself in between curses. *Surely he couldn't have left.*

And then, from the cabin's window, she spotted him. He was approaching the parked Blazer, keys in hand. A halo of vapor circled his head and she saw him lift the collar of his parka against the cold.

Frantically, Molly scrambled back toward the bed. From the chest at its foot, she snatched up her clothes and hurriedly threw the sweater over her head. She grappled with the zipper of her jeans as she raced back to the window, half expecting to see the Blazer's taillights as Mitch drove off.

But he hadn't left. He stood next to the vehicle with one hand on the door handle. He stayed there for a moment before glancing back at the cabin, as though undecided, and finally Molly saw his shoulders sag. He shook his head and jammed his hands into the pockets of his parka. A wave of sweet relief rushed through Molly then as she watched him turn and start back to the cabin.

And it was in that same breath of relief that Molly's eye caught the glint from the thick woods beyond the bordering cabins. Something momentarily flickered in a ray of sunshine that pierced the heavy canopy of pines and found its way into the thick tangle of brush.

Instantly she felt the familiar edginess, a sharp coil of fear at the pit of her stomach. From the windowsill she snatched up a pair of binoculars and lifted them to her eyes. She tried to steady the cumbersome field glasses, sweeping their field of view across the far row of cabins and beyond the parking area. Already suspicion plucked at her nerves, causing her hands to shake as she fumbled with the focus, training the glasses toward the spot where she'd seen the glint.

A heavy spruce bough swayed. A sapling shook. And a clump of snow slipped from an overhead branch. All very

clear signs pointing to the man hiding in the snarl of undergrowth. Even then it took some doing for Molly to pin-
point him, dressed in heavy camouflage with a green-brown
toque on his head. He half crouched behind an enormous
snow-covered log, wedging himself against its rotted
stump.

And then, even though she'd already suspected it,
Molly's heart stopped when she saw the object that had
only seconds ago reflected the sun—the scope on a high-
powered rifle.

Adrenaline coursed through her, yet shock threatened to
paralyze her. Through the lenses she saw the sniper ready
himself, bracing his shoulder more firmly, cocking the
weapon and finally cradling his cheek against the black
nickel as he brought his eye to the scope.

The binoculars clattered to the floor, striking the scarred
pine planks a mere second before Molly was out the door.
She almost slipped on the porch, her stockinged feet instantly wet as she charged down the steps. Again she almost
fell at the east side of the cabin as she stormed around the
corner. She caught herself with her left hand as her right
clenched the rubber grip of her Glock.

"Mitch!" She yelled his name even before she'd
rounded the building. Several vacationers stopped at the
sight, but Molly was aware of them only as obstacles.

"Mitch!" She flew down the slope toward the parking
area, her feet threatening to go out from under her. "Mitch,
get down!"

The cold air felt like knives in her lungs as she took in
more air and was about to yell again. But Mitch had heard.
In one split second she saw shock register on his face as
she waved madly toward the sniper's hiding spot, and in
the next, Mitch was on the ground.

And somewhere in between the two there was the loud
crack of a bullet exploding from the sniper's rifle.

For one fearful moment, Molly believed the worst. She was still charging headlong toward Mitch when she saw him move. He was already scrabbling back to the cover of the car by the time Molly reached him.

"Thank God," she gasped, pausing only long enough to place a hand on his shoulder and meet his upturned gaze. "There's a sniper. In the woods," she managed to say between gulps of freezing air.

"Then get down." He clutched at the sleeve of her sweater, and she heard fear in his voice.

"No, Mitch. I have to go after him." She didn't wait for his protest. She yanked her sleeve from his grasp, circled the Blazer and plunged into the dense underbrush.

It was Mitch's turn to yell. Behind her he shouted her name, but over the pounding of her heart, she barely heard him. She stumbled over snow-covered branches and hidden rocks, thrashing through the thick weave of low branches. With her eyes fixed on the spot where she'd seen the sniper, she readied her weapon. Not that she expected any kind of gunplay now. There were too many potential witnesses at the resort; one round was all the sniper could afford. One well-aimed round.

And if she hadn't spotted him and raised a commotion by racing out of the cabin, that one round from the high-powered rifle would have been more than enough to kill Mitch.

Molly stopped. In a clearing only a couple yards from where she'd seen the sniper with his weapon, she strained to listen over her ragged breathing for any sound of him. The log that he'd huddled against was empty. She let the black muzzle of her Glock lead the way, but as Molly neared the log, she could see he was gone. The snow had been packed down by his weight. Standing within inches of where—only moments ago—the sniper had raised his rifle in a near-successful attempt on Mitch's life, Molly was left with a deep chill. Mitch could have been killed.

The idea of harm coming to Mitch churned her stomach and made her nauseous. She thought she might throw up, and swallowed hard against the sudden taste of bile.

They'd let their guard down. No, *she* had let her guard down. She should not have allowed Mitch out of her sight.

The sound of a revving engine and then the slam of a car door was the only evidence Molly needed to know that she would not be catching the sniper. Between the pine trees and the dense undergrowth there was the dark blur of a vehicle driving away on the road a good fifty yards off. Molly watched it through the vapor from her breath, but there was no way to make out the driver or even the model of the vehicle.

Shoving the cold Glock into the back waistband of her jeans, she pulled her sweater over it and turned. Her feet were numb with cold, and it was almost painful to walk as she picked her way through the snow back to the resort.

Mitch was waiting at the edge of the woods. He offered her his hand, guiding her from the snarl of branches.

"Are you all right?" he asked. He gave her hand a squeeze but didn't let go, as though he needed to hang on to her.

"I'm fine. But we have to get out of here."

"You think he'll—"

"No, the sniper's gone," she explained as they started back to their cabin. "He won't make a second attempt here. Not with all these witnesses."

Worry marked the faces of the few guests who hadn't already scurried back to their cabins. Molly attempted to ease their concern as she and Mitch passed, assuring them that she was police.

"We need to get out of here before the local authorities arrive," she added. "They'll have questions, and frankly,

I don't think we have the time to answer them. If they take us in to the station for statements, there's no telling what might happen. I honestly don't trust that the local sheriff can protect us against Sabatini's men.''

"But how did they find us?" Mitch asked as they mounted the cabin steps.

"Who knows? Maybe they figured we wouldn't go too far. Maybe they spent the entire night scouting out local motels and resorts until they found your truck. Maybe they just got lucky. And then they waited.''

Molly closed the door behind them. When she turned, Mitch stood in the middle of the cabin, his gaze fixed on her. Concern or anxiety or, more likely, both were firmly etched on his face. For a second Molly imagined crossing the room to him, taking his hands in hers and kissing that incredible mouth of his, erasing all those lines of tension.

"It'll be all right, Mitch," she offered, unmoving.

He nodded, and she thought for a moment that he appeared lost somehow. Rattled. But then why shouldn't he? No doubt Mitch realized how close he'd come to losing his life moments ago.

"Honestly, Mitch. We'll get out of this. I promise." However, Molly wondered how much comfort her words could offer. She heard the waver in her voice, knew it stemmed from her own realization of how close she'd come to losing him. And as they started to pack their few belongings, Molly hoped that Mitch didn't notice the way her hands shook.

For seven hours they'd driven in relative silence south from Cheboygan County, taking lesser highways and back roads. Molly had been reluctant to stick to the interstate for fear that Sabatini's thugs would be more able to conceal themselves in the heavier traffic.

Once The Pinery was behind them by a good hundred

miles, Molly had opened the conversation. The shift into detective mode had been so smooth, Mitch hadn't even noticed until he'd found himself answering questions about the night Emily died. Eventually though, like last night, Molly gave up, and silence had prevailed once again.

Neither brought up the subject of the kiss they'd shared last night or Molly's confession of her feelings. Mitch had wanted to say something about it, *and* about the way she'd saved his life this morning, but with his concentration divided between driving and keeping an eye on the rearview mirror, he hadn't known what to say.

Then, just outside of Big Rapids, after they stopped at a roadside diner for lunch, Molly had taken the wheel and refused to let Mitch back into the driver's seat. She'd demanded he get some sleep. He had done that, off and on. And every time he woke he'd glance over to see Molly studying the rearview mirror. Now, as the light of day started to wane and the first few large snowflakes drifted down, Molly seemed more relaxed behind the wheel, even affording him the occasional smile.

"How'd you sleep?" she asked. The corners of her mouth turned up and Mitch felt an involuntary surge of emotion as those glittering dark eyes met his for a brief moment.

"Fine." Mitch stretched the stiffness from his muscles and tried to straighten his left leg. The ten-month-old injury normally caused little more than mild discomfort. Cramped within the confines of the Blazer, however, unable to be extended, the shattered knee that had been practically rebuilt after the accident became far more than a gentle reminder of that fateful night.

He massaged it now, and Molly took note.

"Does it hurt?" Concern replaced the smile.

"No. Just stiff."

"It happened in the accident, didn't it?"

Mitch nodded. "Yeah. It wasn't too pretty."

"I'm sorry, Mitch."

"What's to be sorry about?"

"I'm sorry I...that I didn't come to see you. While you were in the hospital."

He shrugged, letting his gaze scan the rolling countryside as they drove past snow-covered orchards. The rows of dwarf trees were dark and gnarled against the gray-white horizon.

"It's okay, Molly. It wasn't as though I was in any mood for visitors, anyway. So...where are we?"

She glanced across to meet his gaze, obviously wondering if she should push the former topic further. But she didn't. She seemed to recognize that it was a time he would much rather forget.

"We just went through Dowagiac," she answered, studying him for a moment longer. "We should be in Sister Lakes soon."

"And you've been to this resort?"

He caught her nod.

"A few years ago. It's a small resort on Dewey Lake. Shady Shores. Tom's family has owned it for a couple of generations. It's secluded and on one of the smaller lakes, and since it's mostly a summer place, I don't think there'll be much in the way of guests this time of year, so we'll have some privacy."

To his left were more orchards, and then a closed-up fruit market covered with snow and ice. Beyond that were barren fields, the remnants of cornstalks piercing through the heavy white blanket that covered them. And finally, there was the lake.

As Molly slowed the Blazer at a T in the road, Mitch glimpsed the wide-open expanse of ice through a row of mature pines. Turning right, she followed the narrow road that twisted and meandered its way along the lakeshore.

Dusk pressed down on the small lakeside community, bringing with it a grayness that made the frozen landscape appear even colder. Mitch glanced across to Molly. The silvery evening light gave her face a pale appearance and he was reminded of this morning. Her complexion had been white when she'd come charging down the hill with her gun in hand, screaming her warning of the sniper; whiter still when she'd returned from the woods and joined him at the truck.

He'd thought then that it was panic or adrenaline. But when she'd taken his hand and he'd felt how tightly she held on to him, Mitch realized it was fear that had overcome Molly. She'd been afraid for his life, afraid of harm coming to him. And not because he was a potential witness against a criminal she'd wanted for over a year now, but because she was in love with him.

How could he have accused her last night of kissing him as a means of persuasion? How could he have even *thought* it?

"What is it, Mitch?" Molly must have noticed him staring.

"I just...I want to apologize for last night," he mumbled. "When I suggested that our kiss was some kind of a persuasion tactic. It wasn't fair of me. I hadn't realized you were—"

"Forget it, Mitch." She stopped him before he could say more, as though she knew he'd been about to bring up the subject of her feelings for him. "It shouldn't have happened in the first place. Persuasion or not."

She nodded past the windshield and slowed the Blazer.

"This is it," she said, turning the vehicle in beside a white-clapboard, cottage-style home.

She let the engine idle for a few moments and stared at the house with its warmly lit windows.

"I haven't seen them since the funeral," she said quietly.

He sensed a new anxiousness from her now, an apprehension that tightened her mouth and caused her to hesitate before finally turning the key in the ignition and reaching for her door handle.

And that anxiety only seemed to grow as they mounted the steps and Molly rang the bell.

Chapter Nine

Tom Sutton's parents had welcomed them both with open arms, and Lily Sutton—still wearing her apron from having prepared the evening meal—hugged Molly at least three times that Mitch counted. There had been no refusing dinner as Tom's mother set places at the table and served up ample helpings of warmed leftovers.

Molly's restlessness had eased somewhat as they ate and filled in the Suttons on Mitch's situation and the case. But a half hour later, as Irwin Sutton ushered them into the living room and turned down the volume on the Bulls game, Mitch could almost *see* the tension that curved Molly's shoulders and caused a muscle to twitch along her jawline.

It was the photos on the mantelpiece of the unused fireplace that caught and held her attention. He was probably the only one who saw her waver for a moment, before making her way across the room to confront the pictures. When Mitch joined her, she managed a quick smile, but he could clearly see how upsetting it was for her to look at the photos of her dead partner and friend.

"That's Molly and Tommy when they were patrol partners," Lily Sutton murmured, coming up behind Mitch and pointing out the framed print for him.

They stood beside each other, next to a white patrol car,

Molly leaning against the front fender, and Tom—easily a foot taller—looming over her as he used the roof of the radio car to brace his elbow on. They were both in uniform, both smiling. And Mitch couldn't help thinking that the Molly caught on celluloid looked more like the girl he'd left behind than the woman who stood next to him now. Her hair was longer in the photo, tied back into a ponytail, but still gleaming in the sunshine as she wedged her cap with its distinctive black-and-white checkered band under one arm. Her face glowed with enthusiasm and ambition, a smile of conviction, untainted by the yet-unseen horrors of the job or the brutality of Sergio Sabatini.

Watching her now, engrossed in the photos of her friend, Mitch could see how the job had worn at her since those early years on patrol. Even though there was still that light in her eyes, she smiled less. She looked exhausted, her face drawn, her complexion pale. And she was thinner now than she had been in all the years he'd known her.

"Best partner he ever had," Lily Sutton told him. "That's what Tom always said about Molly. Said she was the best cop he knew in all of Chicago."

"No," Molly said quietly as she settled an arm around Lily's small shoulders. "No, that honor was Tom's."

He saw her struggle then to keep her emotions in check. She reached for the detective's shield displayed on the mantel and traced one edge with her fingertip. Mitch saw her chin quiver slightly, and thought he saw the glisten of tears in her eyes.

He wondered if the Suttons knew the whole story, if they were aware of Molly's feeling of guilt at not being able to save their son's life, and her sense of responsibility in the faulty search-and-seizure warrant that had allowed Tom's killer to walk free.

In that moment, Molly looked incredibly fragile. Mitch fought the urge to step in front of the mantel, blocking her from the upsetting photos, to take her by the shoulders and tell her it wasn't her fault. He wanted to hold her tight, comfort her and ease the tension he saw stiffen her stance. And he wanted to kiss that mouth of hers, to taste the passion he had tasted last night, and allow them to drown in their longing for one another and for the past, when life hadn't been so painful.

"So this Sabatini who's after Mitch..." It was Lily Sutton who broke the silence. "He's the same man who killed Tommy, isn't he?"

Molly nodded. "Yes, he is."

"He has to be stopped," Lily said, so softly Mitch wasn't sure she'd spoken at all.

But Molly had. She nodded again, and this time her shoulders straightened and her chin lifted.

"You're right, Mrs. S. He has to be stopped."

Mitch caught her quick glance. He couldn't be sure what he saw then in those dark eyes, but it looked like renewed and fierce determination.

"Can you give me directions to the library in Dowagiac?" she asked Lily Sutton. "I have some work to do."

SEEING TOM'S PARENTS had been difficult enough for Molly. But the photos on the mantelpiece had been the proverbial straw. She'd needed to get out. Away from the memories and the guilt. *And* she needed to be doing something. *Anything.*

Running wasn't the answer. But until she managed to convince Mitch to testify, she couldn't leave him, no matter if the answers were back in Chicago. No, her hands were tied, and her resources were limited.

But there *were* resources.

In the basement of the Dowagiac Public Library, Molly mounted another reel into the microfiche machine. Mitch's chair squealed in protest as he leaned back. The sound broke the dark quiet of the small room, and Molly glanced up in time to see the librarian peer over the heavy frames of her glasses from the counter of the reference desk. The woman, with her painfully thin figure and her pinched face, had had her curiosity piqued by the two latecomers, even more so when they'd asked for the past eighteen months worth of the *Chicago Tribune* on microfilm.

That had been almost two hours ago, and now, as she saw the librarian check her watch, Molly didn't doubt they were on the verge of overstaying their welcome.

However, the gaunt woman wasn't the only one losing patience.

Mitch's chair squealed again as he let it snap back into position. He cleared his throat. "What exactly is it you're looking for, Molly?"

"I won't know till I see it." She fed the film into the empty spool and reeled it forward to begin her search through another week of the publication. "I only know that there's got to be something, Mitch. I know that after the incident in Mackee you think Adam's the leak. But I don't agree. Still, I *do* believe there is a police leak somewhere. *Someone* is feeding information to Sabatini. It could be anyone on the force. Anyone at the office could have overheard Adam on the phone with me, seen him write down the name of the town. And that same anyone could have overheard me asking Sarge for a vacation, and tipped off Sabatini on the likelihood of my coming to look for you."

"So you think it could be someone in Homicide?"

"Not necessarily. There are always other detectives from other units milling around the offices. It could be anyone."

"But how are you going to find them through newspaper articles?"

"I don't know yet, but right now it's all I've got, okay? There *has* to be something in all these Sabatini-connected cases. Some common variable, or something that doesn't ring true, that might point me to someone." She reeled through the local section, pausing, scanning, then reeling again.

"But going through months worth of the *Trib?* Come on, Molly, we'll be here all night."

"Well, how else do you expect me to investigate this?" Her tone was sharp, but it was the level of her voice that caused the librarian at the desk to clear her throat and shoot Molly a warning glance.

She lowered her voice. "How else am I supposed to figure out who the leak is when I'm a hundred miles away from Chicago? I'm helpless out here, Mitch, but I've got to do *something,* all right?"

She wanted to demand that he come with her to Chicago. *Tonight.* But she didn't have to. By his expression, it was clear that Mitch knew damn well what scenario she would prefer, and voicing it now would only add to the tension.

She tried to soften her tone as she turned back to study the microfiche screen. "Listen, if you want to go, just go. You can pick me up in another hour, or I'll get one of the Suttons to come get me."

"I'm staying, Molly. Let's just keep going." He nodded to the screen when she looked at him, but Molly knew the real reason he refused to leave her. It wasn't because he believed she would actually find anything. It was because he worried about her safety. As much as she worried about his now, after this morning's attack.

He'd not mentioned the incident during the entire drive from The Pinery, and while he'd been behind the wheel, she was certain there were times that he was about to broach the subject, to thank her for once again saving his life. But he'd been silent. Had it been pride that prevented him from doing so? Or was there something more?

She sneaked a side glance now, quickly studying that strong profile, and wondered about the expression on his face this morning once they'd returned to the cabin. It had definitely been fear. But was it for himself? Or for her?

"There's the funeral," Mitch pointed out.

Molly directed her focus back at the glowing screen as Mitch took over the control and reeled to the *Tribune*'s full-page write-up on the memorial. A grainy black-and-white photo of Tom in uniform appeared at the top right corner of the article. Molly knew the picture was at least ten years old.

"He was a damned good cop," she said softly. "Probably the best undercover detective on the force." She tried to take her eyes off his photo, but couldn't. "You know something? He was so good his sergeant and fellow detectives rarely knew what he was working on until he made an arrest. That's why I never seriously considered the possibility of a police leak. No one really knew what Tom was investigating. So I assumed he must have somehow given *himself* away, and that's what got him killed. But maybe there *was* a police link to Sabatini. Maybe someone knew what leads Tom was following. And that someone was, and obviously still *is,* being bought."

"Who are all these people?" Mitch pointed to a photo taken at the cemetery. Mourners gathered around the small podium where Lieutenant Mackenzie had delivered his graveside service to a crowd of hundreds—police officers, city officials, family and friends of Tom's.

"They're mostly brass," Molly explained. "Lieutenants, Tom's sergeant, and fellow detectives from Vice. That's Colonel Keel, and Police Commissioner Ward." She pointed the men out, and in spite of the washed-out quality of the black-and-white photo, Molly could remember everything about that day in the most vivid detail: the clear, cobalt-blue sky, the fluttering reds and golds of autumn leaves that caught in the wind and danced across the vibrant green grounds, and the shimmering red, white and blue of the flag draped over the gleaming cherry casket. She'd never forget the almost unearthly silence that had fallen over the cemetery, broken only when the rhythmic thump of helicopter blades began to reverberate through the air as ten police choppers cruised low in formation overhead.

"And her?" Mitch pointed again. "Who's she?"

"That's Rachel Messina. Tom's last partner in Vice."

Soft-spoken Rachel, her blond hair tied back and her face startlingly white in contrast to the black suit she'd worn that day. Molly had gazed across the open grave several times that afternoon to see Rachel biting her lower lip as though fighting back tears. Tom had always voiced an unflinching respect for the detective, but Molly had often wondered how such a delicate, almost demure woman had ever worked her way up the ranks that far. Molly had resolved that there was obviously something about Rachel Messina she was incapable of seeing. After all, the woman carried a ninety-percent clearance rate and was consistently winning convictions on her cases through apparently keen detective work.

"They didn't work much together," she told Mitch. "With Tom doing most of his investigative work undercover, they pretty much did their own thing on most cases."

"So she didn't work with him on the Sabatini case?"

"Probably not, otherwise I think he would have gone to her for help. Not me. But I can't say for sure."

"Could you say that she was the closest person to Tom? On the force, I mean?"

"No, not necessarily. I know he enjoyed working with her, but I'm not sure how close they were. I talked to Rachel briefly a couple of days after the funeral, and she said she knew very little about his investigation into Sabatini. I remember she cursed him for not telling her, for not asking for her help."

"And you believed her?"

When she looked at Mitch, he pulled his hard gaze from the microfiche screen to meet hers. "Just call it a gut feeling," he said, giving her a shrug and the hint of a smile.

"No, you're right. Why not Rachel?"

Rapidly, Molly reeled back the spool and returned it to its box. She scanned the littered tabletop and the boxes of microfilms strewn across it before she spotted the one she needed.

"That one," she told Mitch. "Let me look at last March again. There was a case that Rachel investigated. It was definitely connected to Sabatini, and I know for a fact that the charges there never stuck, either."

She cranked the film forward, scanning for the story. Her eyes were bleary and her head felt thick from the hours behind the glaring light of the machine. But on the trail of a lead, there was no slowing her down.

Pages upon pages of columns whizzed across the screen, until finally Molly found what she'd been searching for. Mitch leaned forward with her as well now, skimming the article.

"Sabatini was up on charges for running an illegal gambling ring out of that little Italian restaurant over on Eastern Avenue. Salvatori's," Molly explained for him as she ran her fingertip across the article. "And Rachel was the assigned detective. From what I remember, the investigation started on a rumor that apparently didn't amount to much. The charges were dropped almost immediately."

She read further. "Here. Listen to this. Detective Rachel Messina with the Vice Unit has concluded her investigation into the alleged gambling ring, stating that, although earlier rumors may have had some foundation, the charges against Sergio Lorenz Sabatini have been dropped. 'At this time we have no witnesses to any kind of illegal gambling on the premises of Salvatori's restaurant, owned by Mr. Sabatini. Without witness testimony and without solid proof, we have no grounds to hold Mr. Sabatini. But I can assure you, this matter is not over. If there is any illegal activity—gambling or otherwise—connected with Salvatori's, the police department *will* intervene,' promises Messina.''

''Sounds on the up and up to me,'' Mitch offered.

''Yeah? Except for the fact that there *were* witnesses. I remember that.''

Molly reeled back a day, then another and another, until she found the small story a full week earlier. It was barely three paragraphs long.

''The only reason I remember this one at all was because I'd been to Salvatori's for dinner shortly before I read the story. See, it's written by the same reporter. Jim Lane. And he's saying there were at least two former employees of Salvatori's who were ready to go public on illegal gambling activities connected to Sabatini.''

''So what are you thinking, Molly?''

She shook her head, reading the story a second time. ''I don't know. But I think it's worth a phone call.''

Rummaging through her shoulder bag, Molly took out her cell phone and punched out a number from memory.

''Yes. Alex Turner, please,'' she said softly when the line was finally picked up.

''Who are you calling?'' Mitch asked, and she saw a flicker of apprehension cross his face.

''Just someone who owes me a couple of favors at the *Trib*.''

She waited for the call to be put through, and when it was answered, relief swept through her.

''Alex, Molly Sparling here.''

''Detective Sparling. How nice to hear from you.'' Sarcasm resonated in the deep voice of the *Trib*'s lead crime reporter. ''You got something for me?''

"Not exactly. This time I'm hoping you'll have something for me."

There was a moment's hesitation, then he asked, "What is it?"

"Jim Lane."

"Yeah?"

"Tell me about him."

"Don't know much. He was with us for a few years, but only did the crime reporting for a few months before he quit."

"He quit? When?"

"Early April, I think. Yeah, end of March, early April."

"Any particular reason?"

"Not that I know of."

Suspicion sparked along Molly's spine. Could there be some connection between the stories Lane wrote about Sabatini and the reporter's early departure from the paper?

"So where's Lane now?"

"Not sure, really. He moved to Indiana. I think he had a job lined up with a small paper in Salem or someplace, but don't quote me on that."

"I need his number, Alex."

"Now, Molly, you know I can't—"

"You owe me, Alex. One number. That's all I'm asking for. It's important."

There was another pause, followed by the sound of shuffling papers. Finally he grunted, "You didn't get it from me, all right?"

"Never," she promised as she jotted down the Indiana number he read to her, and then thanked him before hanging up.

"Where are you going with this, Molly?" Mitch asked, as she started to punch out Lane's number.

"I'm not sure yet, but Lane quit the *Trib* just after that story ran. Do *you* think it's a coincidence?"

Mitch was about to reply, but Molly held up a finger to stop him when the other end of the line was picked up. A child's wavering voice broke through the static of the cell phone.

Molly cleared her throat. "Hi, is your dad home?" she asked.

"Yup. Daddy!"

The phone clattered for a second, and in the background Molly could hear the voices of other children and the faint pulsing of music as though from a television. And finally, a smooth male voice. "Jim Lane, here."

"Mr. Lane. I'm sorry to bother you at home. I'm Detective Sparling with the Chicago Police Department, and I was hoping to—"

"How did you get this number?" His voice lowered suddenly to a harsh whisper, the fear in it obvious.

"From a friend, Mr. Lane. Someone who knows you. And someone who trusts me," she added, sensing that the fear she heard in his voice might cause him to hang up. "Please, I need to ask you a couple of questions. It's very important."

No response. The only sound over the crackle of her cell phone was that of Jim Lane's children in the background.

"Please, Mr. Lane."

"It's about Sabatini, isn't it?"

"Yes, and the illegal gambling ring. You wrote a piece on it last March."

"Among others related to Sabatini, yes."

"You had a source, didn't you? Someone told you about the gambling ring before the police got wind of it, right?"

"I had two sources." Reluctance slowed his words and deepened his tone. "Two former employees of Salvatori's. They came to me separately, both wanting to expose Sabatini for using the restaurant as a front."

"And you took that to the police?"

"No. The police came to me."

"Did you give them the names of your sources?"

"Of course I did."

"And do you know if they questioned them?"

Molly heard a grunt over the phone that sounded like a sarcastic laugh.

"Questioned them? I guess that's one way of looking at it," he said.

"What do you mean?"

"They're dead, Detective Sparling. Or at least the one is. The other, last I heard, was still filed as a missing person. I would have thought you'd know this."

"I'm afraid I'm only just catching up on the case, Mr. Lane."

"As far as I'm concerned, the police had all the evidence against Sabatini they needed with those two witnesses. And they were definitely alive and safe before…before I gave their names to the police."

Molly detected remorse in Jim Lane's voice.

"So, is that why you quit the *Tribune?*"

"Not exactly. I've learned to roll with the punches this job tends to throw your way."

"Why then? Was it related to Sabatini? To the stories you wrote?"

"No, Detective Sparling, I quit because I love my family, and because I value them far more than my career."

"I'm not sure I understand."

"Well, I suppose if it was *your* spouse and children who were forced off the road by another vehicle in broad daylight, you'd understand damned fast."

"You're saying Sabatini made an attempt on your family?"

"Not necessarily."

"Who then? I don't understand, Mr. Lane. If Sabatini wasn't behind—"

"Look, I'll spell it out for you, Detective Sparling, because I don't *ever* want to be bothered by you or any one of Chicago's *finest* again. I've been in the reporting industry for twenty years now. I thought I'd seen it all. On occasion I've been asked by detectives to lay off a witness or to cut back on certain details I was about to put in print. Almost always I've conceded. I've also been threatened before in my line of work. It's nothing new. You grow to expect it, especially when you're doing crime writing. But when it comes to my family…"

"Who threatened you, Mr. Lane? If it wasn't Sabatini, then who?"

Molly struggled to hear over the static, wondering for a second if Jim Lane had hung up. But she could still hear the television in the background.

"Mr. Lane? Are you saying it was a *detective* who threatened you and your family?"

There was more static over the line and then she heard him release a long breath. "Yes," he admitted at last. "And not just with Sabatini's gambling charges."

"The same detective in each case?"

"Yes."

"And you believe this detective was on Sabatini's payroll?"

"Most definitely."

"I don't suppose you would give me a name?"

"You must think I'm stupid, Detective Sparling. I quit the *Trib* the day after those two witnesses went missing, and I was out of Chicago by the end of that week. I'm not about to put my family in jeopardy again."

"Was it Messina, Mr. Lane? Was it Detective Rachel Messina?"

The only answer he gave her was silence, then the phone's receiver slamming into its cradle.

MITCH WONDERED if it was his imagination or if he'd actually watched Molly turn two shades paler in the cold glow of the microfiche machine. There was definitely no mistaking the slight tremor in her hand as she switched off her cell phone and lowered it to her lap.

"It's Rachel?" he asked her.

She nodded slowly, and when she met his gaze disbelief widened her eyes.

"All this time. It was her." She shook her head. "Lane didn't come right out and say it, and there's no way you'd ever get a testimony out of him, but...he answered my question."

She was still shaking her head as she put her cell phone away and started to rewind the reel of microfilm.

"She set Tom up. It had to be Rachel. It makes sense. I mean, who else? She had the most likely access to Tom's reports, even if he didn't keep her informed of his investigation. *And* being in Vice gives her the perfect opportunity to access *other* detectives' cases. Given the kinds of charges that were generally brought against Sabatini, Vice is the main unit that dealt with him."

Molly shook her head, as though making yet another harsh realization. "And Tom's murder. My God, the search-and-seizure warrant I wrote up. If she'd really wanted to, Rachel could have seen a copy of it. She could have gotten to Sabatini in time to warn him we were moving in, and inform him of the warrant's contents. That's how he'd known he'd get away with the murder weapon under his car seat."

"And what about now? Could she be the one behind the information getting to Sabatini regarding your whereabouts?"

Molly seemed to think for a moment, then nodded. "Of course. She was there that morning—in the Homicide Unit—when I asked for time off. I'm sure she was. And boy, Rachel knows damn well how badly I want Sabatini. She could have tipped him off. *And* it's not unlikely that she may have been in the Homicide Unit when I was on the phone with Adam from Bass Lake.''

It was anger now that punctuated each movement of Molly's—the snap of the reel from the machine, the brisk way she shoved it into its box and then the flurry with which she gathered all the films into her arms.

''It makes so much sense. Who else could it be?'' Molly asked again, her voice an almost violent whisper now. ''She found out about Tom's undercover investigation and *knew* he was about to expose Sabatini. She went to Sabatini with the information. Sold out her partner. And *she* got Tom killed.''

Mitch picked up her knapsack and followed her to the audiovisual counter.

''Molly, can you be sure?''

''Oh yeah. I don't have any evidence…yet. But I'm pretty sure.''

The anger he saw darken her face then made Mitch wonder what Molly might have done if Rachel Messina had been standing before her at this very moment.

''And I'll get the evidence, Mitch. Trust me, I'll get the evidence.''

At the counter, Molly let loose her armload of microfilms. They clattered across the countertop, almost spilling over the other side.

Molly muttered an apology to the librarian, but it did nothing to alter the woman's impatient expression.

''I need to use your Internet service,'' she stated to the woman, her voice flat and formal.

And when the librarian gave her a blank stare, Molly's tone became even more rancorous.

''You *do* have a computer with Net capabilities, don't you?''

"Yes, but I'm afraid we're closing."

Both he and Molly followed the librarian's nervous nod at the clock to her left. It was five minutes to nine.

"Well, you're not closed yet." Molly lifted the edge of her sweater and took from the pocket of her jeans her detective's shield. She flipped open the leather wallet and slid it across the counter. "I need to use your computer," she stated flatly.

"Certainly. It's…it's right this way."

Chapter Ten

Forty minutes later, Molly was still glued to the computer screen. Mitch's eyes had long since gone bleary trying to focus on the pages upon pages of police reports that Molly brought up over the Internet. She'd logged into the Chicago Police Headquarters through a complex series of passwords until finally accessing the mainframe, which housed the individual detectives' case files and electronic reports.

Even there she'd been met with further requests for passwords. She'd told Mitch she was logging into Tom's past investigations, explaining how the files were never deleted from the mainframe, even once a case was closed. She'd only been guessing, but having been Tom's partner and having shared passwords all those years, she'd gotten his right on the first try.

From there it had been a dizzying blur of reports. One after the other.

Mitch leaned back in his chair, his eyes closed as he massaged the bridge of his nose with his thumb and forefinger. He admired Molly's stamina, and the fire that consumed her now that an answer seemed near. Her fingers flew over the keys, pausing only as she scanned the report displayed on the monitor, before sending the page to the printer. And with each press of the print key, there seemed a tangible aura of triumph about her.

"I think I've got enough," she said after another fifteen minutes of flurried typing and printing, and she began logging out of the system. "So many reports. It's unbelievable. Rachel has had Tom's password all this time. It doesn't surprise me, since he often asked for help on the computer. I've always known his passwords. No doubt Rachel was in the same boat. Anyway, the contents of some of these reports have obviously been tampered with, changes that lead to glaring technicalities that apparently caused the various charges against Sabatini to be thrown out."

"So why didn't Tom catch them himself?"

"Because he was already dead. These changes to the files…most of them were done after his death, but you wouldn't know that unless you logged into Tom's files yourself using his password. It's just the way the system's set up, unfortunately. Otherwise, someone else might have caught this a lot sooner."

"You're saying she was directly tampering with Tom's files."

"Who else, besides me, would have the password? And there's no telling how many other instances of falsifying reports or tampering with evidence she's responsible for. It might not be just Tom's Sabatini-related investigations. There are plenty of others she may have had a hand in, including the gambling ring."

"And do you think you have enough to prove this?"

Molly stood now, stretching as she did. Due either to the heat of her discoveries or the temperatures rising in the library's basement, she had long since stripped down to her T-shirt. Now Mitch couldn't resist taking an admiring look at the lithe figure beneath the formfitting top: the gentle swell of her breasts, the gradual tapering of her delicate rib cage and slender waist.

"No, this probably isn't enough evidence on its own," she said, reaching for the stack of pages the printer had spewed out, "but I certainly think I've got enough to take to the D.A.'s office to convince them to sign a search-and-seizure warrant. I'm sure Rachel's own case files will be rather revealing, not to mention what we might find in her bank statements."

She straightened the pages into a neat stack before sliding them into her knapsack, and when she reached for her sweater and anorak, Mitch could see a glimmer in her eyes.

"I've got her, Mitch. And with enough on her, she may turn evidence against Sabatini, too. Either way, there's a really good chance I'll have them both."

Victory lifted the corners of her mouth, but Mitch barely had time to see it. Instead, he felt it. She closed the gap between them and in an instant he felt her smile against his own lips. With one hand on his cheek and the other grasping the knapsack with her precious evidence, Molly kissed him. It was a celebratory kiss, meant to express the triumph of her success. But to Mitch there was far more behind it.

It was a reminder of what last night's encounter had been. And it was a taste of more. Much more.

Mitch's body reacted almost immediately, and he was certain Molly was aware of it. But given the look of mild surprise in her eyes when she finally pulled away, Mitch couldn't help thinking that her *own* reaction was more than she'd bargained for.

"Come on," she said, clearing her throat. "Let's get out of here."

And Mitch wondered if there was more than her investigation behind Molly's anxiety just then.

THE MOUNTING SNOW made the drive back from Dowagiac somewhat of a test. A good six inches covered the roads to Dewey Lake, making the surface greasy. The thrashing wipers barely kept up with the heavy snowfall. If not for the rush she'd gotten from discovering Rachel's part in Tom's murder, Molly would have gladly given up the wheel to Mitch. As it was, she was wired.

Even a warm shower at the two-room cabin Tom's parents had given them did nothing to alleviate the surge of impatience that coursed through her. She wanted to be in Chicago. Wanted to go to the D.A.'s office right now, even Internal Affairs, talk to a judge, get a warrant signed. *Anything*. She wanted to act.

Instead, all she could do was pace, and she'd done a pretty good job of that. In spite of the age-worn floorboards of the cabin's main room, Molly was certain she'd already contributed more than her share to their wear. Beneath her stockinged feet, the old pine boards creaked and moaned as she beat a path from the corner cabinet, past the queen-size bed, between the trunk at its foot and the stone hearth, and then to the other side of the main room.

And the entire time, she churned over in her mind the information she'd printed at the library, imagining the search-and-seizure warrant she would write up, and then what was needed to convince a judge to sign it.

"Maybe you should have a drink."

Mitch's voice broke the urgent string of thoughts, and Molly stopped pacing. He handed her a tumbler holding a measure of the Scotch he'd accepted from Mr. Sutton before they'd headed up to the cabin not long ago.

"Thanks." The liquor warmed her throat. Almost immediately she could feel its affects on her nerves, and she took another sip from the glass.

She was about to start pacing again when Mitch stopped her. One broad hand settled on her shoulder, turning her, while with the other he tucked a finger under her chin and tilted her face up so she looked into his eyes.

"Are you all right, Molly?"

His hair was still damp from his shower, and the fingered-back spikes reminded her of summertime, of the beach and Lake Michigan. She could almost smell the lake air. But the concern she saw in his brown eyes was nowhere near the boyish expression attached to the memory that flitted through her mind just then.

"Yeah, I'm fine." The smile she offered didn't seem to satisfy him. "I just wish there was something I could do."

"You've done a lot already. Why don't you just relax for tonight?"

He stepped behind her, placing both hands on her shoulders, and started to massage the tension that had manifested itself in her muscles. She stared into the fire Mitch had lit in the small stone fireplace, and felt the stress of the day melt away under his expert touch.

"You've got your evidence against Rachel," he continued, his voice almost too low, too seductive. "Like you said, you can take that to the D.A.'s office and you'll get a warrant. From there, isn't it only a matter of time before you get Sabatini as well, through evidence and through Rachel?"

"I would hope, yes."

"So, there's nothing you can do about any of it tonight, Molly. Just relax. And tomorrow morning...tomorrow we'll head back to Chicago."

Molly stiffened. Had she heard right?

"Mitch, are you saying..." She spun around to meet his dark gaze. She didn't need to finish the question. He was already nodding.

"I'll come back," he said quietly, and she thought she detected a hint of defeat in his voice. "You need my testimony."

And suddenly, Molly realized they were standing too close. *Far* too close.

It was too easy to throw her arms around him and pull

him against her as relief swept over her. He was coming back to Chicago.

"Thank you, Mitch," she whispered. "Thank you."

Mitch shifted then, as though to take weight off of his bad leg, but he didn't let her go. He closed an arm around her waist and drew her even tighter against his hard body. With her cheek pressed to his wide chest, she could feel the rapid rhythm of his heart. Almost as rapid as her own. His breathing deepened and his hand moved up from her waist, along her back, and finally to the nape of her neck, where he let his fingers comb through her hair.

It was when his finger caressed her chin and he withdrew slightly that Molly knew he was going to kiss her. He lifted her face again, only this time he lowered his mouth to hers. She welcomed the intoxicating brush of his kiss, and drew him tighter as his lips parted hers. He tasted of Scotch and smelled faintly of musk.

Somewhere deep inside, Molly felt the hot coil of desire. It gathered force, as it often had during the past couple of days, and threatened to consume her entirely. And there was no mistaking Mitch's reaction, as well. She felt the length of his erection press against her belly through the fine knit of her sweater, and she sensed the restraint that tightened every muscle along his back as her hand swept lower to his waist, resting at the top of his jeans.

And then, as their kiss deepened, Molly realized that the relief she felt now at knowing Mitch would return with her had nothing to do with the case or his testimony against Sabatini. It was purely to do with the fact that Mitch would be safe. In Chicago, he would be protected, and Sabatini couldn't harm him.

She eased back, intending to thank Mitch again, when the resounding knock on the cabin's door made them both start. A grunt of disappointment slipped from Mitch's throat.

"Do you want to get that?" he asked, running a hand through his damp hair with a definite look of frustration.

Aftershocks of desire pulsed through her like a ripple effect on a lake, and her lips still tingled from his kiss as she crossed the room to the door. She unlatched it without thinking, swinging it wide to a gust of winter air. Only once she saw Ray, Tom's brother, standing at the porch's railing, a cardboard box wedged against one hip, did Molly realize how absolutely careless she'd been.

For all she'd known, it could have been Sabatini's men at the door. It had to be Mitch's kiss. It had completely robbed her of caution. Silently, Molly cursed herself for once again letting her guard down. She couldn't let it happen again. It could get them both killed.

"Ray." She struggled to smile.

Ray Sutton was almost the spitting image of his younger brother, and even when Tom was alive, Molly had found the similarities between the two unnerving. Now, as Ray nodded a greeting and stepped forward to give her a half hug, Molly fought back the memories.

"How're you doing, Molly?"

"Fine, under the circumstances. You?" She ushered him in.

"Good," he said, stepping through the door with the same slightly bowlegged gait that had punctuated Tom's stride. He stomped the snow from his boots and lowered the box to the small wooden table. When he saw Mitch, he gave him a quick nod.

"Ray, this is Mitch Drake," she said as the two men shook hands. "Mitch, Tom's brother Ray."

"Good to meet you," Ray said. "But look, Molly, I won't stay long. I'm sorry to bother you two so late but Ma said you went into Dowagiac, and when I saw the cabin lights on, I figured I should catch you before you turned in for the night. Thought you might be interested in this,'' he said, indicating the box.

''What is it?''

''Some of Tom's stuff. After the funeral, I went to Chicago to clean out his apartment. Anyway, most of it was just regular stuff, you know? Clothes, furniture, dishes, that sorta thing. But when Ma told me about you and Mitch, what you're going through—this whole Sabatini mess— well, I got to wondering if maybe you should look through this.''

He opened the box for them to see.

''It's just stuff he had crammed in his desk.''

''His desk from Headquarters?''

''Oh, no. We never saw any of that. I figure the police kept it all. No, this is from his desk at home.''

Ray started to rummage through it, while Molly joined him.

''It's mostly junk, I guess. I packed in kind of a hurry, but I went over the paperwork and didn't find anything that seemed to be related to his police work. Still, it's all in there if you want to go through it. Oh, and then—'' he rummaged some more, closer to the bottom of the box, and pulled out three microcassettes ''—there are these.''

He handed them to her and she turned them over in her hand, hoping to find some kind of inscription. There was none.

''You don't have a—''

''—tape player?'' Ray finished for her. ''Nope. Otherwise I might have listened to them. As it was, with none of this other stuff related to Tom's work, I didn't figure there'd be anything useful on 'em. But who knows? If you think it's worth it I'm sure you'd be able to pick one up in Dowagiac tomorrow.''

Molly studied the tapes again. Like Ray said, they could be nothing. Or…they could be vital. In their years of partnership, she'd never known Tom to use a tape recorder, even when interviewing suspects. But then, she'd never worked with him when he'd been undercover, so maybe...

"Anyway, look, I'll get out of your hair. It's late. But if there's anything you need, you give me a call. You know I'm just around the corner."

"Thanks, Ray."

He gave her one of those tilted Sutton nods then, lifting his hand to his forehead as though to right a crooked baseball cap. "I'll see you two later. Take care."

Another blast of frigid air and he was gone, closing the door behind him.

"So what do you think?" Mitch asked as the last of the cold air swirled in the far reaches of the cabin's main room.

"I think I can't wait to listen to these tomorrow. And I think I have to make a phone call."

She didn't need to see his face to know she would find the glimmer of suspicion there. She laid a hand on Mitch's arm before he could protest.

"Just my father," she told him. "You'll trust *him*, won't you?"

She waited for Mitch's nod before she took out her cell phone and punched in the number.

Her father picked up on the third ring, clearing his throat as he brought the phone to his chin.

"Sparling here."

"Sparling *here*." It was an on-going joke between them, only tonight Molly had trouble finding amusement in the crisp familial salutations.

"Hey, Sunshine. Where the hell you at?"

"And what kind of greeting is that, hmm, Pops?"

"Well, wadda you expect when you don't return my calls, and then I gotta hear from your sarge that you're on vacation? And since when the hell does a Sparling take a vacation, anyway?"

She knew he was smiling through the gruffness, but she could also hear the worry in his voice.

"I needed to do something, Pops."

"And...didya find him?"

Leo Sparling might have retired from the force five years ago, but he was still one of the sharpest minds Molly knew.

"Yeah. I did."

"He with you?"

"Mm-hmm."

"And you're going to bring him in, right?"

"I think so." She shot a quick glance to where Mitch stood by the fire, his arms crossed over his chest. Given the gravity of his expression, she was certain he knew exactly the content of her conversation, and he didn't appear entirely convinced it was the best thing.

"Good. So get back here so I can give you a decent what-for for thinkin' you can take on this son of a bitch Sabatini single-handedly. What the hell are you thinking, girl?"

"Pops, listen, it's more complicated than that. I need your advice."

"Well, there's a first."

"Seriously. I've got some evidence. It's not hard, though, but it might be enough, and I need to know what is admissible and what isn't."

She told him everything: where they were, how she'd spoken to Jim Lane in Indiana, then about the tampered reports, and about the real likelihood of Rachel's involvement. What she *didn't* tell him was how close Sabatini's men had come to success over the past couple of days. And still he worried. She heard it loud and clear, with each word.

"All right," he said once he'd listened to everything. "I'll do what I can from this end, okay? I've still got some contacts. I'll ask some discreet questions and see what I can find out on where we go with this evidence, what we can use and how much we can do with it. But you had better get your butt back here, girl, and fast.''

''I will.''

''And say hi to Mitch for me. You two be careful.''

''We will. I love you, Pops.''

''Yeah, me too.''

Molly switched off her cell phone. She could count the number of times her father had actually told her he loved her, and yet every time they saw each other or even spoke over the phone, she knew. In his own way, he always made sure she knew.

''So what does your dad say?''

''He says we should get back as soon as we can. And he's going to see what he can find out about how to handle the evidence against Rachel. There's no way I'm willing to hit a snag in the legal system now. Not after all this.''

Mitch nodded and tossed back the last of his Scotch as he stared into the flames.

Outside, the wind must have died down. There was no battering at the shuttered windows or whistling at the door, only the low crackle of the fire. Turning off the cabin's main light, Molly crossed the room to join him.

It would have felt perfectly natural for her to slide her arms around his waist then, and rest her head against his back, Molly thought as she neared him. Or maybe turn him around so he faced her and she could kiss him again.

But she didn't.

There was a darkness in Mitch's expression that warned her against it, a distance that made her wonder if the intimacy she'd felt in their kiss moments ago had only been her imagination.

''So...you *are* coming back, right?'' she dared to ask, standing at his side.

He nodded, avoiding eye contact as he set his glass on

the mantel. He brushed past her then, and lowered himself to sit on the wooden trunk at the end of the bed, favoring his left knee as he did so.

For a moment she stood there, watching the glow of the fire warm his features as he leaned forward with his elbows on his knees.

"Can I ask what changed your mind?" she asked, joining him on the trunk.

Mitch let out a long breath. "A number of things, I guess. Mostly, I realize that you're right about Sabatini. He has to be stopped. And if I'm needed to see that end, then...I'm coming back to Chicago."

His hands were clasped together, the fingers laced, the knuckles almost white with tension. Molly eased her hand over them and felt them ease somewhat.

"I promise it'll be okay, Mitch. I promise to have the best in protection for you."

He nodded. "I know you will."

His gaze never left the fire. But it wasn't the flames he was looking at. Molly could tell that. His eyes searched far, *far* beyond the glow of the hearth.

"Mitch? What is it?"

"It's nothing." But his feeble attempt at a smile didn't fool Molly.

"There's something else, isn't there? Another reason you've finally agreed to come back to Chicago."

He nodded, the movement so subtle she thought she'd only imagined it.

"What is it?" she prompted softly.

There was the slightest waver in his voice when he finally spoke, and Molly could feel his hands begin to twist again under hers.

"The night Emily died..." he began. "There's...there's something about that night that...something I haven't told you yet, Molly."

When he finally looked at her, Molly was startled at the pain she saw in his eyes. It was deeper somehow, darker than any she'd seen there before. It tightened his mouth and worked a series of lines across his forehead and into a knot between his brows.

"What, Mitch? You can talk to me," she prompted when he fell silent again.

"We left the opening earlier than we'd planned. Emily wasn't feeling well and I wanted to get her home. She was..." He shook his head, the memory too unbearable.

Molly wrapped her fingers around his hands, prying them apart and holding them in both of hers now. "Mitch?"

"You see, she...*we*'d been trying for years to get pregnant. It was Emily's dream, to write at home, raise a family. She wanted children so badly. That's why the first miscarriage...it almost killed her. Emotionally, I mean. It was almost the end of our marriage, too. It hit her hard. It hit *us* hard."

Mitch closed his eyes for a moment, but this time Molly waited for him to go on.

"The second wasn't as shattering. She miscarried a lot earlier in the pregnancy, and it didn't hit so hard. But Emily...she was starting to lose hope. I could see it in her...the changes. I knew she thought that we'd never be able to have a child. And then, like a miracle, it happened. Just when *I* had started to think it would never happen..."

"Emily was...she was pregnant the night of the accident?"

Molly almost choked on her disbelief as she watched Mitch nod.

"Seven and a half months," he said, his voice barely a whisper. "Seven and a half months. It was a girl."

"I'm so sorry, Mitch."

"The doctors, they tried to save her, you know? But...there were too many complications."

"I'm sorry," Molly said again, wishing there were other words that could possibly offer more comfort. "I'm so sorry."

"So you see, Sabatini and me...well, if you're talking thorns, I think I've got yours beat, Molly. The son of a bitch took everything from me. Emily, my daughter, my career, my whole goddamn life."

"You can rebuild it, Mitch. I promise you."

It took him a long time to nod then, searching her eyes as though he'd believe the truth in them and no place else.

"Nothing you do can bring Emily back. Or your daughter. Nothing can ever give you back the life you had. But if you testify against Sabatini, if he's behind bars, you *can* start over, Mitch. I promise. You have your work, and you can make a life for yourself again. You just have to do this first."

"I know," he whispered, and Molly felt his hand turn under hers so that his fingers wove through hers. He caressed the inside of her wrist with his thumb, staring at their entwined hands for a long time, and Molly couldn't help thinking that he looked lost.

It was unbearable to see him that way...to see Mitch— the one person with more drive and stamina, more courage and lust for life than anyone she'd known—now appear so vulnerable, so defeated.

Molly lifted her other hand and pressed her palm against his freshly shaved cheek. She wanted to erase that look. She wanted to fill those dark eyes with the kind of light and hope she'd always seen there. But then, who was to say *she* was the one to do it? Who was to say *anyone* could do it after he'd suffered such an incredible loss?

"You'll be all right," she said again, risking sounding like a broken record. "I know you, Mitch Drake. You're strong. You'll come through this."

For several heartbeats, he stared into her eyes. Then he

nodded. And when he tilted his head and pressed his lips longingly to the sensitive skin of her palm, Molly's breath caught. He kissed her again. And again. Working his way to her wrist, and with each kiss, the shocks of yearning drove deeper.

''Mitch.'' She murmured his name, or maybe it echoed so strongly in her mind that she simply *thought* she'd spoken it. For twelve years she had whispered his name, in the dark of night, curled up in her bed, wondering.... And in those twelve years, even though she'd hoped for it, she never once believed in the possibility of something like this. The two of them...together.

She reached for him, bringing her hand to the back of his neck, drawing him to her so she could feel that mouth on hers. And Mitch obliged. Eagerly.

His kiss was even hungrier than before, more demanding, more fervent. His own breath was as ragged as hers, and she heard a raw, hoarse sound come from deep inside his chest. He pulled her closer, his wide hands moving from her face down over her shoulders, past her rib cage to the curve of her waist. His fingers tightened around her hips, and his kiss deepened as he shifted even closer to her.

There was a desperation in the way his mouth consumed hers, but Molly's was no less ravenous. Her hands followed the wide outline of his shoulders and then moved down across his chest, her fingers fanning over the hard muscles beneath the cotton of his shirt. The top button slipped easily from its hole, almost without her doing, and Molly couldn't deny her urge to touch him. She slid one hand under the soft material, skimming over the mat of hair and finally pressing the length of her hand against his hot skin. Her breath hitched. But then, so did Mitch's.

Under her palm she could feel the clamoring of his heart, and the low vibration of his groan before she heard it.

He drew back slightly, resting his forehead against hers,

and Molly swore she could still feel the wet heat of his mouth on hers.

"Molly, I want you so badly."

The whispered confession shot an arrow of heat right to her core.

"Mitch…"

"I *need* you," he murmured, as if he thought she would protest.

But protest was the furthest thing from her thoughts.

"I need you, Molly, but if you…if there's someone else…someone in your life, just tell me. Because if—"

"There's no one," she whispered, touching one fingertip to his moist lips. *No one but you,* she wanted to say, but didn't. How could there be any other man when it was Mitch she'd been in love with all these years?

He let out a long breath, and she felt its heat trace across her lips, beckoning her back to his mouth. With his hands at the nape of her neck, he pulled her into his insatiable kiss. Then he drew her up with him from the trunk and guided her to the side of the bed.

Molly swayed against him, needing his solidness to hold her up. Her knees felt so weak. Weaker still when she felt the fullness of his arousal crushed against her belly.

His hands found the edge of her sweater and he lifted it over her head. She was already tugging at her T-shirt, pulling it off as well, before the sweater hit the floor. And then Mitch's hands were on her—hot, wide, skillful hands, skimming across her skin, leaving behind quivering shocks of desire.

When he gazed down at her, she saw an unmistakable sense of marvel in his eyes. And in that moment, Molly could see the anxious seventeen-year-old in him—breathless with wonder as he'd touched her body for the first time. Only now, maturity had taught Mitch patience, and appreciation. And that appreciation was amply visible in his devouring stare. He lifted his hands to cup her lace-clad breasts, deliciously kneading one in each hand.

Relentlessly, he circled the hardening nipples just beneath the white lace with his thumbs. The sensation drove another wave of heat through her, and Molly grasped the waist of Mitch's jeans to balance herself. She heard his deep intake of breath and watched him hold it as his hands finally slipped to the back of her bra and undid the clasp.

It was Molly's turn to draw in a shuddering breath as her bra dropped to the floor and she felt him take her naked breasts in his hands. She saw the faintest glimmer of a smile tug at the corners of his mouth then as he shook his head in apparent disbelief.

In one fluid motion, he eased her back, pulling away the covers and lowering her to the cool sheets. He moved onto the bed with her, kneeling over her as he raked his gaze across her body. His eyes stopped at the strip of white gauze just above her hip, and Molly saw his mouth tighten, as though he were remembering that night and the fear he'd so obviously displayed when first seeing her injury.

Molly reached for his chin, guiding his gaze back to hers. She saw longing there, so intense that it came close to mirroring her own. Desperate now, she reached for the buttons of his shirt, her fingers shaking with anticipation, and she fumbled with each one.

There was no restraining her moan as she brushed the shirt from his square shoulders and let her fingers trail over the hard angles. Her memory had been accurate. *So* vividly accurate, she thought now as her hands swept across the fiery familiarity of his skin. She could feel the power of his body above her, feel the incredible restraint locked in each muscle that quivered in response to her anxious touch.

Mitch lowered his mouth to her neck. Skillfully, he caressed the sensitive spot with his lips. She arched against him, wanting to feel the heat of his skin against hers, and when she did, the shock of his nakedness against hers was almost too much to bear. She felt a sob trapped in her throat.

It was too easy to forget the warning she'd heard so clearly in her mind last night. She didn't care if she was made a fool of herself a second time. She wanted to be with Mitch. Needed his passion, his touch…as though making love to him would give reason to all those unanswered dreams she'd lived with for the past twelve years.

Only…it was *Mitch* who was making love to *her*.

His hand glided between their hot bodies, down past her stomach to the tops of her jeans. Blazing a trail of kisses from her shoulder to her breast, he took one nipple into his mouth, embracing it with his tongue as he unzipped her jeans. His hand slid easily under the heavy denim barrier, and then her panties. She was liquid fire long before his strong fingers found her wet heat and began their slow, delicious stroking.

He kissed her again, his mouth clamped over hers with such urgency that Molly couldn't determine where one sensation began and the other ended. She reached for him as well now. Hungrily, she caressed the hard length of his erection. It strained against the thick denim, and Molly felt the overwhelming need to have him inside of her. Yet what he was doing with his fingers…she didn't want Mitch to stop. The rhythm of his tongue worked in sync with his skillful fingers, threatening to drive her to the brink before she was even able to unzip the fly of his jeans.

But then, as she felt the extreme restraint that rippled through his body, Molly realized Mitch had no intention of satisfying himself…not yet. He moved over her, his kiss somewhere between gentle and devouring, his touch increasingly insistent until her body was rocking beneath him, begging for release.

And when release came, it was greater than anything

Molly had ever experienced. Heat exploded through her. She melted at every point where her body touched Mitch's, shuddering as his name rose from somewhere deep inside of her and escaped from her throat in a final breath of ecstasy.

WHEN HE HEARD MOLLY gasp his name, Mitch couldn't remember if he'd ever heard a sweeter sound. Certainly he'd never heard anything that came close to creating the kind of raging desire he felt right now.

Gradually her body eased beneath him. Her embrace relaxed as her breathing deepened, and her hands settled on his waist. He placed a light kiss on both eyelids, and once he had, Molly opened her eyes.

Her mouth formed his name again, but no sound came out as she held his stare.

He propped himself further up on his elbows and studied the prefect lines of her face, tracing a finger across the angles and the hollows, and following the sharp definition of her jaw.

He didn't know why he should be so shocked at her driving hunger, her overwhelming passion. Last night she'd admitted to him that she'd never stopped loving him. That's why Mitch had wanted to please her first. He'd wanted to make her climax at just his touch. And he'd wanted to watch her when she did.

She was beautiful: her face, the magnificent curves and angles of her body, the hot silkiness of her skin, and the way her body moved. Nothing had ever turned him on more than the way Molly's body moved against his. It was like they fit together. Always had. Even now, both still wearing their jeans, there was nothing quite like it, Mitch thought.

He let his gaze travel lower, raking over the sumptuous mounds of her breasts, the flat stomach and the gentle, enticing rise to where her jeans splayed open on her hips. Her skin shimmered in the warm glow from the fire, as though tempting him to touch it.

He did. Splaying his fingers across her warm flesh, he caressed each curve, stopping only when his eye caught the edge of the bandage on Molly's waist. He looked at it, the white gauze a sharp contrast to the olive color of her skin. It was a cold reminder of the risks Molly had taken to protect him, of how close she'd come to losing her life that first night when she'd found him.

Mitch shuddered now as he thought of that happening. The intimacy they were sharing now, the reunion of their passions…they would never have had the chance to explore these if that bullet had been just one inch closer.

"Mitch?"

There was concern in Molly's eyes when he met her gaze. He hadn't realized he'd stopped caressing her, as though his hand had been paralyzed by the horror of his thoughts.

Molly trailed her fingers down the length of his back, then up again, past his shoulders and through his hair. Pleasure appeared to turn up the corners of her lips.

"Mitch," she whispered again. "Please. I want you inside of me."

The sound of her voice alone was enough to send another flood of longing through him. Mitch felt the urgency of his own arousal, pressing almost painfully against its denim barrier.

Molly grappled with the button, then the zipper, and when she slid her hand beneath and took hold of him, it required every ounce of restraint for him not to come in that instant. Easing away from her, Mitch gripped the waist of her jeans, and when Molly lifted her hips, he tugged the jeans free. Then his own. He moved onto the bed with her again. Nothing between them now. Just skin against skin. Flesh against willing flesh.

Anxiously, she shifted beneath him. Her hands slid down his back, stopping only when they reached his buttocks. There she urged him, drawing him closer, as though desperate for him.

His mouth found hers and she answered his kiss with an almost savage desire. The smell of jasmine filled his senses. The movement of her body seduced him. Then there was the feel of her wet, inviting heat.

And finally...finally Mitch entered her. Slowly. Wanting to experience every second to its fullest, every sensation to its absolute height. Little by little he filled her, each gentle thrust exhilaratingly unique, until eventually he was engulfed by her hot sweetness.

Everything faded then.

The months.

The years.

There was only him and Molly. Together. Nothing else mattered. Only their union.

Her body moved with his, falling into their familiar rhythm. She whispered his name, clutched him to her as each thrust brought him closer and closer to a brink he'd not experienced in a very long time. And when he felt the first shudder of release, when he wanted nothing more than to bury himself deep inside of her and lose himself, Mitch withdrew. Instead, he pressed himself against the soft heat of her belly, buried his face in her hair and cried her name as the blinding pulse of his climax shattered through him.

Chapter Eleven

It looked like they were in for more snow. The morning sky was as gray as yesterday's. Bordering on oppressive, Molly thought as she stood at the edge of Dewey Lake and surveyed the heavy, bruise-colored clouds that crept along the horizon. Across the lake, far past the half dozen makeshift ice-fishing huts, she could make out several cottages along the distant shoreline, sheltered by the same type of tall pines that graced the grounds of Shady Shores.

She lifted the collar of her anorak against the wind. It came from the east, stirring up the freshly fallen snow and creating miniature white twisters that danced along the lake's frozen surface. She watched them for a moment, welcoming the cold as though it might clear her head.

From the moment she'd slipped out from under the covers, her mind had been a chaos of thoughts. Quietly she'd gotten dressed, snatching glances of Mitch as he slept, one arm splayed across the empty space where she had lain. His face had held an expression she would have described as peaceful—one she hadn't seen from him until this morning. She'd wanted nothing more than to kiss him awake, to touch him and feel the power of his body against hers all over again. But to disturb that apparent peace...

She'd left instead. Sneaking out the cabin door into the

fresh morning air, still not completely awake and still not convinced she should leave the warmth of his embrace.

But she'd needed to think. She'd needed perspective.

Down at the lakeshore, gazing at the barrenness of the frozen landscape, Molly had started to draw some conclusions. Last night had been like a dream—the same one she'd had countless times over the years, and one she'd never believed could ever possibly come true.

But then…it hadn't come true. Not really. Not when she considered the circumstances, the situation, and especially, what Mitch had been through during the past ten months. The dream she'd always had was one of passion—*mutual* passion—and love. But how could Mitch possibly be capable of love right now? How could last night have been anything more than sex for him?

Yes, what she'd sensed from Mitch last night had felt passionate, felt like love. It had *felt* as though being with her was the only thing that had mattered to him. But after the loss of Emily, his daughter, the life he'd worked so hard for…how could he have any idea what he wanted or what mattered anymore?

Last night she'd been lost in the passion. Yet this morning, with the light of day, Molly couldn't escape the realization that what Mitch had *really* been seeking through their intimacy was comfort. Maybe, more than the passion, he'd been answering a need to feel alive again.

And if that wasn't enough to convince Molly that last night meant more to her than Mitch, there was the issue of time. It wasn't just the hurt that had separated them, but the years as well. *Twelve years.* They were different people now than the young adults they'd been, with different values, different wants and desires. And even though Molly felt the same connection with Mitch she had all those years ago, was it just fantasy? Was it one-sided?

No, one night of passion did not a future make. She had

to allow reality to play its hand. *And* she had to allow Mitch the time he no doubt needed to heal, before he could ever know what it was he wanted in life and in a partner. She'd seen the love in his eyes when he'd talked about Emily, and she'd seen his pain when he'd spoken of the daughter he'd lost. She couldn't claim to know the kind of love that grew through eight years of marriage, but if it was anything close to what she'd felt for Mitch all those years ago, there was no way he could give himself to her yet. Not completely. And not sincerely.

Molly turned from the lakeshore and headed back in the direction of the resort. She'd toyed with the idea of simply enjoying Mitch while she could, of not worrying so much about whether he was ready or not. But could she honestly deal with that kind of hurt a second time, if he decided to leave again?

Yes, she'd drawn some conclusions, all right. And at the end of all those, she was no further ahead. She *still* wanted to be with Mitch. She'd slept better last night than she had in years—an indication of how right it felt for her to be with him, to be sleeping in his arms. How could she ignore *that?*

Molly exhaled her frustration into a heavy cloud of breath vapor. She mounted the steps leading from the frozen beach to the roadway that separated the resort from its waterfront access. At the snow-covered road, Molly stopped, waiting for two snowmobiles to speed by. Thick clouds of snow churned in the air behind them, and quickly the high-pitched whine of their motors was swallowed up by distance and the snow.

Then Molly heard something else. Someone calling her name.

Across the road and down the resort's drive, a man stood next to a dark sedan.

Molly stopped, uncertain if he was the source until he lifted an arm and called her name again.

Suspicion flared through her and all her senses were sparked. Who could know she was here?

Moving slowly, she crossed the road, her eyes never leaving the figure next to the car. The weight of her Glock at her hip was of little comfort. It was tucked under so many layers of clothes there was no hope of getting to the weapon quickly. Molly's pulse kicked up a notch.

The man didn't move. With his hands buried in the pockets of his long tweed car coat, he waited for her by the car. There was something familiar about him, though, and as the wind whipped at the edges of his coat and suddenly snatched his red scarf from his neck, she heard him curse.

"Sarge?"

She watched him spin around, grabbing for the scarf before the wind could carry it away, and when he turned back to her he was shaking the snow off it and wrapping it around his neck once again.

He was still cursing mildly as she closed the distance between them.

"Sarge, what are you doing here?"

"What do you think?" he muttered, his face tightening into a grimace against the biting wind. He wasn't at all dressed for the elements. The open car coat blew back in the wind, and his short, salt-and-pepper hair provided little protection from the cold. "I was just about to go into the main office and ask for you," he added.

"But how did you—"

"I was at your dad's last night when you called," he explained, crossing his arms over his barreled chest in an effort to keep his coat closed. "What the *hell* are you doing, Molly?"

"Sarge, I—"

"Do you have any idea how concerned your father is? The man's worried sick about you."

"I told him I was all right."

"Against Sabatini's men? I don't think so. Good God, Molly! If I'd known what you were up to, I would *never* have approved your vacation request. Do you realize the risks you're taking? Not to mention the violations that'll end up on your record?"

"Sarge, listen to me. I had to find him. I had to bring him in. We need his testimony."

"Of course we need his testimony, Molly. And that's why we have a Fugitive Unit. They're handling the case. Damn, they're running around looking for him right now, and he's hiding out with *you!* Tell me how long you figured you'd get away with this?"

"I only just convinced him to come back to Chicago, Sarge."

"All right then. So let's go. Get Drake. Get your stuff. And get in the car."

Molly dropped her gaze to the ground, where she kicked at a chunk of ice. Mitch would never go for it. She might have finally convinced him to return to Chicago with her, but how many times had he voiced his mistrust of the police? It wouldn't matter to him that this was her sergeant, that this was a man she trusted explicitly. If he saw any sign of any other cop, Molly was certain Mitch would change his mind. And she was not about to risk that.

"Sarge, I…I can't."

"What? What the hell do you mean, you can't?"

She shook her head. "It's Drake. After the explosion…he doesn't trust the police."

"But he trusts you?"

She nodded.

"So, if he trusts you, then you tell him we're heading out in ten minutes." He turned to take hold of the car's door handle. "It's an order, Molly," he added, when she failed to move.

"I can't."

"Listen to me, Molly. I've just spent four hours driving through this crap to find you. I promised your dad I'd bring you home safe. So I am *not* leaving here without you and Drake."

Molly cast a quick glance in the direction of the cabin. Mitch wouldn't go for it. She knew him.

"I can't, Sarge," she said again.

Impatience darkened his face when he turned to look at her again. "Molly—"

"He's not with me right now," she lied.

"What the hell are you talking about? You told your father—"

"That was last night.

"So where the hell is he?"

"I...I'm not sure. I mean, I think I know."

"Molly, you either have Drake or you don't. Which is it?"

She took in a breath of cold, raw air. *Could he see she was lying?*

"Molly?" he prompted again.

"I don't have him. He took off, Sarge. This morning."

"Where to?"

"I...I'm not sure yet."

"All right, then—" he opened the sedan door and hit the button for the power locks "—get in. We'll go find him together."

"Sarge, I can't. I—"

"Molly, I'm getting tired of this. Get in the car and let's go."

"No. Listen to me, Sarge. Please. Trust me. Drake will never agree to go with both of us. I know him. Only *I* can bring him in."

"Then I'll treat him as a hostile witness for the prosecution and—"

"—and he'll never testify for us, Sarge. *Please.* When have I ever let you down in the past? Just trust me on this one. I'll have Drake back to Chicago tomorrow. I promise. Just give me one more day."

The deep lines etched across Sarge's face appeared to soften somewhat as he studied her. Then he looked away, scanning the resort and the cabins through the trees. *Did he believe her? Or was he searching for any sign of Mitch?* Finally he turned his hard gaze back on her.

"You're telling me the truth when you say you don't have Drake here? Right now?"

One more time Molly took in a breath, nodding and silently praying he couldn't see through the lie.

"But you're sure you can bring him in?"

She nodded again.

"All right," he said at last. "You bring him in then. But you have one day, Molly. After that I can't promise what will or won't be written into your record."

"I understand, Sarge."

"I hope so."

He appeared to give the resort a final, doubtful scrutiny.

"Your dad told me about the evidence you have on Rachel Messina. Tampered reports?"

"I don't know if it's enough, Sarge, but yes, there's evidence in the police computer system."

Molly explained briefly the files she'd printed on the various cases Rachel had been connected to. As he listened, Karl Burr turned up the narrow collar of his coat and hunched his shoulders against the cold as he shifted his weight from one foot to the other.

"I'm going to look into it as soon as I get back," he assured her. "I'll talk to Garrettson in the D.A.'s office and see what we can come up with."

"Thanks."

"Just get Drake, Molly."

"I will."

Behind his stare, Molly thought she saw skepticism.

"Trust me, Sarge," she added.

"It's not that I don't trust you, Molly. I'm just worried about what your father will do to me if anything happens to you."

"Nothing's going to happen to me. I promise."

With one final long, hard stare, Karl Burr turned at last to the salt-stained sedan. He folded his large frame into the driver's seat, and Molly caught a brief whiff of leather and cigarettes as the car's warning system chimed softly.

"I'll see you in Chicago. Tomorrow. And Molly, be careful. Be damned careful," he said before pulling the door shut and turning over the engine.

She stood in the resort's main entrance as Sarge slipped the large vehicle into reverse and gave her one last warning look through the windshield. She watched him maneuver the car through the heavy snow, steering it onto the road and in the direction of Dowagiac…and Chicago.

One day. She had one day. Molly headed up the path leading to the cabins along the slope. If there was anyone she couldn't let down it was Karl Burr. No matter what, she *had* to have Mitch in Chicago by tomorrow. And as her hand closed over the handle of the cabin's front door, Molly hoped that, after last night, Mitch hadn't changed his mind.

She stepped inside, her gaze immediately going to the rumpled sheets of the bed. Then to the unoccupied bathroom, and to the empty hook where Mitch's coat had hung. And, finally, Molly saw the open back door.

She tried to tame the panic that already had her heart hammering against her ribs. But in the same instant she heard the stuttering ignition and then the scream of a snowmobile engine. It had to be one of the Suttons' own machines, she realized, parked in the small shelter behind their cabin. Irwin Sutton had pointed them out last night, offering their use to her and Mitch.

Surely Mitch wouldn't leave without telling her.

Molly charged through the cabin, disbelief growing with each racing stride. And when she reached the back porch, she saw him.

He was just lifting a helmet onto his head.

"Mitch?"

Over the roar of the engine, he didn't appear to hear her shout.

"Mitch!" she yelled louder now, waving to him as she struggled through the fresh snow.

And then he saw her.

But instead of flipping up the helmet's visor as she expected him to do, Mitch hurriedly buckled the strap. He straddled the machine's wide seat and opened the throttle. And when he looked at her again, Molly could have sworn she saw something akin to fear flash in his eyes behind the heavy visor.

"Mitch, wait!" she called out again, but it was useless. There was the thick odor of burning oil and gas, and then a spray of snow as he sped away.

Shock and confusion threatened to immobilize her. And yet she couldn't afford to waste a second. Zipping up her coat, Molly ran to the shelter. She snatched up a helmet and rammed it onto her head. And as she jumped astride one of the two remaining machines and reached for the ignition key, Molly prayed she remembered enough from her one experience on a snowmobile to see her through this.

She couldn't lose Mitch. But as she careened the machine out of the shelter, he was already no more than a fading trail of swirling snow.

MITCH CURSED HIMSELF for what had to be the hundredth time within the past five minutes since he'd first seen Molly with the man at the resort entrance. He'd been a fool. Such a *damned* fool!

He *knew* better than to trust the police. *Knew* they couldn't protect him. On top of which, last night he'd seen for himself the very real links between the Chicago Police Department and Sabatini's felonious circle. How on *earth* had he let himself believe Molly was any different?

No, Mitch thought again. There was no mistaking the man with Molly moments ago.

Wind tore at his parka and battered against the helmet. The snowmobile beneath him vibrated as he gave even more gas to it and left the maze of pine trees behind. Now in an open field, the machine's skis plowed through the light snow, skipping and thudding over the uneven surface beneath.

He had no idea where he was headed. No bearings, no sense of direction. No idea even how much fuel he might have in the tank. Only a steadily growing conviction that he had to get the hell out of there. And fast. Sabatini's men could have descended upon him at any moment.

A quick glimpse over his shoulder assured him that he was hardly in the clear yet. Molly was after him. And gaining.

He'd seen her mount one of the other machines seconds after he'd sped away. He hadn't given her credit for knowing how to operate it, but when he'd seen her blast out of the shelter in hot pursuit, Mitch knew he'd have a run for his money. And now, gauging the narrowing gap between them, he was beginning to wonder if she'd lucked out with a better machine, or if she was making this her kamikaze mission.

His own machine thundered across the white expanse of the field, leaving behind him a cloud of snow that almost

obscured the headlamp of Molly's machine. But he knew
she was there. Mitch gave even more gas. He had to lose
her. She was one of them. Not to be trusted.

He angled the snowmobile to his right, bearing steadily
toward the lake. He'd already decided he had to avoid the
roads. Sabatini's men could be posted anywhere along the
lakeshore drive. But the lake…if he could get to the frozen
lake and cross to the other side, to the more remote cottages
and summer homes that the Suttons had told them about
last night, he'd stand a much better chance of losing Molly
and whatever other men Sabatini had watching the resort.

He cursed himself again. How could he have so readily
believed Molly last night? She'd printed pages upon pages
of so-called evidence from the police's electronic files, but
how was he to know the real content of the documents?
Everything Molly had excitedly churned out at the library
could just as easily have been bogus, or maybe even evidence she herself had planted in Tom's files. Molly had
suggested it was Rachel Messina who had betrayed Tom to
Sabatini and gotten him killed. But wasn't Molly—a former
partner of Tom's—just as likely a candidate? Could it not
have been *Molly* who had put Sabatini onto Tom?

God, anything was possible.

Mitch should have stuck to his conviction a few days
ago. Standing in the sunshine outside Barb's house, he'd
told her he couldn't trust anyone. Why hadn't he heeded
that inner voice that had warned him so loudly back then?

No, instead he'd trusted Molly. He'd let himself believe
that the years hadn't changed them, that he could trust her
the same way he had over a decade ago, when—in fact—
he hardly knew her at all.

Mitch saw the road. He slowed only enough to check for
traffic before steering his machine down the steep embankment to the shore. Gripping the snowmobile's tank with his
knees, Mitch eased the machine over crevices and jagged

ice crags, and when his skis at last touched the smooth surface of the frozen lake, he leaned forward and opened the throttle.

Molly was right behind him. She'd gained some distance in the field, and seemed to take little notice of the rugged shoreline as her machine bucked and twisted. Now it didn't seem to matter how much he gunned the machine, Molly was catching up to him. With quick glances over his shoulder, he could see the distance between them close. And then she was steering to the right, clearly aware that she had the superior machine and by coming alongside him she could cut him off.

Other snowmobilers had made the lake their raceway. Countless tracks intersected one another, especially near the middle of the lake, and Mitch had to concentrate to keep his machine on an even keel as it thumped across opposing trails like a water-skier skipping over cross waves.

Another side glance, and he saw Molly lean into her machine, her lithe figure hugging the snowmobile's gas tank as the vehicle careened over the ice. Involuntarily, images from last night filled his thoughts: the way he'd made love to Molly, the way she'd made love to *him*. He'd felt then—more than ever—that he knew her, that he was connected to her. Feeling her body move with his, sensing the passion flood through her, holding her in his arms...

But he'd been fooled.

He banked his machine to the left, hoping to put some space between them. It was going to be impossible to lose her here, in the open, but if he could maintain some distance and reach the other side, he might stand a chance. With some strategy and maneuvering he might lose her in the trees that crowded the opposite shore.

This time when he jammed the accelerator all the way with his thumb, he felt the machine shudder for a split second beneath him, then surge forward. The shore loomed.

Another hundred yards and he'd reach the safety of the woods.

It was then, with a last shred of hope, that Mitch looked over his shoulder again.

But instead of the relief he expected to feel at seeing Molly lose some ground, Mitch's heart stopped. In one second she was banking her own machine to the left in an attempt to counter his maneuver, and in the next her snowmobile was airborne. He saw the skis strike a nearly invisible rift in the ice, saw one snap in two, and then saw the wide track propel the machine up—it had to be eight…ten feet in air—twisting as though in slow motion while Mitch watched in shock. And then Molly…flailing off the machine, hurled through the air, finally landing on the ice and rolling like a lifeless rag doll.

Chapter Twelve

"Molly!" Inside his helmet, Mitch screamed her name. His breath fogged the visor and he flipped it open as he swung his snowmobile around.

"Molly!" he shouted again.

But there was no response from her. Her body lay motionless, sprawled on the ice a good fifteen feet from the battered snowmobile. With his heart in his throat, Mitch gunned his machine, throwing up huge chunks of snow and ice behind him.

He came to a skidding stop near her prone body. In seconds he was off his machine and crossing the ice. His legs were shaky, and he knew it was from fear. He could taste it in his throat—a sour bitterness. His heart raced, and there was a fist around his lungs, threatening to squeeze out his next breath.

He yanked off his helmet. It clattered to the ice. The wind was sharper here, raw and relentless, blasting across the open expanse of the frozen lake, biting into his numbed skin and tearing at his hair.

"Molly?" He dropped to his knees next to her. "God, Molly. Come on."

She was on her stomach, her head turned to her right, unmoving.

Mitch tore his gloves from his hands and reached between the collar of her anorak and her helmet. His fingers fluttered across the silkiness of her skin, searching frantically for a pulse.

It was there. Faint, but there.

The inside of her helmet's visor was fogged. He wanted to see her face, wanted to tear her helmet off, but what if she'd broken her neck? Or her back?

Frantically, Mitch scanned the lake. If anyone had seen the accident, they'd be here. They'd have called for help.

But there was nothing. No sign of anyone.

He turned back to her.

"Molly? Can you hear me?"

Practically lying on the ice himself now so he could see her, he lifted the helmet's visor. Her eyes were closed, her mouth open. Her breathing was shallow.

"God, Molly, please." He reached into the helmet, touching her cheek with shaking fingers. Her skin was cool and her complexion pale.

"Come on, honey." Panic threatened to steal his voice.

Suddenly the idea of Molly connected to Sabatini didn't matter. Mitch almost didn't care if the kingpin's thugs came charging across the ice right now for him, if they ran him down in cold blood in the middle of this barren landscape. As long as Molly was okay.

"Please, Molly, you have to be all right."

Not knowing the full extent of her injuries, he fought the urge to scoop her up into his arms, to cradle her in his lap and hold her tight against him.

"Come on, baby, you're okay. You *have* to be."

He touched her again, taking off her glove and squeezing her hand in his.

"We finally found each other again," he whispered, his voice even shakier now. "You're not leaving me. I'm not letting you. I love you, Molly. Do you hear me?"

If not for the helmet, he would have kissed her cold lips.

"I love you," he said again, chanting it as though only those three words could pull her from the darkness that consumed her. "Molly, do you hear me? I said I love you."

His fingers trembled as he pressed them to her lips.

Mitch wasn't certain if he heard her groan first or felt it against his fingertips, but the sound sent a shock of relief through him.

"Molly? Can you hear me?"

She stirred. Her hand tightened around his, and then her eyes fluttered open.

Disorientation swam in those wide, dark eyes, and Mitch wondered if she knew where she was and how she'd come to be here.

"Can you move?" he asked her.

Her gaze flitted up, locking onto his, and two lines of confusion deepened above the bridge of her nose.

"Mitch?"

"Molly, can you move?" he demanded again. "Is anything broken?"

She shook her head and gathered herself. Still holding Mitch's hand, she pulled herself up from the ice. She leaned heavily against him for a moment and then eased back, as though intending to stand on her own. If not for Mitch catching her, she would have been back on the ice.

"Are you hurt anywhere?" he asked her, holding her at arm's length so he could look at her. With her helmet on, he couldn't be sure, but Mitch was certain she'd turned another shade paler.

She was shaking her head, her hands gripping his shoulders tightly. "No. I think I'm fine. Just…shaky."

Again she tried to stand on her own, and again Mitch had to catch her.

"Come on." Still supporting her, he managed to snatch up his helmet. He slid her arm over his shoulder and put his own around her waist as he guided her to his snowmobile. "I'm getting you out of here," he said, even though he had no idea where.

He knew he should probably take her to a hospital, but that wasn't an option. Not now, with Sabatini's men in the area. He needed to get off the lake, to find shelter, get Molly warm and take a closer look for injuries.

But less than a half dozen staggering steps from the snowmobile, Molly suddenly sagged. Her body was instantly limp, and Mitch tasted fear all over again.

He shouted this time. "Molly, no! Listen to me. I need your help here."

She came to, clutching at his parka and drawing herself up once again. She mumbled something that Mitch couldn't make out.

"Come on, Molly. We have to get out of here."

Several more shaky steps and they were there. He eased her onto the wide seat of the snowmobile and placed her hands on the bars.

"Hang on," he ordered, as he straddled the seat behind her, half expecting her to pass out again. And with one arm wrapped around her waist, his knees gripping the gas tank, Mitch nosed the lumbering machine toward the shoreline and the trees.

MOLLY'S AWARENESS returned to her in faint whispers. First there was the crackle of a fire, then its warmth. She felt the softness of the blankets around her and the hard floor beneath. She heard the wind outside, blowing through trees. And then there was the smell—Mitch.

The scent of his aftershave lifted off the collar of the sweater she wore. With her eyes still closed, she drew it closer to her nose, the wool scratching her skin as she inhaled deeply.

Her head throbbed and her body felt stiff. And as she took in another breath of his scent, Molly opened her eyes.

She had no idea where she was. It was early evening. Dusk darkened the small square windows. The old stone fireplace blazed, lighting up the interior of the one-room log cabin. Above the mantel, glaring down at her with a full rack of horns, hung a stuffed deer head. Complimentary hooves were mounted on either side. Farther back in the shadows, several other trophies adorned the far wall. The glow of the fire reflected in their glass eyes and gleamed off a collection of antique rifles. And if these weren't enough evidence, the furnishings of the small cabin were definitely à la hunting lodge—tasteless, marred, and over-shellacked knotty pine.

Where the hell was she?

Frantically, Molly tried to piece together what had happened. She remembered the snowmobiles and the lake. And she remembered Mitch shouting at her, carrying her, and then his soothing voice whispering through a haze of memories.

Molly drew herself up so she sat on the small island of blankets before the hearth. To her left, Mitch leaned back in a rocking chair, his head lolled to one side, his eyes closed.

He'd brought her here. Carried her. Vaguely she remembered his struggle with the door as he'd held her in his arms. He'd set her down, demanding that she stand when all she'd wanted to do was close her eyes. And she remembered him searching for a key, finding it over the window frame as she clung to him.

But where was here? And why?

"Mitch?"

She'd barely whispered his name and he jolted awake. She thought she saw a flicker of panic in his eyes for a split second before he seemed to realize where he was.

"What time is it?" he asked.

"I don't know. Evening."

His gaze went from the windows to the fireplace, and then back to her. There was a wariness there that she didn't understand.

"How are you feeling?" He leaned forward, his elbows on his knees as he rubbed his face.

"Fine, I guess. My head hurts a little. What happened?"

"You don't remember?"

"Well, I remember being on snowmobiles. Driving across the lake and…" Molly shook her head.

"And you hit a rift in the ice," he finished for her. "You could have been killed." He stood, picking up a poker and rearranging the logs on the grate. "I thought I'd have to take you to a hospital. You've been out for hours."

"You woke me." Her memory stumbled over itself.

"Every hour. I didn't know what else to do. You were in and out of consciousness. I thought…. You had me scared, Molly."

She wished she could see his face, but he refused to look at her, as though unwilling to let her see the emotion she heard in his voice.

"So where are we?"

"Across the lake. I didn't know where else to go. Shady Shores isn't safe anymore. So I broke into this place."

"What do you mean, Shady Shores isn't safe?"

When he turned at last to face her, there was no mistaking the mistrust that flashed in his eyes. And then she remembered. It was the same look he'd given her back at the resort an instant before he'd jumped astride the snowmobile and taken off.

She'd chased him. *That's* why they'd been on the lake. She had tried to stop him, and he'd been running…from her.

"Mitch, I don't understand what's going on. What do you mean, Shady Shores isn't safe?" she asked again.

He studied her for a long moment, the warmth of the

firelight doing nothing to soften the hard look he gave her. "It's not safe because you let them know we were there."

"Them? Who's them?"

"Sabatini's men, who else? You're connected to him, aren't you, Molly?"

"What the hell are you talking about?" Exasperation lifted her voice. "What's going on, Mitch? Why did you run away from me?"

He slid his hands into the pockets of his jeans, but she could still see the fists he made.

"You asked me the other night if I'd be able to remember the faces of any of the men that night," he began, his tone low, his words coming slowly as though he deliberated over each one.

"Yes?" She drew herself up onto the small, threadbare sofa, her head spinning even from that small effort.

"The man you were talking to this morning at the resort…"

"That was my—"

"He was there, Molly. The night Emily was killed. He was under the overpass, standing next to Sabatini when he shot that detective."

"No, Mitch, you're wrong. Maybe you didn't see him properly this morning. The distance—"

"There was a pair of binoculars in the cabin, Molly. I saw just fine."

"But you couldn't have. You—"

"*I saw him, Molly.* It was *him,* all right? Don't tell me what I did or didn't see. *You weren't there!*"

"Mitch, the man you saw me talking to this morning, he's my sergeant. Karl Burr. I've talked to you about him, when we were kids. The man…he's my dad's best friend, his former partner. He's like an uncle to me. I've known him practically my whole life."

"I don't care how you know him, Molly. I'm telling you

he was there that night. Standing next to Sabatini. He jumped into a car along with the rest of the sons of bitches and ran us off the road.''

Molly lifted a hand to her temple, massaging the slight throb. *He had to be wrong.* Karl Burr hadn't been there that night. He wasn't connected to Sabatini. Next to her father, the man was the finest cop the Chicago PD had to offer. Of anyone, Karl Burr was the last officer who could be bought.

Yet the fierce certainty in Mitch's expression was difficult to argue with.

''Look, Mitch, maybe you saw him at Headquarters when the detectives questioned you. Maybe—''

''I was never at Headquarters, Molly. The detectives interviewed me at the hospital. And I can guarantee you, no sergeant ever talked to me. A lieutenant, maybe. But no sergeant. And definitely not Karl Burr.''

''But—''

''No, Molly. No 'buts.' It was him. I'm positive.''

''But we've already proved it's Rachel who's the leak. How—?''

''Who's to say Sabatini doesn't have more than one cop on his payroll? And why *not* a sergeant, someone higher up? Maybe it costs Sabatini a bit more, but it would explain a lot of leaks over the years, no? You're always wondering how all those charges against Sabatini get thrown out on technicalities. Well, I'm sure they were being thrown out long before Rachel Messina ever got her detective's shield.''

Molly stood now. She needed to think, needed to move, in spite of the room threatening to whirl. Her legs were shaky, but gradually she gained her balance as she paced from one end of the cramped cabin to the next.

''Okay, Mitch, if you're right—''

''I'm right, Molly.''

"Fine. But you saw Sarge with Sabatini that night…then what was this morning about? Why would he drive all the way from Chicago?"

"Well, I can guarantee you it wasn't a social visit."

"What then? If he came to kill us, then why didn't he, hmm?"

"Because maybe he wasn't sure I was still with you. He needed to be sure."

Molly felt her pulse quicken. He was right. She'd told Sarge Mitch wasn't with her, that she'd find him, bring him in. In the blink of an eye she could envision the way Sarge had looked past her shoulder then, disbelieving. Searching? She'd been so worried that he'd sense her lie that she hadn't paid full attention to his reaction. But maybe…maybe Mitch was right. Maybe Sarge *had* come to deal with Mitch. And to deal with her.

The thought sent a chill through her.

"So why did he drive away then, Mitch?" she asked, still clinging to disbelief.

"He didn't. I called Irwin Sutton, to tell him about the snowmobile on the lake. He said a dark Illinois-plated sedan had driven by the resort several times this morning."

"I don't get it." She shook her head. Too many possibilities. Even more implications.

Karl Burr? *Sarge?*

"What's to get, Molly?"

"Well…he knew where we were. Why wouldn't he call Sabatini's men and have them deal with us, instead of driving all that way?"

"How should I know? Maybe after their failed attempts, your sergeant decided he wanted to take care of it himself. After all, I can ID him as well as I can Sabatini, right? Maybe he's more concerned about himself right now than his mobster buddy."

Molly struggled against the sudden urge to be sick. The

idea of Sarge driving four hours from Chicago with one intent, to kill Mitch—and to kill her, most likely—was horrifying.

"Molly, listen to me." He stepped in front of her now, blocking her path, and took her shoulders in his hands.

"I'm right about this," he said. "I saw him. You have to trust me. Please."

She searched his dark eyes, wishing…praying he was wrong.

"Trust me, Molly, in the same way you're asking me to trust you…to trust that you have nothing to do with Sabatini yourself."

"What? No, Mitch! Please, you can't think that. How can you? After last night…after what we shared, you can't possibly—"

"I don't." He stopped her, squeezing her shoulders so hard she thought she might find bruises there in the morning. "I don't, Molly. I did…this morning. When I saw you with that man, I believed…I don't know what I believed, exactly. But I trust you."

Maybe they were standing too close, maybe the situation was too emotionally charged, or maybe Mitch felt the need to kiss her then in order to convince her. But when he did, Molly didn't doubt his words.

His kiss was deep. Consuming. Passionate. There was none of the hesitancy she thought she'd sensed from him before, but instead, a confidence and a determination that felt like the old Mitch.

And how easy it would be to let their kiss carry her away. Mitch drew her closer against his hard body, and Molly felt his desire as keenly as she felt her own settle deep in her core.

But—more immediate than her desire—lives were at stake. *Their* lives.

"Mitch." She drew back slightly, reluctantly, feeling the

lingering heat of his lips on hers. "You're still coming with me to Chicago, right?"

He didn't answer her, and in his eyes she could see that the most recent events had shaken his resolution to do what was right. What was safe.

"Now, more than ever, we need protection. *Both* of us. If you're right about Sarge...if he really is connected to Sabatini, then this situation is even more dangerous than either of us can imagine. Who knows where the connections end? And unless I'm in Chicago, there's nothing I can do to stop any of them."

Still he didn't answer. He lowered his forehead so it rested against hers, and Molly felt the heat of his breath whisper across her lips as he exhaled. Nestling her palms against the roughness of his unshaved cheeks, she tilted his face so he looked at her.

"Mitch, you have to go back. Please? I don't want anything to happen to you."

She waited for his nod.

"Thank you," she murmured, and placed another lingering kiss on his moist lips.

"I don't think we've got much fuel left," he warned.

"That's all right. I have a plan."

"WELL, YOU'RE RIGHT," Molly said ten minutes later, replacing the phone's receiver into its cradle. "Shady Shores is definitely not the place either of us wants to be right now."

While she'd spoken to Ray Sutton on the phone, Mitch had rummaged through the cabin's cupboards and boiled some water. Now he handed her a steaming cup of tea.

"Ray says there have been a couple of Illinois-plated vehicles cruising by the resort at staggered intervals. One of them's a black four-by-four."

"Sounds as though your sergeant turned us in to Sabatini's thugs, after all."

Molly nodded, wrapping her hands around the hot mug and standing before the fire. She knew she should sit down. Her body felt drained. Yet she was wired, wanting to take action.

"So what's the plan?" Mitch asked, joining her.

"We're heading to Chicago tomorrow. Ray says there's a train that leaves from Niles at noon. He figures he'll wait till dark to go to our cabin in case Sabatini's men are still lurking. He'll get our stuff, and pick us up in the morning to take us to the station."

Mitch stared into the fire. He looked a million miles away.

"Mitch?"

When he turned to her, Molly couldn't help thinking that he looked rattled.

"And what's the plan once we're in Chicago?" he asked.

"I'm not sure yet. Get you into protective custody to begin with. Then I can figure out what to do with the evidence I have on Rachel, and try to get something on Sarge. We need more proof on his connection to Sabatini than just your eyewitness testimony, and if I can do that, I—"

"And what about *your* safety, Molly?"

She started to shake her head, wanting to tell him not to worry, but the worry was already there.

"As far as I can tell," he continued, "you're just as wanted by Sabatini as I am now."

"Mitch, I'll be fine."

"No, Molly, that won't cut it. Not when…" He shook his head, as if incapable of finishing the thought that darkened his expression.

"What, Mitch? What is it?"

"When I saw you… When that snowmobile crashed, and

you were on the ice…not moving… I thought you were dead, Molly.''

He didn't need to explain further. The fear was so evident it darkened his eyes and put a quaver in his voice. And eventually he turned away, as though unable to look her in the eye. *He thought he'd lost her;* that's what he'd intended to say.

Molly touched his arm and felt the tension in his muscles.

''You know, you talk about not wanting anything to happen to me,'' he said, so quietly she had to strain to hear. ''Well…I feel the same about you, Molly. What you've brought to my life…you've shown me hope. And let me tell you, I've been pretty slim on that these past few months. In fact, I don't think I knew what hope was anymore, to be honest. Without it, I certainly wouldn't be agreeing to return to Chicago…for you or for anyone.''

''Mitch.'' She tightened her grip on his arm, drawing him around so he looked at her. ''I'll be careful,'' she whispered. ''I promise.''

He seemed to study her for a long time then, clearly not trusting her word. And when she lay a hand against his cheek, she felt the brief flexing of a muscle along his jaw. Gradually it eased, as did the tension in his face.

She couldn't resist a smile then as she considered Mitch's obvious concern. Lightly, she traced the pad of her thumb over his lower lip, wanting to feel its curve against her own.

''I'm glad I was able to give you hope again,'' she said, watching the reflection of the flames in his eyes. ''And I'm glad you finally believe that you have a life. Because you *do*, Mitch.''

He opened his mouth as though to say something, but then stopped himself.

Instead, he kissed her. There was a fierceness to it, echoing the fear she'd seen in his eyes moments ago when he'd spoken of her accident. He reached for her hips and drew her close, as if desperate to feel the full length of her body, to prove to himself that she was alive.

His hands slid to her buttocks, holding her against him so that there was no question as to his intent. Or his need. As keen as her own now.

"Thank you, Molly," she heard him murmur between their kisses. "Thank you."

Deftly, he tugged the sweater over her head, then worked the buttons of her shirt. His mouth never left hers—sweet yet insistent, gentle yet relentless. There was no telling who led who now; both were driven. Both remembering last night, and both wanting more...much more.

When Molly felt Mitch's hands on her skin, blazing across her flesh, taking hold of one breast and massaging it as his hips ground into hers, she thought she'd forgotten to breathe. She heard her own gasp and felt the tripping of her heart as an undeniable desire settled deep inside her.

But it was more than physical. And it was more than the here and now, Molly realized. She wanted Mitch...forever. She wanted to be with him, to show him life again, and to share it with him.

And as she drank in his eager desperation, Molly felt for the first time that she might actually have a fighting chance with Mitch, that the dream might be more than just some wild fantasy left over from her girlhood. Mitch felt real. His passion felt real.

Her own hands moved anxiously over him, splaying across his wide chest, then down to the bottom of his sweater and beneath it. She lifted it over his head, even as he worked the button of her jeans and slid his hand under the denim barrier. This time it was Mitch's groan she heard as his fingers found her wet heat.

Longing drove them. And fear—the very real fear of

losing after finally finding again. Molly tore at Mitch's clothes with the same fervor, until both were naked. The heat of the fire was nothing compared to the heat of Mitch's body against hers. He lowered her to the blankets before the hearth, his mouth still devouring hers, as she grasped him, drawing him to her, *needing* him inside of her.

And when Mitch entered her there was none of the patience or the hesitancy she'd felt from him last night. Only a driving assuredness. A sense of right. A sense of belonging. And a sense of future.

She moved with him, their rhythm familiar. She arched against him, clutching him to her as she felt the rise of his climax. And as her own hot release reached its edge, and she felt Mitch about to withdraw, Molly held him tightly.

"No," she begged. "No, Mitch. I want you."

The plea had barely left her lips when she felt his release, shuddering through his body and vibrating into her very core as he cried out her name.

Molly wasn't sure how long they stayed like that—her arms around him, his body covering hers. It could have been hours, and it still wouldn't have been long enough. Eventually Mitch shifted. She felt his reluctance.

Nestling behind her, he drew her into his embrace, her body fitting easily into the angles of his. He cradled her head in the crook of his arm, pulled up one of the blankets and held her as night darkened the windows. Gradually Mitch's breathing deepened, and as Molly watched the flames lick at the logs, she thought for sure he was asleep.

She wondered if he thought the same of her then, because when he spoke, his lips nuzzling against her ear, his words sounded more like a private confession.

"I love you, Molly," he whispered, holding her a little tighter. "Not a day's gone by in my life when I haven't loved you."

Chapter Thirteen

Mitch and Molly had showered and were ready by the time Ray showed up at eleven o'clock. They waited while Molly searched her pockets for a few dollars, leaving the money on the coffee table along with a scribbled note of thanks to the cabin's owners, and within five minutes they were on the road.

From the dash of his Buick, Ray handed them a paper bag containing two egg sandwiches. Both were devoured before they'd even left the Sister Lakes area.

He'd informed them of his success in retrieving their belongings from the cabin without detection, and assured Molly several times that he wasn't followed around the lake to their hideaway. Still, they drove in relative silence for the first fifteen minutes, all three of them on alert for tailing vehicles.

It had snowed again in the night, and Mitch squinted against the glare of the sun on the new snow. It blanketed rooftops and clung to tree limbs, turning the rolling landscape into a postcard vista. But from the passenger seat of Ray's car, Mitch found little enjoyment in the ever-changing panorama. His nerves were on edge. As were Molly's. He sensed it from her: in the way she'd fidgeted in the back seat.

Even Ray seemed more than a little uptight, his grip visibly white around the steering wheel.

Bracing her forearms across the top of the bench seat, Molly leaned forward between them. She seemed to pick up on Ray's uneasiness as well, and settled one hand onto his shoulder.

"I can't thank you enough," she said, flashing him a genuine smile when he glanced quickly back at her.

"It's not a problem, Molly. Nothing is, if it means seeing Tom's killer behind bars."

"We're going to get him this time. I promise you."

Ray only nodded, fixing his stare out the windshield as they entered Niles.

Silence again, only this time it was Mitch's shoulder Molly placed a hand on. The simple touch sent a quiver of longing through him. With Molly leaning so close, he could smell the traces of jasmine just under the staleness of old car upholstery. The scent triggered sweet memories. There had been an ardent desperation to their lovemaking last night. Not just from him, but from Molly as well. An indescribable need to be together. And an incredible feeling of "right."

After eight years with Emily, after loving her all that time, Mitch had never imagined touching another woman. He'd never thought he'd be able to, especially after losing her. He'd believed he'd be racked with guilt.

Yet there was none of that with Molly…neither this morning nor yesterday. Nothing felt more right than touching her, than being with her, inside her, connected to her. There was no trace of the guilt he'd expected, but instead an extraordinary sense of approval, as though Emily would have offered him her blessing.

And it was that sense of "right" that had led him to confess things to Molly last night, things he probably shouldn't have voiced, things that might now put undue pressure on her emotionally. Yet there was more...much more he'd wanted to say to her as he'd held her in his arms.

Yes, Molly had shown him that he did still have a life, even after Emily and the shattered dreams. But *being* with Molly was what had allowed him to *believe* it. Still, he hadn't dared to voice that, not when Molly might have different plans or hopes. There was no knowing what Molly was feeling. Yes, she'd admitted she'd never fallen out of love with him. But how was he to know her intentions today? Ultimately, could she forgive what he'd done to her twelve years ago? Was it possible to start fresh, with a new set of dreams? And did she even *want* someone in her life right now?

If it was the old Molly—the Molly he'd understood almost better than himself—Mitch would have known the answer. He would have known that, for Molly Sparling, love—the kind he'd felt from her through their lovemaking—*that* kind of love superceded all else. But they were different people now, with twelve years of past that didn't include one another. You couldn't just pick up where you'd left off with a person, let alone expect them to cling to the same ideals and desires they had all those years before.

No, for now, Mitch thought, some things were better left unsaid.

Snow crunched under the Buick's tires as they turned into the narrow parking lot of the Niles train station. The century-old building looked more like a movie set than a functioning station. Quaint and authentic, it harkened back to the romance of rail travel, contrasting sharply with the sleek, high-tech train that crouched next to the eastbound platform.

Mitch passed an apprehensive glance across the lot, half expecting to see a black four-by-four sitting in the corner, waiting. Or maybe Molly's sergeant's sedan. But there was no sign of Sabatini presence.

Ray put the Buick in park and turned off the engine. "You want me to go in and buy the tickets?" he asked, already unbuckling his seat belt.

"No, Ray. You've done more than enough. Thank you," Molly said, scooping up their knapsacks from the seat next to her. "We've got time. We'll get them."

"All right. Well, maybe you'll want this then." Ray reached under his seat, rummaging for a second, before he came up with a plastic bag. "Went into Dowagiac before I picked you guys up. Thought you might need it."

He handed Molly the bag, watching as she pulled out a package. Inside, behind the plastic bubble wrap, was a black microcassette player.

"There's batteries in there, too," Ray added.

"You're a real hero, Ray, you know that?" She smiled and leaned over the back of the seat in order to place a quick kiss on his cheek. "Just like your brother."

When she sat back again, Mitch caught the brief flicker of sadness behind those smiling eyes.

"All right, Mitch. You ready?" she asked him then, reaching for the door handle.

He thanked Ray himself, telling him he'd call to make arrangements for Barb's Blazer, and opened the door. The cold snatched his breath for a second as he circled the car to join Molly, but the sun warmed his skin. A plume of vapor hung in the still air between them, and through it Mitch watched Molly scan the parking lot. There was tension in her face and wariness in her stance as she handed him his knapsack and shouldered her own.

The smile he'd seen on her lips moments ago was gone now.

"Molly? Are you okay?"

She nodded, turning those dark eyes on him.

"Sure," she murmured. But she looked far from okay as she scanned the lot a final time before starting toward the station doors.

THERE SEEMED TO BE no shaking the nervousness that clawed at the pit of Molly's stomach. Even once the west-bound train had cleared the tracks and left the town limits of Niles a good fifteen minutes behind, Molly felt her pulse racing.

Mitch must have sensed her anxiousness. He'd been silent since they pulled out of the station, sitting across from her in the private compartment they'd managed to secure. He reached over now and took her hand in his.

"Relax, Molly," he told her, massaging the back of her hand with his thumb. "You're in control. You have the evidence. You have your witness."

She shared his quick smile.

"They're not onto us," he continued. "We'd have seen them. They would have made a move by now."

Molly wished she could take comfort in his words. But one thing she'd learned about Sabatini over the years was that besides being ruthless, the man was completely unpredictable. There was no telling what move his men would make next. And now there was Sarge to contend with as well. Karl Burr might very well be working on his own, so all of a sudden there were *two* threatening forces to dodge instead of one.

She looked up to meet Mitch's stare. In a million years, Molly thought, she could never tire of looking at him—those strong angles, the handsome lines and those mesmerizing, dark eyes of his. They could consume her in a single glance, make her forget all her fears and her doubts…make her forget the rest of the world, in fact.

His face was like home to her. In the same way his body had been last night. And in the same way his voice had sounded when he'd whispered his love to her. She wondered still if Mitch had known she was awake when he'd uttered his confession.

She considered telling him that she had been. She wanted to ask him, in the light of day, what his intentions were, what his feelings were about the future, *their* future, and if she should even allow herself to consider one with him.

But she couldn't. It was too soon, she reminded herself. Mitch needed time. The past few days had been a blur of emotions, made even more intense by the attacks and threat of Sabatini's men. Hardly the circumstances under which two people should consider a future together...

No, she needed to take her focus off Mitch and concentrate on keeping him out of Sabatini's clutches.

Mitch seemed to know what she was thinking then, because they both reached for the microcassette player on the seat next to her.

"Maybe we should listen to those tapes," he suggested. "Who knows, you might have more evidence right here."

She spent the next half hour listening and fast-forwarding through the three cassettes Ray had found in Tom's desk. Mostly they were notes to himself. His voice whispered over the hiss of the tape, and there was street noise in the background and the occasional rustle of paper. As she listened, Molly could envision Tom in the front seat of his unmarked car, sipping coffee from a paper cup and crumpling takeout wrappers as he sat through long hours of surveillance.

The memories flooded back. She'd done her share of stakeout assignments with Tom. In fact, her first had been with him. That's when they'd really gotten to know each other, sharing the front bench seat of an unmarked car through the dead of night, taking turns sleeping, and exchanging far too many personal anecdotes in an attempt to fill the long hours.

But harder than the memories was hearing Tom's voice again. Even the poor quality of the recordings couldn't mask the familiarity for Molly. She didn't need more incentive; keeping Mitch safe, seeing him reclaim his life was enough to drive her. But hearing Tom's voice, after all this time... If she'd been able, she would have speeded up the train. She wanted Sabatini so badly. She wanted to see the man with a life sentence—and then some—for what he'd done to Tom.

Mitch seemed to sense the affect Tom's recorded voice had on her. When the tape player reached the end of the cassette and Molly sat, unmoving, with the small machine resting in her lap, Mitch placed a hand over hers. He didn't prompt her, only sat quietly next to her as the train rocked and lilted along the tracks below.

"Are you all right?" he asked eventually.

Molly nodded.

"You up to listening to the other side of this one, or would you like me to do it?"

"No. I'm fine, Mitch. Really."

She popped out the cassette, turned it over and pressed play.

Immediately Molly knew they'd found something. The quality of the recording was different than the others; it was more staticky, with voices in the distance. Intermittently the player's tiny speaker squawked and hissed as though the recorder had been jostled.

Molly turned up the volume and strained to listen to the distant conversation behind the interference.

There were two men. Their voices were muffled, and echoed as though they were meeting in a warehouse, or a cavernous room. But in spite of the poor quality, Molly recognized the voice of her sergeant.

And the other—without a doubt—was Sergio Sabatini.

"...not necessary, Mr. Sabatini," she heard Sarge say,

his tone anxious even through the distortion of the recording. ''I'll take care of it.''

''I take care of my own trash, Sergeant.''

''But killing him… It's not necessary, I tell you. I can talk to him. He's reasonable.''

''You also told me some time ago that he was a good detective. Now, which is it? Is he a fine, upstanding cop, or is he someone you all of a sudden believe can be bought off?''

''I think I can talk to him. He's young, you know? And maybe just the right amount stupid. He's single, so it's not like he's got a family he's concerned about. Just…damn it, just give me a couple of days, all right? There's no need to make such rash—''

''Rash? I'm not being rash, Sergeant. On the contrary, I think I've been extraordinarily patient. Sutton's been a pain in my ass for some time now. I knew he was police before you got around to informing me. Sooner or later I knew I'd have to deal with him. It was just a matter of time. And the time's come.''

Molly heard more scuffling on the tape recorder, and she could almost see Tom—crouched behind something, taking cover in the shadows, desperate to capture every last word on tape, but scared senseless of being found out. And the whole time, listening to the two men discuss his own murder.

There were mumblings, inaudible remarks and then what sounded like swearing.

''…of a bitch. You're going to get more flak from something like this than anything. I can't…how much more do you expect me to do, Sabatini, hmm? How many more files and evidence…Goddamn police reports do you expect me to doctor up for you? How many cases do you honestly think I can control? I'm with the Homicide Unit, for crying out loud! Do you have any idea the kinds of risks I run when I have to mess with reports or evidence from another unit for you?''

''Well, I'll be sure this one ends up a homicide, then. I wouldn't want to make your job too 'risky,' now would I, Sergeant?''

Molly heard more expletives, and then a sharp click—Tom turning off the recorder. Then the hiss of blank tape.

Molly thought she might be sick. The thought of Tom listening to—*recording* the plotting of his own execution by two men, *one* of whom he'd trusted—brought a sour taste to her throat.

''No wonder Tom called me,'' she said, trying to control the quaver she heard in her own voice now. ''He must have taped this within days...maybe even hours of his murder. He *knew* Sabatini was going to have him executed. He knew Sarge was in on it.''

Letting her gaze glide over the white, rolling landscape rushing past the compartment's window, Molly relived those last days before Tom's murder. He'd had evidence. *Hard* evidence. Maybe not enough to put Sabatini away for anything more than conspiracy, but at least enough that he could have given Molly a copy for safekeeping.

Molly cursed him then. She cursed Tom for always being a supercop, for believing himself a one-man crime unit, thinking he could bring in anyone single-handedly, including Sabatini. She cursed him for letting the job be more important than his own life. But then, wasn't Tom just like her? Wouldn't *she* have done the exact same thing in his position?

The frightening thought was quickly followed by a galvanizing realization.

''Sarge was the lead investigator into Tom's murder,'' she said, standing, needing to pace even if it was only the four-foot length of the train compartment.

When she turned and caught the questioning expression on Mitch's face, she explained.

"The search-and-seizure warrant I wrote for Sabatini's residence... I lost the murder weapon. Had it in my hands, but then the D.A. threw it out because I hadn't included Sabatini's car in the warrant. But I had, Mitch. I *had* included it, I'm positive."

"It was an emotional time, Molly. I'm sure—"

"Of course it was emotional. And that's why I let myself think that I must have *forgotten* to put Sabatini's car in the warrant. But I didn't forget it, Mitch. Sarge erased it. *That's* how Sabatini knew the murder weapon would be thrown out. That's the *only* way he could get out of the charge. He *knew* the warrant wasn't good for the car because Sarge told him. Because *Sarge* tampered with the warrant."

It was as though a weight had lifted for her. Months of guilt, of blame... And it hadn't been her fault.

"It wasn't because of me that Sabatini got away with Tom's murder, Mitch. I did all the paperwork on that case, but it was up to Sarge to approve everything. I typed the search-and-seizure warrant on the computer for Sarge to look over. He had to print it out and sign it...but he must have made some changes first."

"And this tape?" Mitch asked. "Is there anything you can do with it to bring new charges against Sabatini for Tom's murder?"

"Maybe. I'd have to take it to the D.A.'s office first...but there might still be a way to see that bastard pay for Tom's murder."

MITCH HADN'T THOUGHT it possible for Molly to sleep on the train. With Chicago still a couple of hours away, she'd been so wired, so ready for action after hearing the tape. She'd spent fifteen minutes pacing the small compartment, and when that wasn't enough, she'd taken to walking the length of the train car. She'd left under the guise of finding them something to drink, but it had taken her so long that Mitch had known she'd simply needed space.

When she'd returned, she sat next to him and talked about the various options she had with the tape as evidence, with the printouts of tampered reports implicating Rachel, and with Mitch's ability to place Sarge at the scene of Sabatini's last cop execution. In time, after batting around the possibilities, Molly seemed to tire.

For over an hour now she'd been asleep, lying across the cushioned seats with her head resting in Mitch's lap. Unconsciously his fingers threaded through her hair and stroked the silkiness of her skin as he watched the winterscape speed past in a blur of white.

Nothing in his memory had felt more natural, more perfect than this. Along with hope, for the first time in months Mitch felt contentment. He felt whole somehow, as though Molly enabled him to see not just life again, but *himself* after these long months of darkness. And right now, if there was any way he could have made the entire Sabatini situation go away, Mitch would have done it. He'd give anything—even his career—to be on a train with Molly to *anywhere* but Chicago.

There was no way to even guess what awaited them in the Windy City. Molly seemed to have her plan intact, but who could say what Sabatini's plan was? Or Sergeant Burr's? Anything was possible. And contemplating the dangers was chilling.

Unbidden, the thought of harm coming to Molly entered Mitch's mind. He looked down at her peaceful expression and reflexively slid his hand across her shoulders to draw her tighter against him. She stirred, but did not wake. Not then.

It was ten minutes later that Molly woke. Her cell phone, in spite of being buried in her knapsack, pierced the rhythmic thudding of the train against the tracks. Molly sat bolt upright on the second ring.

The moment of disorientation was a mere flicker across her face as Molly looked from Mitch to her knapsack. Within a second she was digging for her phone.

"It must have gotten switched on when Ray packed our things," she muttered, as she clambered to shake off the sleep.

And by the time she yanked the compact phone from her pack, Molly's voice was solid and assured.

"Sparling here." Her eyes flashed to Mitch's. "Sarge?"

Mitch saw the color visibly bleed from her face as he listened to the one-sided conversation. Her grip on the small cell phone tightened and her other hand trembled as she lifted it to massage the bridge of her nose, the instant flare of tension furrowing deep lines of concern across her brow.

"No." She shook her head. "No…I can't…. Yes, we're on our way but—"

She was silent for what felt like forever, listening as Mitch saw fear, then anger darken her expression. And when she spoke again, her voice was low and filled with a rage Mitch couldn't remember ever hearing from her.

"You what? No…no…you son of a bitch. I swear to God, if you do *anything* to him I'm—"

Again she was cut off. Mitch touched her shoulder, shocked at the rock-hard tension he found there. She appeared to be straining to hear, but Mitch realized then that it was more a case of Molly trying to contain herself.

When she spoke again, her voice was so low Mitch had to struggle to make out her words over the thumping of the train. Her tone held the sound of defeat.

"Okay," she said at last. "Yes, I understand…yes. We'll be there."

Molly switched off the phone. It was the only movement

she seemed capable of as she stared at the opposite wall of the compartment.

"Molly?" Mitch took her hand, surprised at how cold it felt all of a sudden. "Tell me what's going on?"

Her voice came out sounding flat. Desperate. "He has my father."

"What?"

"Sergeant Burr is holding my father hostage."

"Why would he—"

"In trade for you, Mitch. He'll let my father go if I bring you to him." When she turned her eyes to him at last, Mitch worried about the despair he saw there.

"Wait a second, you're telling me he's threatening your father's life if you don't hand me over to him?"

Molly nodded.

"But that's insane."

"Is it? Come on, Mitch, Sarge knows me. He knows Pops. He knows I'd do anything for him."

"Okay, but does he actually think he'll get away with this? That he'll let you and your dad go and you won't say anything?"

"I doubt it. Sarge isn't thinking too straight right now. He's desperate, Mitch. There's no telling what he'll do. But I'd guess Sabatini's not involved with this. I think Sarge is working on his own now. And maybe that buys us an edge."

"How?"

"Because maybe, without Sabatini's thugs around, I can still talk reason into him."

Mitch stood. Roughly, he ran a hand over his hair, as he looked out the train window and released a long breath. "God, I don't believe this. It's like a bad dream. How...what happened to push him to this? How does he even know that you're aware of his involvement with Sabatini?"

He turned in time to catch Molly's shrug.

"I don't know. When I saw him at Shady Shores, I told him about the evidence I had against Rachel. Maybe… maybe the two of them are working together and he's worried I'll get to her and she'll turn evidence on him. Maybe he felt he needed to make the first move before I had an advantage, even if it meant revealing his association with Sabatini himself."

"So you've agreed to meet with him then?"

She nodded.

"But you're not going to go by yourself, right?"

"Of course I am. That's his demand."

"No way, Molly." He shook his head. "No way you're doing this without backup. It's suicide."

"He'll kill my father, Mitch."

"And you don't think he's going to try to do that anyway? You, me, your father…we're all on his list now. With any one of us alive, he risks exposure. You go in there, Molly, with me, and I guarantee you he's not planning on letting *any* of us go."

"But force isn't the answer. And if I go to IAD you can bet they'll send in a full tactical unit. It's too dangerous. This is my *father* we're talking about, Mitch."

"I understand, Molly, but—"

"But nothing. We have two hours. I have to play by Sarge's rules. It's the only chance I have of saving Pops."

Chapter Fourteen

Mitch said nothing for a long time. He seemed to realize there would be no convincing her to get police backup, so, for the next twenty minutes after the phone call from Sarge, it had been Mitch who silently paced the length of the train compartment.

But just within the city limits, he stood suddenly as though struck with a plan. Without explanation, he gathered their things, took Molly's hand and wordlessly led her from the compartment to the car's exit. Other passengers were disembarking as well, several stops before Union Station. They waited silently with them.

Molly didn't question him.

Even as Mitch led her through the station to the street and hailed a cab, she didn't ask his intentions. And, after a fifteen-minute ride, when the cabbie pulled up to the curb on Chapman Avenue, Molly knew where they were.

She looked across the street to the three-story stone and wood-siding house. Mitch's house. She'd driven by it twice over the years. The first time had been by accident, but the second had been out of curiosity.

It sat back from the street, fronted by two large sycamores and a tangle of small, snow-covered hedges. The drive was cleared, as was the curving walkway that led to the wide, wraparound porch and the double front doors.

Behind several windows, lights glowed through the grow-ing dusk. Someone had obviously been keeping up the house in Mitch's absence, attempting to give it an inhabited look despite ten months of sitting empty.

Mitch said nothing as he paid the cab driver and crossed the street. Only when she'd followed him past the garage to the back of the house and waited as he retrieved a key from under a concrete planting pot did Molly ask him his plan.

"We need a bargaining chip," he explained, unlocking the back door and ushering her into the relative warmth of the kitchen. "If you hope to convince your sergeant to let any of us go once we get there, you're going to need some pretty convincing leverage."

"You mean the tape?"

Mitch nodded. He stood for a moment in the middle of the kitchen and cast his eyes over the room. Molly followed his gaze, taking in the white ceramic tile floor, the maple-and-glass cabinetry and the modern stainless steel appli-ances and countertops. But it was the knickknacks and plants on the various shelves, the framed photos hanging on the wall over the breakfast nook, and the more intimate items—a sweater draped over the back of one chair, a pair of slippers next to the door, a felt hat, no doubt Emily's, perched on the corner of a pine bench—that gave the room a personal feel, a sense of the lives that had once made this house a home.

Molly could almost see the memories wash over Mitch then. She couldn't begin to imagine what he must be feel-ing, stepping into the house he'd shared all those years with Emily, a house he'd not set foot in since the accident took her from him. Molly knew how protective custody worked; more than likely the police hadn't even allowed Mitch back to the house to retrieve a few belongings and clothes. They would have asked him to make arrangements for a friend to do it, which would mean that the last time he'd been here was probably the night of the accident.

Molly imagined the scene: Mitch in his tuxedo, and Emily dressed in something that suited her stunning beauty, whisking out the door on their way to the celebration of Mitch's biggest achievement in his career. How could anyone have expected the terror that put an end to all that love and happiness only a few hours later?

Molly looked to Mitch again and placed a hand on his shoulder. She thought he was about to say something in regards to the loss she saw so clearly in his face. But he didn't. Instead, she saw that old Mitch Drake dam come up on his emotions.

"We need to make a copy of that tape," he told her, and nodded to the corridor past the kitchen.

She followed him to the front foyer and up the wide oak staircase that curved to the second floor. And when they reached the open doorway of what must have been Emily's office, Mitch flipped the light switch and paused again. Molly could see the desk past his shoulder. A green banker's lamp spread its glow across stacks of papers on either side of a computer.

She was aware of Mitch taking in a breath before he stepped into the room and crossed over to the desk. He rolled back the high-back leather chair and sat down. Even that seemed to cause a moment's hesitation, and again Molly felt compelled to place a hand on his shoulder. She wasn't surprised at the tight knots she felt there.

"I know Emily's got a tape recorder," he mumbled, and launched a search of the drawers.

Molly scanned the top of the desk. She'd known Emily wrote for *Inside Chicago* magazine, but somehow she hadn't imagined that the freelance work was such a production. Stacks of files covered the desk, as well as countless reference books. But Molly's gaze passed over all of these and fixed on the framed photo next to the computer monitor.

It was a five-by-seven of the two of them—Emily and Mitch—both dressed in casual, flowing white shirts. Emily stood behind Mitch, her chin nestled against his temple and her arms around his shoulders. In front of Mitch's chest, their hands entwined, the gold wedding bands gleaming against the white backdrop. But it was their smiles that shone the brightest, lighting up their faces and their eyes.

Whether the photo had been taken with a timer or by a photographer friend of Emily's from the magazine, the camera had captured the intimacy and the love between them. It was almost tangible.

"Here it is." Mitch withdrew a microcassette recorder from the bottom desk drawer and rummaged for a tape.

For the next ten minutes he set up, taped and double-checked the recording of Sabatini's and Sarge's chilling conversation from more than a year ago. Molly paced silently across the carpeted room. The sound of Sarge's voice, however muted and distorted by the recording, sent shivers through her as she imagined him at the waterfront warehouse address he'd given her. He was there now, most likely, with her father. *Was he tied up? Did Sarge have a gun to his head?*

Molly fought back the nausea that curled in her stomach. She checked her watch. They still had time. But there was no calming her anxiousness.

And then Mitch was searching drawers again. This time he pulled out a small padded envelope and handed it to Molly.

"To your Internal Affairs Department," he said, handing her a pen as well.

"You want me to mail it?"

"The copy, yes." He nodded. "We'll take the original with us, let your sergeant hear it for himself, but if anything happens to us, Molly...I want *someone* to know who's responsible.''

There was an uneasiness in Mitch's expression then, and she couldn't be sure if it was there because of what they were about to do or if it was a reaction to being in his house again. More likely, Molly thought as she started to write out the address, it was a combination of both.

She'd barely completed the address when Mitch took the envelope from her. He tossed in the copy before sealing it. Tucking it under his arm, he handed Molly the original cassette and the tape player.

''You ready?'' he asked.

Molly nodded and was about to turn from the room when Mitch stopped her. He slid one finger under her chin and tilted her face so she looked at him. In the dim glow of the banker's lamp she could see the concern in those dark eyes of his.

''Are you okay, Molly?''

She managed another nod, even though she knew Mitch could see through her front. He'd always been able to read her like a book, Molly thought. Even when they were kids. How was it that she thought she could mask her fear from him now?

''I'll be fine when this is over,'' she told him.

He cupped her cheek in the heat of his palm, and a smile tugged weakly at the corners of his mouth.

''You're very brave, Molly. And I...I love you.''

She thought he was about to kiss her, could see in his eyes that he wanted to. But he wouldn't, Molly realized. Not here, in the house he'd shared with Emily, in her office.

''Come on,'' he said instead, as though needing to banish the urge. ''Let's go.''

MITCH HAD BEEN SURPRISED and relieved when Emily's car actually started. After sitting unused in the garage for ten months, the luxury station wagon ran a little rough at first. They stopped only briefly to drop the envelope into a mail box, and by the time he steered into the heavy traffic along Elston Avenue, the car was purring along.

It felt more than a little strange to be behind the wheel of Emily's station wagon. Stranger still to have been in the house. For months he'd dreamed of being back there, of going home. But he'd never imagined the overwhelming emptiness he'd felt the second he set foot through the back door, or the incredible sadness that had flooded over him when he'd stepped into Emily's office. He'd almost expected to see her there, sitting in her chair, her long, slender fingers flying over the keyboard as she wrote another column on her computer. He'd expected the chair to swivel around, and to be met with the radiant smile that had always greeted him in the past.

So empty.

Mitch set the wipers on high to combat the driving snow. He couldn't think about Emily. Not now. He needed to focus on Molly, and on what they were about to walk into.

For close to twenty minutes Molly had been silent in the passenger seat, staring ahead through the windshield at the sea of red taillights. Her tension was almost palpable. Mitch imagined he'd feel it on her, like a second skin, if he reached over to touch her. It had started on the train, but he'd noticed it more when they were in Emily's office. Molly had paced the floor behind him as he'd made a copy of Tom's tape, and when he'd finished and turned to look at her, Mitch could remember only one other time that he'd ever seen Molly so anxious, so on edge.

It had been near the end of his final year at high school. Molly was barely seventeen. The hospital had called the school. And Molly had called him. He'd driven to the hospital and sat with her for what felt like hours as they waited for word on her father.

It had been a minor heart attack, yet no matter how hard the doctors and nurses tried to convince her he would be fine, Molly had been frantic. But in a quiet way. In the Sparling way.

Mitch would never forget how she'd worn a path into the tiles of the hospital corridor. She'd chewed her nails to the quick, and even when Mitch had been able to make her stop pacing, she hadn't sat still. He'd known she was scared, but more than that she was anxious, desperate to do something, but acutely aware of her helplessness at the same time. It was on that day that Mitch realized just how incredibly connected Molly was to her father.

In fact, if it hadn't been for Leo Sparling and his heart attack that year before college, Molly probably wouldn't be a cop today, Mitch thought. She'd never have gone to the Police Academy. Before the heart attack, Molly and her father both had talked about her getting a law degree. There'd been talk of her joining Mitch in Boston to study. And when Molly had announced that she was staying in Chicago to pursue a law-enforcement career like her father, Mitch had known it was because of the heart attack. He'd known it was because Leo Sparling was the only family Molly had and—after the fright of the heart attack—the thought of being too far away from him was impossible for her to live with.

Now, with Sergeant Burr threatening her father's life, there was no way for Mitch to comprehend the kind of fear she must be going through as they sped north across the city. Snatching quick side glances, he could see her tension; the soft glow of the car's dash lights could do nothing to soften the harsh lines of worry.

Mitch placed a hand over hers. Her skin felt cold.

"We'll get him, Molly."

In the brief gaze she shot him, Mitch wished he'd been able to see more hope in those dark eyes. But there was only fear. Still, she nodded, and a muscle along her jaw flexed as she lifted her chin with an almost defiant air.

"This is it." She leaned forward in her seat, straining to see through the heavy snowfall. They were the first words she'd spoken in so long, her voice cracked.

Mitch took a right, steering the station wagon down the ill-lit street. They drove by several blocks of rundown apartment complexes, their courtyards deep in snow beyond their low, chain-link fences. The wind seemed to pick up. It churned the snow into thick whirlwinds that whisked across the wet pavement in the light of the streetlamps. And then came the warehouses. One after the next. Some still operating, others abandoned.

Both he and Molly leaned forward to study the street signs past the thrashing wipers, following Sergeant Burr's directions, until at last they found the building he'd described. Mitch steered around to the rear of the two-story warehouse with its darkened windows, and at the back loading docks they spotted Burr's dark sedan.

Mitch pulled the station wagon up alongside it, letting the engine idle as they both looked up at the brown-brick structure.

"No other cars in sight." Mitch broke the uneasy silence.

"I figured he'd be solo on this one."

Molly gave the building and its vacant lot one final scan. She checked her pocket for the tape recorder, then lifted the edge of her anorak and slid her gun from its holster. As she removed and doublechecked the gun's clip, Mitch felt the Walther strapped to his ankle just above the top of his boot.

Molly hadn't asked him about her off-duty weapon, whether he had it on him or if it was still in his pack, and Mitch considered telling her. But if he did, he was certain Molly would have demanded it back. She'd want to protect him, wouldn't want him to take risks. And she'd probably have good reason: he wasn't trained like her. There was no guarantee he'd know how to handle a confrontation, with a gun, with their lives at stake. At the same time, there was no way he'd step into that warehouse without it. The semi-automatic in its ankle holster was the only shred of control he had in the situation right now.

Molly took in a deep breath, and Mitch could hear the shakiness of it.

"Are you ready?" she asked.

He gave her a silent nod and reached for the door.

Snow blasted around the side of the building, biting the exposed skin of his face and hands. Molly, too, flinched at the harsh cold, but Mitch could see her caution. With her gun in her right hand, lowered against her thigh, she followed the path through the snow, up the steps to the loading dock and the back door.

He watched her hand close over the knob. She paused for a second as though steeling herself.

"I want you to stay behind me, Mitch," she told him. "No matter what happens, I'm in charge, okay?"

There was no sense arguing. Nothing to do but nod and follow her lead.

The warehouse wasn't much warmer than outside, but at least without the wind it was bearable. Mitch eased the door shut behind them. A long, dimly lit corridor stretched out before them—the only possible route.

Molly moved slowly, even though Mitch could sense the urgency she felt. Cautiously, she headed down the corridor, her gun at her side. Through the plume of vapor from her breath Mitch could see beyond the mouth of the corridor, could just make out the faint light and stacks of crates. And when they reached the mouth, Molly paused. He heard her take another deep breath before she stepped into the main area of the warehouse.

She saw him before Mitch did.

Edging around the corner of the first stack of crates, Mitch watched her lift her gun, holding it with both hands. She shifted her grip, her fingers clenching and unclenching around the gun's butt. Mitch couldn't help thinking then that the black Glock looked far too heavy, too unwieldy in her small hands.

"Show yourself, Sarge," she called out, the boldness of her voice belying the fear he knew had to be coursing through her.

Over her shoulder, Mitch spotted Leo Sparling. He was bound, but not gagged, sitting at least forty feet away in a chair surrounded by walls of crates. The dim light from the high overhead lamps shimmered off of the full head of white hair and made his complexion seem pale.

"Show yourself, damn it!" Anger sharpened Molly's tone. Her knuckles were white around the grip of the gun, and she took another cautious step forward, all the time scanning the cavernous space of the warehouse searching the shadows.

And then, using Leo Sparling as his cover, Sergeant Burr stepped from behind a stack of crates. His own gun was raised.

Mitch clamped down on the icy bitterness that rammed through him at seeing the man's face again. Molly seemed to sense it. She whispered to him, "Stay behind me, Mitch. Please."

"I'm sorry, Molly," Karl Burr offered, the muzzle of his gun trained on her father's head.

"Like hell you are."

"I didn't want it to have to come to this."

Mitch wondered how the man could adopt even the shred of apology he heard in his tone. Then again, perhaps it was desperation that caused the waver in his voice.

"I need you to put the gun down, Molly," Burr demanded, standing next to her father now.

But she didn't. Instead, Mitch could see her fingers tighten around the black, rubber grip of the Glock. Determination set in her expression, and a muscle in her jaw quivered.

"Put the gun down, Molly," Sergeant Burr warned a second time.

Still she didn't.

And then it was Leo Sparling's voice that cut the thick silence of the warehouse.

"Molly, don't—"

But his attempt to advise his daughter was immediately silenced with the muzzle of Burr's revolver. It pressed into the senior Sparling's temple, causing him to wince visibly.

"You son of a bitch!" Molly lunged three steps forward, stopping only when Burr shouted.

"Drop the damned gun!" The demand echoed through the cavernous expanse.

Mitch heard Molly curse under her breath again as she finally lowered the semiautomatic. Crouching, she set the weapon on the floor and slowly straightened.

"Now kick it over here."

Without protest this time, she did his bidding. The gun skittered across the concrete floor, spinning in two slow revolutions as it came to rest within inches of the chair. Burr kicked it himself, sending it backward into the shadows of the crates behind him.

"Your off-duty weapon, too, Molly."

"I don't have it on me."

"Show me."

She lifted the cuff of each pant leg, revealing nothing over the leather ankle boots.

"And the jacket," Burr demanded.

She lifted the edge of her anorak and the sweater beneath

to reveal nothing but her slim waist and the jeans that hugged her hips. "Satisfied?" she asked.

"All right then." Burr seemed to relax by a degree. The muzzle of his gun eased away from Leo Sparling's temple then, and as though Molly expected him to turn the revolver toward Mitch, she took one sideways step, putting herself between him and Karl Burr.

"All right," Burr said again. "Let's talk."

"Yes, Sarge. Let's," Molly stated calmly. "Because we've got a lot to talk about."

Chapter Fifteen

Molly pushed back the nausea that swept through her. The sight of her father—bound to the chair, with Sarge's gun jammed against his temple with such force that his head was craned to the side—threatened to immobilize her. But she couldn't afford fear right now. She needed to be cool. To remain calm. In control.

She met Sarge's stare. His cold, seemingly emotionless eyes revealed so little. Yet they revealed everything Molly needed to know. Mitch was right. Sarge had no intention of letting any of them go tonight. He fully intended to shoot all three of them in cold blood. How he hoped to get away with it was beyond Molly, though.

The snub-nosed revolver looked lost in his huge grip, giving it the appearance of a toy. But Molly wasn't fooled. She knew what the .357 was capable of. More than that, she could see what Sarge was capable of in his desperation.

"Where's Sabatini?" she asked him.

"He's on his way."

"So what is it? He didn't want to waste his time? He wants to be sure you could lure us here before he bothers to show up?"

"Something like that."

Molly wondered how much time they had. She had hoped Sarge would tell her this was *his* deal, that Sabatini wasn't involved. But if the mob king *was,* that gave her even less time to convince Sarge of his insanity.

"Then I think I should show you something before he gets here," she suggested, inching her hand to the pocket of her anorak.

His revolver's muzzle tightened against her father's temple once again.

"Relax, Sarge." She attempted a calming tone, but it appeared to have little affect.

The expression on his face flickered from despair to ruthlessness and then back again. It was impossible to tell what fears were plaguing him now or how far they would force his hand. And Molly was hardly about to test them.

"Please. I'm unarmed," she said. "I just need to show you something."

Gingerly, between thumb and forefinger, Molly withdrew the microcassette player from her pocket. It dangled there in her grasp for a moment as she waited for Sarge to relax his stance.

When he did, she took several more steps forward. Only ten feet separated them now...separated her from her father. She could see the anger in Pop's face, and something that looked to her like embarrassment. But there was also a calm in those dark brown eyes of Leo Sparling's, a calm that told Molly he trusted her, had faith in her ability to get them all out of this mess.

She prayed she could live up to that faith.

Suspicion flickered across Karl Burr's face when she looked at him again. Quickly it faded to defeat the second she pressed Play and he listened to his own voice in the malevolent dialogue with Sabatini.

"It's up to you how this goes down, Sarge," she said when the recording ended. "If Sabatini shows up, you know we're all dead. Including you. Don't fool yourself."

His mind raced with a million possibilities. Molly could

see it in the lines that snaked across his wide, glistening forehead, and in the slight waver of the gun he held to her father's head.

"*Or* you could shave some time off your sentence and maybe buy some lenience from the D.A.'s office by testifying against Sabatini," she continued. "Either way, IAD's all over this tape as of the morning. This one's just a copy."

She switched off the recorder and pretended to offer it to him.

He didn't move, his eyes riveted on the small, black recorder.

"Not a lot of time here, Sarge."

"Karl, listen to her," her father advised, fidgeting against the rope around his wrists. "You know she's right. Sabatini comes in here and you're the first one on his list."

Karl Burr shook his head, a look of disbelief washing over his pallid face.

"Consider it, Karl. You can turn in the entire organization."

Still he said nothing.

"What the *hell* is stopping you?"

Her father's bellow echoed through the maze of crates, and Molly thought she saw Sarge's grip slacken slightly on the gun.

"What the hell does Sabatini have on you, Karl? It's not just the money. I *know* it can't be just the money. Not for all this. What is it? Is it your daughter? Is it Amy?"

He shook his head even more now, cursing under his breath. "I'm in too deep, Leo," he said at last. "I'm in too deep."

"What? What's he got on you?"

"For God's sake… He said…he's going to kill Amy if I don't pull this one off."

Molly couldn't help thinking he was on the verge of tears. He was almost blubbering as he went on.

"I curse the day I took that first payoff. The son of a bitch... My life was over that day. I never meant for it..."

And then the gun lowered. Karl Burr brought up his free hand and held his head, still shaking it in defeat. Molly stepped forward and carefully laid her hand over his. The revolver slipped easily from his grasp.

She was aware of Mitch moving behind the chair and loosening the restraints that held her father as she uncocked the Smith & Wesson.

"Help us, Sarge," she said, working to find even a shred of compassion for the man. She placed a comforting hand on his shoulder, when all she really wanted to do was hit him. She wanted to put him on the floor, even though he easily outweighed her twice over. "Help us put Sergio Sabatini away before he kills even more innocent people."

He was nodding—blubbering and nodding—and Molly wished she could feel sympathy. But even if she *had* been able to conjure up an emotion for her sergeant then, she didn't get the chance.

Mitch cleared his throat suddenly and loudly. And when Molly looked to him, she caught his wide-eyed nod toward the corridor behind her.

Instantly, she felt a hot prickle of dread crawl up the back of her neck. Her spine stiffened, and for a split second her grip tightened around the .357 in her hand.

"You can drop the gun, Detective Sparling."

The voice was unmistakable. It sounded every bit as smug and coldly self-assured as the man it came from.

She heard the hard-soled shoes against the concrete floor, grinding grit beneath them with each step. Without turning, Molly knew there had to be at least three or four henchmen—maybe more—surrounding Sergio Sabatini as he crossed the loading bay. And they would all have their guns drawn. It was suicide to consider hanging on to the revolver at her side. She'd be dead before she brought the .357 up into her other hand.

With her back still turned, Molly hastily eyed the walls of crates. They offered the only available cover; even then, it wasn't much. That was assuming, of course, she could get Mitch and her father behind them before the bullets started flying. And then what?

"As you know, Detective, I'm not a man of patience. So I'll say it only one more time—"

She heard the distinct sound of metal sliding on metal. A semiautomatic being cocked. Had Sabatini come prepared to do some of his own cleanup?

"—put the gun down and turn around."

The footsteps stopped. They were close. Only a couple of yards behind her, she guessed. Molly bent down to place the revolver on the floor. And when she cautiously turned around, she was shocked to find him standing so near.

Sergio Sabatini wasn't as large in person as he was in every cop's imagination. Especially Molly's. Whenever she'd dealt with Sabatini in the past, he'd usually been sitting down—behind a desk, at the defense table or on the witness stand in court. Only once had she been face-to-face with the man, at his estate when she'd served the search-and-seizure warrant over a year ago, and even then there had been his shiny Cadillac separating her from his smug grin.

It was his presence that had always made him seem larger, Molly realized. Standing in front of him now, she was actually surprised at how small Sergio Sabatini was. He was a corpulent man, but certainly not of any great stature. Perhaps no more than five-eight or five-nine. His complexion was pasty, and he looked old, with his thinning hair swept over an obviously balding pate.

Her gaze dropped to the gleaming nickel semiautomatic he held firmly in one meaty hand. Instinctively Molly raised her hands from her sides, and started to back away. She needed to get as close as possible to the relative safety of the crates.

Through the corner of her eye, she could see that Mitch had managed to undo most of the cords that bound her father. Pops was up on his feet now, his hands still tied behind him.

Three more steps back and she felt the solidness of Mitch behind her. She nudged him, urging him back a few steps as well, and she wondered if he understood her reasoning.

"That's better," Sabatini said, his voice sounding as cold as his gray eyes.

He stood there for a long moment, studying all four of them—her and Mitch standing together, and her father and Sarge several feet away on either side.

"Looks like I've finally got all my loose ends in one place," he said. "You've been a particular pain in my ass for some time now, Mr. Drake."

Sabatini drilled Mitch with a stare, and Molly prayed that the man wouldn't make any moves to narrow the gap between them. If they were to have any chance at all of getting out of this now, they needed as much space as possible between themselves and the mob king.

"You and the good detective here have certainly done your share of embarrassing my men over the past few days. It's too bad they're still on their way back from Michigan. I know they would have loved to be here.

"And Sergeant—" Sabatini took two steps toward Sarge, the gleaming semiautomatic still thrust before him "—you've turned out to be somewhat of a disappointment. I'd hoped for more from you—a man looking at retirement. I would have thought you'd welcome a little extra subsidy on that meager police pension you'll be pulling in. Not to mention, of course, your wonderful daughter."

Even in the dim lighting from the overhead lamps high

in the rafters of the warehouse, Molly could see the gray pallor that washed over Sarge's face.

"I swear, Sabatini, if you've done anything to her, I'll—"

"Oh, come now. You know me, Sergeant. You know my men will make sure Amy's looked after."

The growl in Sarge's voice was the only warning. The words came from deep in his chest and erupted on his lips. "You son of a bitch!" he snarled, and in the same instant he threw himself at the mob king.

He was easily the larger of the two men, the force of his lunge sending Sabatini back a few staggering steps. But size hardly mattered when a .45 was involved.

The retort of the gun was muffled, shielded by Sarge's body. But it wasn't enough to soften the shock of hearing it go off. Molly's heart was in her throat. As was everyone else's in that split second.

Stunned, Sabatini's men watched as Sarge clung to their boss for a moment, and even before he'd begun to crumple to the ground, Molly sprang into action.

Clutching Mitch's arm, she dragged him in one blind leap to the safety of the crates, the corner of one driving painfully into her hip. She bit back a curse and frantically searched the shadows for her Glock. In one fluid motion, she reached for the gun, wrapped her fingers around the grip and raised it.

The two large sodium bulbs overhead were easy targets and exploded within a split second of each other, raining shards of glass down around the men in the center of the warehouse floor.

Through the dark, she heard expletives. Somewhere to her left, she knew her father took cover as well, and she tried to make out his figure in the shadows. The pale light from a streetlamp outside filtered through a grimy window high above them, and Molly waited for her eyes to adjust to the severely limited light.

With more cursing, Sabatini ordered his men into action. The gunfire began.

There was no telling where it came from, whether his men were fanning out behind them or if they'd decided to simply open fire on the wall of crates. Molly struggled not to flinch at the sound of each bullet.

She felt Mitch behind her, crouching as well. She ordered him to stay down, and in the same breath she hit the floor. Over grit and oil, she elbowed her way to the corner of the outside crate. Peering around it, she could see the silhouettes of the men—all four of them—and the flare of each muzzle as the rounds exploded from their guns.

There would be no fancy aiming. No attempt to disarm. "Center body mass," Molly whispered to herself, along with a silent prayer, as she squeezed off the first round.

It met its mark with sickening accuracy. She watched the man fall, and quickly chose her next target. Her training forced her to count each round that left her gun. Four. Five. Six.

And then the second man hit the floor. But there was no let-up in the storm of bullets that pierced the heavy plywood crates and ricocheted off concrete and steel around her.

Only after the third man cried out in pain and Molly saw his gun skitter across the floor out of his reach did the gunfire abate slightly. It was then that Molly was aware of Mitch, on the move. He came alongside her, and before she could say anything, he hurled himself across the open space to the crates to her left.

Sabatini's men must have seen him. The gunfire erupted anew.

Eight. Nine. Ten.

Molly knew her rounds hadn't met any marks, but it was

all she could do to put up a cover for Mitch. She drew back, crouching still, and leaned against the side of one crate as her eyes searched the distant shadows.

Where was he? And why had he—

And then Molly saw the purpose of Mitch's mission. Through the murkiness, she could just make out her father's figure. Mitch must have untied the last of his bindings. She saw a gesture from her father that looked like a thumbs-up, and then she saw the gun in his hands. The dim light gleamed off of it for a split second, but it was enough for her to recognize her off-duty Walther.

Mitch must have had it on his ankle the entire time, Molly realized as her father joined her in returning Sabatini's fire. *But where was Mitch?*

Several frantic glances into the shadows beyond her father revealed nothing to Molly. There was no sign of Mitch. *Could he have taken a bullet? Was he lying on the dark floor someplace, bleeding?*

Molly considered dashing across the opening herself. But Sabatini's men had her pinned, and they would definitely be better prepared for her sudden rush than they'd been for Mitch's. She'd be dead for sure.

Fourteen. Fifteen. Sixteen.

Molly drew back from the corner of the crate. One round left in her clip. She had to make it count. Closing her eyes for a second, she tried to imagine where she'd seen Sabatini's figure last in the dimness of the loading area. If she stood now, exposing herself to the henchmen's bullets, she would have a much better chance at finding a target…at finding Sabatini. But she'd have to find that target before one of their bullets found her.

Taking in several deep breaths, Molly gathered herself. And in the same second she was about to stand, the gunfire ceased.

It was Sabatini's booming voice that filled the silence as

the last echo of gunfire died in the far reaches of the warehouse.

"All right. All right!" he bellowed, and there was the sound of a weapon clattering to the floor.

"Tell them to back off." It was Mitch's voice. "I want them out of here."

Relief spread through Molly. Mitch was okay, but what the hell was he doing? She dared to snatch a quick glimpse around the corner of the crate, expecting a shot to ring out.

Nothing happened.

And then—illuminated by the thin shaft of light that filtered down from the high window to the floor—there was Mitch. He stood behind Sabatini, the collar of the man's leather trenchcoat clenched in one hand and a gun in the other. Its muzzle was pressed against the back of Sabatini's head.

"You're outnumbered, Mr. Drake," Sabatini hissed.

"Oh yeah? Then why am *I* the one holding a gun to *your* head, you son of a bitch? Now, I said I want them out of here. Now!" Mitch shouted, giving the gun a shove as though to make his demand clearer.

With a barely perceptible flick of his wrist, Sabatini dismissed the last two standing men. They paused only long enough to help one of their comrades to his feet on their way out.

As their footsteps faded down the corridor, Molly stood. Mitch's rage was more than apparent. It tightened his expression, and even in the dim light Molly could see the white-knuckled grip he sustained around the gun. It was one of Sabatini's men's guns, she realized then. Had to be. Mitch must have used the crates as cover and circled around the group of men while she and her father held their positions.

She shared a brief look with her father, assuring herself that he was all right, before she stepped out from behind

the crates. To her left, the body of Sabatini's man lay unmoving on the concrete floor. The sight of his prone form,
of the dark pool of blood that spread out around him,
should have shocked her. She'd never shot anyone before.
But for Molly, right now, there was only Mitch.

Vaguely she was aware of her father crossing the floor
behind her to Sergeant Burr's side as she approached Mitch
and Sabatini. She expected Mitch to look in her direction,
to exchange a glance at least, but he didn't even seem
aware of her presence.

Without taking his eyes off of Sabatini, he kicked the
man's gun out of reach, and at the same time spun him
roughly around. Sabatini took one stumbling step backward, his arms raised from his sides in a gesture of surren-
der as he returned Mitch's stare.

But it was the intensity on Mitch's face, and in the grip
he maintained on the gun, that frightened Molly. With his
shoulders squared, Mitch held the weapon at arm's length,
its barrel aimed squarely at Sabatini's assured expression.

Molly circled around. "Mitch?"

He didn't respond. Didn't even seem to have heard her,
or realize she'd come up beside him.

"Mitch?"

His focus was riveted on the man in his gun sight. Molly
sensed...no, she *knew* what was going through Mitch's
mind in that moment. It was Emily. It was the child he
would never know. It was the life Sabatini had stolen from
him that bred the startling fierceness she saw in him now.

The gray light gleamed off the weapon in his hand.
Molly considered touching his arm then, urging him to
lower it. And then she saw his finger press the gentle curve
of the trigger, the flesh of his fingertip white from the pressure he held there.

He wanted to kill Sabatini. Standing there, coldly facing

the man, Mitch was ready to pull the trigger. Ready to avenge Emily's murder. His daughter's murder.

Far more shocking than that, however, was the fact that she almost wanted Mitch to do it.

Molly cast an anxious glance around the loading area. Calculating…

Shell casings littered the floor. The wall of crates that had separated them from Sabatini's deadly force was essentially ripped apart from the countless rounds of bullets. One man already lay dead, another three injured. And no witnesses. So what if Sabatini should take a bullet himself? There wasn't a single detective or crime scene technician in the entire city of Chicago who would ever question that one bullet, which gun it came from and by whose hand.

One bullet… Who was to know any better?

It would be so easy.

But Molly knew better. If Mitch pulled that trigger, if Sabatini was killed by his hand, he would never…*never* be able to live with himself. If losing Emily and his unborn child hadn't ended Mitch's life, then killing Sabatini surely *would*.

She couldn't let him do it.

"Mitch?"

THE WEIGHT OF THE GUN in his hand, the promise of the trigger's curve under his finger, and the smug look on Sabatini's face…

It was as though Mitch had waited ten months for this exact moment in time, as though everything leading up to this—the explosion of the safe house, his flight up to Canada, Molly coming back into his life and convincing him to return to Chicago—everything had been for this one single opportunity.

Emily.

He was staring at Sabatini's sallow face, but it was Emily's smile that filled his mind's eye. It was her laughter and the sound of her voice. It was the feel of her hand in his, of her body lying next to him, the softness of her skin and the heat of her breath against his chest. It was the warmth of her round, swollen belly under the palm of his hand, the gentle kick he'd felt and the hope it had signified... *These* were the images Mitch saw as his fingertip caressed the gun's trigger.

All that was left to do was squeeze that curve of checkered steel.

He watched Sabatini's expression, in one moment so full of disdain, and in the next...fear. It was slow to set across his aging face, starting as a twitch at the side of his thick lips, and then at the corner of one cold, gray eye. And then Mitch could see the tension in the man's entire stance as he seemed to understand that Mitch had absolutely nothing to lose by pulling the trigger.

But he did, Mitch realized then. He had everything to lose. All over again. A whole new life. A life with Molly.

Killing Sabatini would destroy that chance. Could he honestly live with himself after killing a man in cold blood, even if it was the murderer of his wife and child?

No, he couldn't. By shooting Sabatini he would let the monster win a second time. Even dead, he would have ruined Mitch's life all over again.

It was Molly's voice that drew him out of the rage that consumed him.

"Mitch. Please."

The gentle touch of her hand on his arm offered him reality...a *new* reality, like a light through the darkness, beckoning him.

"Don't," she whispered, and her fingers wrapped softly around his tense grip on the gun.

His eyes never left Sabatini's. But he didn't need to look at Molly to see the plea he knew etched lines across her forehead and lifted her brows. He didn't need to stare into the depths of those dark eyes to know she loved him, that— more than anything—she didn't want him to compromise whatever hope they might have for a future together.

"Mitch." She breathed his name, and he thought she murmured, "I love you."

Then her hand tightened on his. He allowed her to lower it and slip the gun from his fingers. Only then did he look away from Sabatini, swearing to himself that it would be the last time he'd ever look the man in the eye.

He turned away, needing space between him and the murderer. In his peripheral vision, he was conscious of Leo Sparling's presence. He handed his daughter a pair of handcuffs, and it was Molly who cuffed Sabatini.

Mitch heard her voice—strong, assured.

"No way you're getting out of *these* charges," she told him. "Looks like you just shot your only ticket out of this one, Sabatini." Then Molly's father was on her cell phone, calling for police backup and a medical team. Mitch was aware of his heart racing. Adrenaline still pumped through his body. From the moment he'd decided to make his move, he had acted in a blind rush—not knowing what he could do, only knowing he had to do *something*. He'd been terrified and determined at the same time, but it was when he'd picked up the fallen man's gun and nudged it up against the back of Sabatini's skull…it was *then* that Mitch had felt power at last.

And that sense of power stayed with him even now. He had the power to live his life. Free of Sabatini.

Molly was at his side again.

"Mitch?"

She said his name, but that was all. She didn't need to say anything else. Her eyes told him everything he needed to know. One look into her upturned face, and Mitch knew he'd done the right thing by not shooting Sabatini, even though the anger…the desire to do it would be with him for a long time still.

She lifted one hand, bringing her palm to rest against his cheek as though needing to assure herself that he was all right. He offered her a silent nod. And when he took her hand in his, Mitch wondered if he could ever let it go.

Epilogue

Molly steered the unmarked police car to the curb. With so many overtime hours devoted to the case against Sabatini, there had been no time to even consider shopping for a new vehicle, and the insurance adjusters had long since given up trying to reach her for details on her totaled Jeep in Canada. It had been a blur of long days of gathering evidence and typing reports for the D.A.'s office so they could determine where to start with the endless list of charges against Sabatini. In the meantime, he sat in the city jail. Bail had been flatly denied.

Today, almost three weeks after Sabatini's arrest at the warehouse, Molly was just beginning to see the end of the long road. Still, if it hadn't been for Lieutenant Hendrickson coming down from the seventh-floor offices this morning to personally see to it that Molly took some badly needed time off, she wouldn't be here this afternoon. As it was, she had the next two days off—ordered to stay away from Headquarters.

So she'd handed her files to Adam, walked her last reports over to the district attorney's offices and met her father for a quick lunch at Moe's Diner.

He'd been to see Sarge at the hospital again, Pops had admitted over a plate of greasy onion rings. She'd learned to keep her mouth shut around Pops when it came to Sarge.

They were still partners, he'd told her more than a few times since that night. And that was the end of it.

As it turned out, Pops seeing Sarge every day at Mercy Hospital had been a good thing. Without Pops, Sarge might never have been convinced to finally turn state's evidence against Sabatini. And between that and Rachel Messina's wise choice to do the same, the D.A.'s office had enough hard evidence secured to put Sabatini away for life, if not until he was the ripe age of a hundred and two.

With that assurance and with no sign of retaliation of any kind from the Sabatini "family," Mitch's safety had become a somewhat lower priority on the CPD's list of Sabatini-related items. His testimony was merely icing on an already tall cake, and whatever "family" was left in the Sabatini organization seemed to recognize that as well.

Mitch was safe.

Nevertheless, a posted officer sat in a radio car parked outside the Chapman Avenue address.

Molly gave the uniformed rookie a quick nod as she closed the door of her unmarked vehicle.

The past four days of sunshine and springlike temperatures had succeeded in deceiving most Chicagoans. Even Molly had started to wonder if she'd forgotten to turn a couple of pages on the calendar. With her trenchcoat blowing open behind her, she crossed the street. Several blocks over, she could hear the distinct rumble of the El as it clattered along its steel rails, no doubt thundering south into the downtown core.

Before she reached the opposite sidewalk, Molly noticed the red-and-white Realtor sign on the snow-covered lawn. Its placard swung gently in the damp breeze that wound its way along Chapman Avenue and its rows of stately maples.

Molly hesitated on the sidewalk and stared at the three-story house for a moment. Melting snow dripped from the eaves and onto the asphalt of the drive where the station wagon sat.

Mitch was in.

She was startled by the nervous anticipation that shivered through her. Hadn't she hoped he'd be in? Wasn't that why she'd driven across the city?

Still, to see him again after almost three weeks...

The night of the warehouse shootout and Sabatini's arrest, Mitch had gone to Headquarters separately in a squad car. Only after extensive questioning—detectives with Mitch, and IAD with Molly—had they been allowed to speak with one another again. But the late hour and the shock of the night's events had left little energy for discussion. He'd declined Molly's offer to go home with him, and—accompanied by a police escort—he had driven himself.

He'd needed space. And time.

It wasn't just the shock of having been in his and Emily's home again for the first time in months that had rattled him. No doubt the act of holding Emily's murderer in the sight of a gun, with nothing but opportunity on his side, had shaken Mitch to the core. When he'd said good-night to Molly three weeks ago, she had known that there was still an unmeasurable amount of healing to be done on Mitch's part.

But three weeks?

If not for the demands of the case, Molly might have gone mad with waiting—waiting for the phone to ring, waiting for a knock at her apartment door, waiting to see Mitch walk into the Homicide offices.

In all that time there had been only one contact, and it was Molly who had picked up the phone at last. It had been late, and clearly she'd woken him. Even today, Molly couldn't be sure if the awkward silence was due to Mitch's grogginess or his emotions. Either way, he hadn't called her back.

So here she was today. No longer able to stay away. No longer willing to wait and give Mitch time. After all, *too* much time, Molly thought, could also prove to be a detriment. What if, surrounded by the memories of his former life, Mitch slipped so far into his grief that he once again forgot what life had to offer? What if, in all that grief, he forgot the time they'd shared and the connection they'd rediscovered?

Molly took the curved walk to the front porch. There, she knocked at the double oak doors.

No answer.

She knocked again, this time trying the knob. The door was unlocked. She swung it open, intending to call out Mitch's name, but the state of the house stopped her. Closing the door behind her, Molly stood in the front foyer for a moment, the living room to her left and the dining room to her right. Both rooms were packed up. Boxes were labeled and stacked, and furniture was draped in sheets. Even the kitchen, down the corridor ahead of her, appeared mostly packed up.

"Hello?" Molly called out at last.

But there was no reply.

She took to the stairs then, feeling like an intruder but guessing that wherever Mitch was he couldn't hear her.

"Hello?" She reached the top landing and gazed at the open doorways. Even up here, the rooms had been packed up. Emily's office. The master bedroom, too, Molly noticed at last.

"Mitch?"

"Up here," she heard him shout down from the attic.

He was waiting for her at the top of the wooden stairs. Wearing worn khakis and a loose-fitting white shirt, he stood with his hands buried in his pockets, his unease visible by his stiff stance.

"Hi." His voice was no more than a whisper, and even that sent a shiver of longing through her.

"Hi."

In three weeks she'd missed him like crazy. But looking into his eyes again, smelling the scent of his skin and then standing so close to him she could almost feel his heat…it was enough to make Molly want to throw herself into his arms. She wanted to feel his mouth on hers, to press her body against his and admit to him that she'd been lost these past three weeks without him.

But she didn't.

"You've been packing," she said, noting even more boxes in the renovated attic that obviously served as his home office.

"Yeah. I've decided to sell the house. Already had an offer on it, in fact."

"And where will you live?"

"There's an apartment in my firm's complex. I figure I'll stay there for a while."

Molly nodded as she gave the attic a scan. Not everything had been packed. Across the enormous drafting table were scattered papers and pens, a couple old mugs of coffee, countless sketches and what appeared to be architectural blueprints.

She turned to face him squarely then, letting her gaze drift over him.

Taking one hand from his pocket, he ran it nervously over his hair. It had grown, but he'd kept the clean-shaven look, Molly was glad to see.

"How have you been?" she asked at last, staring him in the eye so there could be no lies.

He took a deep breath, held it for a moment and then released it.

"I've missed you like hell, Molly." There was a detectable waver in his voice. "And you?"

"The same."

She wondered if he was going to kiss her. Instead, he returned his hand to the pocket of his slacks and cast his gaze downward.

"So, I guess if you're going to be living so close to your firm, you'll be able to work even more hours, hmm?"

"Actually," he answered, "the contracts are already rolling in. More work than I can handle. I've started interviewing other architects. I was going to hire just one, but I'm thinking of expanding beyond that even. It's...well, it's not just the contracts. It's that...the thing is, I'm planning on devoting more of my time to other things."

There was an unmistakable flicker in his eyes. Molly couldn't put her finger on what it was exactly, but something in the way he looked at her just then sent a quiver of hope through her.

"The way I see it," he continued, "is I've spent too much of my time developing my career. And now that it's at a place where I can relax with it, well, I figure I should start developing my life a little more. Starting with this..." He gestured toward the desk.

He stepped past her, the mere brush of his shoulder against hers sending a flare of desire through her. Molly took a deep breath, struggling to quell the sensation as she followed him to the long desk under the arched window.

He straightened some papers, pushing them aside to reveal a full architectural plan.

"Do you recognize it?" he asked, and Molly knew his eyes were on her. Expectant.

She shook her head. "No."

"Look at it again," he urged, only this time he withdrew a three-dimensional pencil sketch from the rumpled stack of papers.

She'd never set eyes on the house depicted in the sketch before, yet recognition was immediate: the second-floor turret, the wraparound porch, the rear sunroom connected to the kitchen. She knew the house intimately, as though she'd been inside it, *lived* inside it. And she had. In her dreams, Molly had.

It was the summer before Mitch went back to college and she started the academy. She could recall everything about that afternoon, in the same way she could remember every last detail of the dream house they'd spent the day designing and redesigning in their imaginations. They'd taken a picnic out on the bluffs just north of Waukegan, overlooking Lake Michigan, the same bluffs where they'd spent countless romantic afternoons. And evenings.

Over the years, Molly had often considered driving up there, to see if it had been taken over by the urban sprawl, to see if she could somehow let go of her past by confronting her memories. But she never had.

"I'm going to build you that house one day, Molly," Mitch had promised her that afternoon. He'd been lying across the scratchy wool blanket, his hands folded behind his head as he closed his eyes against the sun. "I mean it. I'm going to design it, and then I'm going to build it for us. I can see it in my head, Molly."

And he'd jumped up then, his sudden enthusiasm almost knocking over the containers of leftovers.

"Right here." He'd stood at the very edge of the bluff then, his arms spread wide as though he were embracing the summer breeze that lifted off Lake Michigan below. "Our house. You just wait, Molly. I'm going to build it."

"Mitch, this is…" she began as she studied the sketches now.

"*Our* house," he finished for her as he settled a hand on her shoulder. "It's our house, Molly."

Disbelief stole her ability to speak. Molly had no idea

what to say. The implications of what he was showing her—

"I've wanted to call you for days now," Mitch explained, turning her within the circle of his arms. "Yes, I needed time. But that wasn't the only thing. I also wanted to get these plans done. I—I wanted...*needed* to show you how much I want to be with you, Molly. These plans...this house, it's a new start for me. A new life. But...it'll mean nothing to me if you're not in it."

Molly knew that if she looked up into those dark eyes of his right now she would be lost. One glance and she would be consumed by the passion she already felt crackling in the narrow space of air that separated them.

So she looked.

The corners of his mouth lifted, deepening the fine lines that bracketed his smile.

"I love you, Molly. I want to be with you."

He closed the gap between them. Sliding his hands beneath the trenchcoat, he wrapped his arms around her waist. The heat of his body was like a beacon, calling to her, drawing her closer.

"Mitch, are you sure?"

"Sure about what? About loving you? There's no question in my mind, Molly. I never stopped loving you."

"But you're sure...it's not too soon."

"No, love, it's not too soon. If anything, it's far too late."

"And Emily?"

There was the slightest hesitation, and Molly didn't doubt that it would always be there in Mitch. Hearing Emily's name, or seeing her picture...it would always have an affect on him, always make him pause.

"I loved Emily," he said softly. Still, his hold on her didn't slacken in the least, nor did his eyes leave hers. "But you've been right all along. I have to move on with my life. Emily would want that as well. She never failed to tell me how much she wanted me to be happy, and you, Molly…*you* make me happier than I have been in a very long time.''

He pulled her tight against him and placed a light, lingering kiss on her mouth. When he withdrew, he traced the line of her lips with his thumb.

''Emily will forever be in my heart,'' he whispered. ''But it's you, Molly, who has always possessed it.''

When he kissed her this time, Molly felt the sincerity of his words. She felt the fullness of his passion—so absolute and unwavering. So whole. So utterly and indescribably complete.

''Now, come on,'' he said, his mouth still close enough that she could feel his smile. ''I want to show you the site.''

''The site?''

''For our house, Molly. Come on, we'll drive up to Waukegan and—''

''You…you didn't. You bought the property?''

''Of course I did. Where else am I supposed to build our home?''

With a broad smile, he took her hand in his. But as he led Molly from the attic, she knew that even without the bluffs overlooking Lake Michigan, even without the dream house…her home was wherever Mitch was. *He* was her home. He always had been. And always would be.

The romantic suspense at

HARLEQUIN®

INTRIGUE

just got more intense!

On the precipice between imminent danger and smoldering desire, they are

**When your back is against the wall
and nothing makes sense, only one man
is strong enough to pull you from the brink—
and into his loving arms!
Look for all the books in this riveting new
promotion:**

WOMAN MOST WANTED (#599)
by **Harper Allen**
On sale January 2001

PRIVATE VOWS (#603)
by **Sally Steward**
On sale February 2001

NIGHTTIME GUARDIAN (#607)
by **Amanda Stevens**
On sale March 2001

Available at your favorite retail outlet.

HARLEQUIN®
Makes any time special ™

Visit us at www.eHarlequin.com

HIOTE

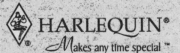
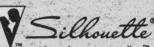

CELEBRATE VALENTINE'S DAY WITH HARLEQUIN®'S LATEST TITLE— *Stolen Memories*

Available in trade-size format, this collector's edition contains three full-length novels by *New York Times* bestselling authors Jayne Ann Krentz and Tess Gerritsen, along with national bestselling author Stella Cameron.

TEST OF TIME by **Jayne Ann Krentz**—
He married for the best reason.... She married for the only reason.... Did they stand a chance at making the only reason the real reason to share a lifetime?

THIEF OF HEARTS by **Tess Gerritsen**—
Their distrust of each other was only as strong as their desire. And Jordan began to fear that Diana was more than just a thief of hearts.

MOONTIDE by **Stella Cameron**—
For Andrew, Greer's return is a miracle. It had broken his heart to let her go. Now fate has brought them back together. And he won't lose her again...

Make this Valentine's Day one to remember!

Look for this exciting collector's edition on sale January 2001 at your favorite retail outlet.

HARLEQUIN®
Makes any time special ™

Visit us at www.eHarlequin.com

PHSM

HARLEQUIN®

A M E R I C A N ◆ R O M A N C E®

and **Muriel Jensen**
present

WHO'S THE DADDY?

*A*t a festive costume ball, three identical
sisters meet three masked bachelors.

*E*ach couple has a taste of true love behind
the anonymity of their costumes—but
only one will become parents
in nine months!

Find out who it will be!

November 2000
FATHER FEVER #858

January 2001
FATHER FORMULA #855

March 2001
FATHER FOUND #866

HARLEQUIN®
*M*akes any time special ™

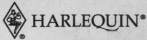